Chronicles of the

G000047008

Amulet

of

Wishes

Rita A. Rubin

Chronicles of the Guardians, Amulet of Wishes.

© Rita A. Rubin 2021.

The right for Rita A. Rubin to be identified as the author of this book has been asserted in accordance with the Copyright Act 1968.

All rights reserved. No part of this publication may be reproduced, stored in a retrieval system or transmitted in any form or by any means (electronic, mechanical, photocopying, recording or otherwise), without prior written permission from the author of this book.

This book is a work of fiction and any resemblance to real people or events is coincidental.

Cover design by Emily's World of Design.

ISBN: 978-0-6450928-0-6

Acknowledgments

Saying that this book wouldn't have been possible without the help of others sounds like a rather generic thing to say. However, I can't think of a truer statement. This book and I wouldn't be where we are today without so many helping hands along the way. I owe my thanks to everyone who read this book its early days and gave me words of advice and encouragement. Who helped me believe that this story had potential. To everyone who expressed their excitement for my world and my characters and gave me the motivation to keep going. To Emily for creating the most incredible cover imaginable for my book child. To my friends and family for their unconditional love and support and a special shout out to my brother for being my number one beta-reader. Maybe one day I'll promote you to alpha-reader status. Maybe.

PROLOGUE

It was raining on the night that Derek Draco's family was murdered.

It had been an unseasonably wet autumn, but after such a dry summer, no one was complaining. Especially not those who lived in the Valley, many of whom grew their own fruit and vegetables, not only to feed themselves but also to earn a living. For them, this rain was like a blessing from the Goddess, Ithulia, herself.

Derek and his parents were in high spirits that night. Their home-grown produce had sold reasonably well at the autumn market in Windfell, the town that sat on the side of the mountain that towered above the Valley. When they returned to their cottage in the Valley, Derek's mother prepared them a feast of a dinner with roast beef, stewed vegetables and a delicious apple pie for dessert.

Later, Derek found himself sitting up in bed, nestled comfortably back against the pillow and his teddy bear in his arms. His father, Alexander, sat on a rickety old chair beside him.

Outside, the wind was howling and the rain lashed the windows. At the sound of rumbling thunder in the distance, Derek clutched his toy closer but didn't voice his discomfort. He would be turning seven in the winter, he was too old to be scared of thunderstorms. So he hugged his bear to his chest and listened to the story his father was about to tell.

"Hundreds of years ago," Alexander Draco began. "Back when daemons still roamed the land, the daemon king, Asmydionn had three sons, Algron, Milrath and Zathral."

"I've heard of them," Derek piped up. "Edgar told me that it was the daemon Algron who created the vampirism and lycanthropy diseases."

His father nodded. The candlelight cast flickering shadows upon his skin and put a reddish tint to his brown hair. "That's right. Or at least, that's how the legend goes. It's said that Asmydionn's sons each left something behind before Aryanna Vir Fortis, banished the daemons from this realm. Algron created the strains of vampirism and lycanthropy. Zathral placed a curse on the earth elves that turned them into wicked creatures we now call grems. And Milrath created an amulet out of three pieces, that when brought together, could grant wishes."

Derek frowned. "Grants wishes? That doesn't sound like such a bad thing." In fact, Derek thought that it sounded wonderful. If he had an amulet like that, he would make a wish to never have to eat vegetables again.

"Ah, but it's not that simple," Alexander said with a knowing smile. "You see the amulet—"

"All right, I think that is enough for tonight," came the voice of Derek's mother from the doorway. Erica Draco was a beautiful woman with long, ink-black hair and fair skin. Derek often heard people comment about how much he resembled his mother. He had the same black hair, the same chin (which confused Derek because didn't everyone's chin look the same?). The only thing he appeared to have inherited from his father was his blue eyes, the same colour as the sky on a cloudless summer day.

His mother was wearing a nightgown that hung loose on her slender frame. Even so, the bump in her stomach was still quite noticeable. In another six months, Erica would give birth to her and Alexander's second child. Derek's first sibling. It had become quite the guessing game in their household as to whether the baby would be a boy or a girl. Both of his parents thought it would be nice to have a little girl, but Derek didn't really mind what the baby turned out to be. As long as it was someone to play with, that was all that mattered to him.

Erica gave her husband a stern look as she stepped further into the bedroom. "Really Alexander? Telling our son stories about daemons right before bed? You will give him nightmares." Erica pushed back a lock of her hair, revealing the sharp point of her ear.

Erica Draco was a wood elf, which made Derek half-elf. The only sign of his elvish heritage was that his ears were slightly more pointed than a normal human's.

"I'm not scared," Derek protested.

"No, no, your mother's right," Alexander said with a sheepish chuckle. "Perhaps that's not the right story for bed. Maybe a different one? What would you like to hear?"

Derek perked up instantly. "Tell me a story about the Guardians!"

The good mood seemed to drain from the room like water tipped out of a cup.

His words had a strange effect on his parents; his mother closed her eyes briefly and rested her hand on her swelling belly, a pained look on her face. Meanwhile, the smile fell from his father's face, his brow furrowing.

It was like this every time Derek mentioned the Guardians. Which he couldn't help but find odd. The Guardians were the heroic protectors of Aloseria, everyone thought so, but only his parents seemed to think otherwise.

"No, Derek," Alexander said softly.

"Why not?"

"Because I said so."

Derek folded his arms, pouting crossly. "It's not fair. You never want to tell stories about the Guardians."

"Derek," Erica said in a warning tone. "That is enough."

"But I should know all about them if I'm going to be one someday."

"Derek, we've been over this." Alexander's voice had taken on a stern edge. "You can't be a Guardian."

"Why not?"

"Because it's too dangerous."

"But you used to be a Guardian, Da."

"Yes," said Alexander. "I *was*. But then I left."

"Why?" Derek pressed.

Alexander sighed and stood from his chair. "I'll tell you when you're older," he said as he came over to kiss his son's forehead. "Sleep well." and he left the room without a backwards glance.

Derek began to fidget nervously with his toy bear. "Is Da angry with me?" He asked his mother.

"No, he is not angry," Erica said as she began the task of tucking him into bed. "He is just . . . Your da does not like to talk about those days."

"But why not?"

"It is not for me to say, *annwynia*," she said adding the elvish word for beloved. Erica often addressed Derek and Alexander with elvish terms of endearment. "That is something your father is going to have to tell you himself one day."

Derek sighed in defeat as he lay down. "Okay."

Erica pressed a kiss to Derek's cheek. "I love you," she said with a smile. "And your father loves you too. So much."

Derek smiled sleepily up at his mother. "I love you too, Mum."

Erica took the candle from the bedside table and carried it out of the room with her, closing the door behind her as she went.

The room was bathed in darkness and within moments, Derek drifted into sleep.

Later that night, Derek got up out of bed to get himself a glass of water from the kitchen downstairs. The air was cool and he shivered in his thin bed shirt and bare feet. He was just climbing back up the attic stairs to his bedroom when he heard a knocking at the front door.

Derek paused, wondering if maybe, in his still half-asleep state, he had imagined the sound. A moment later, there was another knock and Derek saw his parents emerge from their bedroom just down the hall, Erica holding a burning candle in her hand. Her hair immaculate even after just getting out of bed. "Who could it be at this time of night?"

"Maybe Coren's cow got loose again?" suggested Alexander as he went to open the door.

Everything happened so fast.

His father opened the door, Derek could just make out a dark figure standing on the other side, and before his father could say or do anything, there was a flash of silver. A choked sound and Alexander Draco crumpled to the ground like a puppet cut from its strings.

He fell onto his back and Derek could see the long cut along his father's throat, oozing blood onto the floor.

"*DA!*" Derek screamed at the same time that his mother let out a scream that was part, horror, part anguish, part *rage*.

Stepping inside, over Alexander's still body, was a tall man, dressed all in black. His coat dripping wet from the rain. He had long black hair, sopping and plastered to the sides of his pale face.

His eyes were the colour of scarlet and seemed to shine unnaturally in the darkness.

"Who are you?" Erica demanded viciously.

Instead of replying, the man just regarded her coolly and brandished a long, silver knife. Slicked red with the blood of Derek's father.

Erica took two steps forward. She was holding a dagger in her hand (Derek wasn't sure when or where she had gotten it from) and pointed it at the man. *"Answer me!"* She screamed.

Derek had never heard his mother sound so angry. So wrecked.

The man's lips curled slowly into a predatory grin. "No one." And then he lunged.

Erica met the man's blade with her own.

"Mum!" cried Derek.

His mother looked up to where he stood on the stairs with wide, horrified eyes. "Derek," she shouted just as she spun to the side to avoid the man's knife strike. "Get out of here! Go someplace safe!"

"No! Mum, I can't—"

The man's blade and Erica's clanged against each other with a metallic scraping sound. When they broke apart, Erica moved swiftly and jabbed her elbow into the man's chest. The man coughed and stumbled back a few steps. Erica looked up at Derek. The look on her face was some combination of grief, fear and desperation. She looked wild and Derek never thought he would see his mother look like that.

"Go!" She yelled up at him. *"Now!"*

Something in her voice and the look on her face propelled Derek to turn and scramble up the stairs.

When he was in his room, Derek threw the door shut behind him before racing over to the window. He pulled over the chair his father had been sitting on earlier and clambered on top of it so that he could reach for the window latch.

His hands were shaking so badly that he fumbled with it a few times. His heart was beating so rapidly he thought it might break open his chest.

The latch slid open and Derek flung the window wide. The wall outside his bedroom was covered by a garden lattice. He had used the lattice many times before when he wished to leave the house without his parent's knowledge. Derek hopped up onto the windowsill and began to climb down.

The rain had grown heavier, the droplets of water falling against Derek's skin like cold needle tips, soaking his clothes and hair in a matter of seconds. The rain also made the lattice slippery so that Derek struggled at times to find purchase with his hands and feet.

Once he was on the ground, Derek splashed through the muddy vegetable garden, jumped over the white, picket fence that encircled their home, and made for the hilltop at the edge of the Valley.

His mother had said to get somewhere safe and the first place that came to mind was Windfell. There were guards at Windfell, guards with swords that were big and sharp and that would stab that man in the heart if he tried to hurt Derek.

Derek's legs were tired and sore by the time he had reached the top of the hill. He had paused briefly to catch his breath when there was an ear-splitting explosion and Derek whirled around to see that their little cottage, his *home,* was on fire.

The plumes of orange flame lit up the night sky.

Derek sucked in a breath. *Mum.*

But he couldn't linger here. Windfell. He had to get to Windfell. He had to get someplace safe, just like his mother had asked him to. So Derek turned back around and plunged into the forest ahead of him. It was so dark that Derek could hardly see what was in front of him. He stumbled over sharp rocks and twigs that stabbed painfully into the soles of his bare feet.

When Derek finally felt like he could run no more, he collapsed against the base of an old, oak tree, boneless and panting and shivering in his saturated clothing. He closed his eyes and saw the image of his father lying dead on the floor. He could still hear his mother's agonized screams and see his home on fire. He was even sure he could smell the acrid scent of the smoke.

Derek wrapped his arms around his shivering body. *Scared. I'm scared. I want Mum. I want Da. I want to go home. I'm scared.*

The rain had stopped and apart from the singing of crickets and the sound of his harsh breathing and quiet sobbing, everything was still and quiet.

The quiet was broken by the sound of a snapping twig.

Derek spun around and his heart pounded with fear in dread when he spotted the man with the red eyes.

And he was coming straight towards him.

Derek didn't have time to wonder how the man had found him and so quickly. His first instinct was to run and that's just what he did.

Desperate to get away from the one who had murdered his father. Who had probably just murdered his mother.

He fell to the ground when he felt something wrap around his legs. His chin knocked against the hard earth and the taste of blood filled his mouth. Pushing himself onto his elbows, Derek looked over his shoulder at his legs, to see they were bound together by something that looked like black smoke. Only it did not feel like smoke. Instead, it felt as tight as rope, cutting into the delicate skin beneath the fabric of his pants.

As he struggled to free himself, a dark figure loomed over him and Derek looked up into the piercing red eyes of the black-haired stranger.

His heart was hammering in his chest, his body trembled like a leaf in the wind. As Derek stared into those bright, emotionless eyes, he thought of his father. Dead. He thought of his mother. Also probably dead. He thought of how he was about to meet the same fate. And he was *terrified*.

His vision began to blur. He felt as if the ground beneath him was tilting sideways and Derek fell onto his side. He was panting now. He couldn't catch his breath. His chest hurt. He couldn't *breathe*.

He saw the man bending over him. An outstretched hand

reaching for him.

Mum . . . Da . . . Help me.

It was the last thing he thought before everything went dark.

1

Nine Years Later

The front door flew open and Derek rushed out, still adjusting his satchel onto his shoulder and stuffing the last piece of his toast into his mouth.

When he had woken up that morning, he'd taken one look at his clock and had one thought, *shit.*

He'd overslept (again) and now he was running late (again).

Although it was still early, the city of Ember was already stirring to life. Ember was the capital city of Aloseria and by far the largest and most vibrant, with its brightly coloured buildings and lively inhabitants. If one were to look at the city from afar, they would think it resembled a four-tiered cake. The lower half of the city was mostly made up of shops, inns and taverns. The middle was where the city's inhabitants lived. The upper part of the city was where the nobles of the city resided and sitting at the very top, like a crowning jewel, was the royal palace.

Derek sprinted down the cobblestoned streets until he came to the city centre where vendors were setting up their stalls for the open air market. There were the confectioners with their jam tarts and honeyed treats. The butcher had his carcasses hanging up at the back of his stall and neat displays of steak and lamb chops at the front. Next to him, the greengrocers were putting out crates full of fresh fruit and vegetables.

A sudden commotion from up ahead made Derek pause just in time to avoid getting knocked over by two dragons that came barrelling past, knocking over one of the stalls in the process.

The owner of the now ruined stall recovered from her initial shock and turned to the two creatures responsible. "You hooligans!" The woman shouted furiously. "Just look at what you've done! Come back here!" But the dragons had already flown away.

Dragons crashing into unsuspecting market stalls may have made for a strange—perhaps even frightening—occurrence in other places, but not in Ember. Because many of the people who lived in Ember could *Change* into dragons. Derek included.

Guardians. That was what they were known as. Protectors of Aloseria and keepers of the peace.

The source of their power came from their rings. Imbued with an ancient and powerful magic, all they had to do was put it on and they would find themselves transformed into creatures that had been extinct for hundreds of years.

Some said that the rings were given by the Goddess Ithulia to the legendary hero, Aryanna Vir Fortis, and her people to help them defeat the daemon plague. Others said that it had been the work of an extremely powerful mage.

One thing that everyone knew for certain, however, was that only those descended from those very first Guardians could wear the rings, which were passed down through generations.

Derek picked up a doll made of yarn that had landed near his feet when the stall was knocked over. He carried it back to where the woman was collecting her scattered items and muttering angrily to herself about the youth of today.

"Here," Derek said, handing her the doll.

The woman blinked at him in surprise before smiling. "Thank you, dear."

By now, others were making their way over to help the woman pick up her wares and fix her stall, so Derek didn't feel guilty when he took off running again.

He was still late after all.

Guardians weren't made overnight. To become a Guardian, one must first complete years of rigorous training.

That was the purpose of the Academy. Standing proudly near the city centre, the Academy was easily one of the largest buildings in Ember, except for the royal palace, of course. It looked like a miniature castle with white brick walls and looming towers and surrounded by perfectly tended gardens. It was said that the Academy was nearly as old as Ember itself.

Derek pelted through the empty courtyard and up the steps before slipping in through the grand, front doors. Almost as soon as he stepped inside, he was brought up short by the towering figure of a bespectacled woman glaring down at him with stern disapproval. Headmistress Perril was a middle-aged woman with dark skin and dark grey hair that was usually tied into a tight bun at the back of her head.

"You're late *again*, Master Draco," she said.

"I know. I'm so sorry, Headmistress," said Derek, doing his best to look and sound contrite.

"If this happens again, I'll be having a word with your father."

Derek repressed a grimace. "It won't happen again."

The headmistress looked unconvinced but simply said, "Off to class with you."

The halls of the Academy were made up of pristine white walls and polished marble floors. Sunlight streamed in from the arched windows and portraits of former headmasters and headmistresses lined the walls. Derek made his way up a winding marble staircase, taking the steps two at a time until he reached the west tower's top floor. There was only one classroom on this floor and when he opened the door and stepped inside, Derek found that unsurprisingly, class was already underway.

A few other students turned in their seats to look at him, while at the head of the classroom, their teacher, Professor Farrowshire continued speaking as if he had not just noticed Derek.

Out of the corner of his eye, Derek spotted a familiar face with brown skin and wavy, darker brown hair, sitting at a desk by the window and gesturing for him to come and sit in the empty chair beside him. The familiar face was Jared Regalias, Derek's closest friend and the Prince of Aloseria.

"Oversleep again did you?" Jared whispered to him as he sat down.

"Only a little bit," was Derek's reply as he pulled his books out from his satchel.

"You haven't really missed much. Farrowshire's just been recapping the Samweanese conjugations we learned last lesson."

"Did you do the homework?"

"Oh, I did it all right," said Jared. "But it's bad. *Horrendously* bad. I think Farrowshire might even have me thrown out of the Academy for it."

"I doubt they'd expel a prince." Derek grinned. Languages were not Jared's strong point.

"There's a first time for everything."

At some point during the class, Farrowshire had to step out and left his students with the instructions to read quietly while he was gone. Naturally, everyone started talking as soon as he left the room.

Sitting in the row across from them, Derek noticed two girls, murmuring to each other while they snuck glances at him. Jared had noticed the girls too and scowled. "Don't they have anything better to talk about after all these years?"

"It doesn't matter," said Derek. By now he was used to it, the looks and the whispers.

He had endured them since he first arrived in Ember at nine-years-old and even now, he was still something of a novelty to the people of this city; the son of an exiled Guardian and an outcast wood elf. The adopted son of the late Mayor of Windfell. Family murdered. Adoptive father dead three years later and brought to Ember and then adopted by Darus Flynn. People also liked to discuss whether or not he was even fit to be a Guardian because of his elf heritage. Some believed being part elf made him untrustworthy, that the King was foolish to allow him to study at the Academy and even fraternize with the Prince.

Derek could care less what these people had to say about him, but he knew that Jared wasn't so accepting of others talking about him behind his back. Fortunately, before Jared could confront the girls, Farrowshire reappeared and class resumed.

After Languages, his next class was History. Derek didn't mind History, but their teacher harboured a strong resentment towards Derek for nothing other than the fact that he had elf blood in him.

Over twenty years ago, a wood elf had been blamed for the assassination of Queen Josphine. In retaliation, King Gerard sent his own assassins to kill the elf king's family. The attack failed but was successful in starting a war between the Guardians and the wood elves. The war lasted several years, only coming to an end when King Jonathan, Jared's father, took the throne and brokered a peace treaty with the new elf queen.

Even so, Derek knew there were many who still bore ill feelings towards the wood elves.

Professor Carloth lost both of his sons to the war, so it was probably no wonder he seemed to despise Derek so.

In today's class, he had them all reading passages from a book detailing the life of Aryanna Vir Fortis. Derek had read it before and still couldn't help but find it odd that there was hardly any mention of what happened to Aryanna after she defeated Asmydionn and the rest of the daemons. There were many books one could read about Aryanna Vir Fortis, but not one of them mentioned anything beyond that she eventually married and had a child.

Derek had once brought this matter up once in History class a few years ago but the Professor had simply ignored him.

His last class of the day was Combat Practice, which just so happened to be Derek's favourite class. Learning how to fight was an essential part of becoming a Guardian and fortunately, Derek was quite good at it. He excelled at many of his subjects, but none more than Combat.

Their class was held in a large hall with a high ceiling. The floors were carpeted with soft mats and the walls were lined with mounted weapons; swords, daggers, and battleaxes that were not to be touched by the students. Their teacher, Professor Ason, was a stocky, battle-hardened woman with a scarred face. That lesson she showed them how one could disarm and subdue an armed attacker and then paired them off to practice on each other.

"Oh, will you stop that," snapped Rosalie Decorus when she failed to pin Derek and he jabbed her in the ribs with his wooden knife.

"Your form's all wrong," Derek explained, twirling the knife lazily between his fingers. "Your feet should be further apart."

Rosalie pushed some of her dark hair out of her face and scowled. "It's time to swap roles."

"Why?"

"Because I want a go at stabbing you with the knife."

Derek smirked.

After classes had officially ended for the day and almost everyone had gone home, Derek decided to stay behind in the training hall and train alone. It made little difference to him that he'd just spent the last hour training for class. He liked training, there had been times where he'd gone whole days doing almost nothing but train (much to Darus's consternation).

For Derek, training was relaxing, as strange as it sounded. It cleared his mind, made him focus on what he was doing then and there and forget about everything else. And there were many things that Derek wanted to forget.

By the time Derek did return home, it was already well into the evening. He had been too tired to make the trek home by foot but there was a simple solution to that.

Once he had stepped outside of the Academy walls, Derek had removed his ring that he wore on a chain around his neck.

While identical in design, every Guardian's ring was a different colour. Derek's was a plain black band with a small blue stone set in the middle. He'd slid the ring onto one of his fingers and felt the familiar humming within as the Change came over him.

The first time Derek had ever Changed, it had been a disorienting experience and he'd had to lie down afterwards to stop everything from spinning. But he'd been told it was normal to feel that way after the first time, Darus told him that he'd once known a boy who had thrown up the first time he Changed.

Now Changing was as easy for him as slipping on a shoe. When a Guardian Changed there was no tearing of clothes or breaking of bones, just an instantaneous transformation and an almost pleasant thrumming inside that felt like a second pulse.

Before long, Derek Draco stood in the Academy courtyard on all fours as a black dragon. As a dragon, Derek was approximately the same size as a small horse with a body that resembled a cat's. The skin of his wings, chest, and underbelly were a light blue in colour, almost the exact same shade as his eyes.

He made it home in no time, Changing back as soon as he landed in the front yard. He slipped his ring off his finger, back onto his chain, and made his way across the grass towards the double-storey house, made of reddish-brown brick and a blue tiled roof.

Lying stretched out under the shade of the front veranda was a grey tabby cat and as soon as it saw Derek approaching, it leapt to its feet to greet him with insistent mewling.

"Hello, Finn," Derek murmured as he bent down to indulge the cat with a scratch behind the ear. "I'm sure I didn't let you out this morning. If you're out here, then I guess that means he's home isn't he?"

Finn butted his head against Derek's wrist in response.

As he stepped in through the front door with Finn at his heels, Derek noticed the flickering of candlelight coming from the kitchen.

The inside of the house was simple, with wooden floorboards and the walls painted a buttercup yellow. There was a small foyer when you walked in that then stretched into a long hallway, branching off into different rooms. At the end of the hallway was a dark, wooden staircase that led to the second floor.

Before Derek even got the chance to enter the kitchen, however, he suddenly found his arms full of a giant, scruffy brown dog and a wet tongue lapping at his face. It was a good thing Derek was used to the dog's enthusiastic greetings or he'd probably have ended up flat on his back.

"Daisy!" A familiar, deep voice called out from inside the kitchen. "Come here and leave the poor boy alone."

Obediently, Daisy the wolfhound removed her front paws from around Derek's shoulders and padded back over to her master.

Sitting at the table in the centre of the kitchen was a handsome young man with long, golden-brown hair tied into a ponytail. He was dressed in a loose white shirt and tight black pants. A glass of red wine on the table in front of him.

The man looked up at Derek and smiled. "It's about time you came home."

"I could say the same thing to you," Derek said to his adoptive father as he set his satchel down on one of the stools near the kitchen bench and went over to the sink to get a glass of water.

Darus Flynn's grin widened. "Did you miss me?"

"Actually it was nice having the house to myself," said Derek. "I'm sad that time is over."

"And here I was hoping Daisy wouldn't be the only one excited to see me."

"You should know better than to get your hopes up." Derek took a seat at the table beside Darus. "How did the assignment go?"

The humour on Darus's face faded. Derek noticed the dark circles under the older man's eyes. "We managed to capture a few of the bandits, but Durbash still got away."

Durbash. The name of Aloseria's most wanted man. He was also wanted in the rest of the four known lands, Samwea, Ishlav, and Tybenia. He was an ogre from the tropical isles of Samwea, who had started out as an average bandit until he moved onto orchestrating an illegal slave trading industry, kidnapping and enslaving thousands of people from all across the lands. The Guardians had been after him for years now, but so far he had proven to be incredibly good at alluding them.

"He certainly knows how to keep himself well hidden," Darus

said bitterly. "For someone of his size."

"His size?"

"I swear he was carved from a mountain."

Derek chuckled into his glass.

Afterwards, Derek left to wash up in the upstairs bathroom while Darus prepared dinner.

"You better eat all of your vegetables this time," Darus said afterwards as they sat down to a meal of cooked fish, bread rolls, and boiled carrots and potatoes.

Derek looked down at the innocuous-looking vegetables with disdain. "I make no promises."

Darus sighed.

They spoke more while they ate. Darus regaled him with more details about his assignment to capture Durbash. Derek told Darus how things had been going at the Academy while he had been away and how apparently the seamstress's son had gone and gotten himself engaged to a fisherman from White Lake.

"Oh, Bernard got engaged?" said Darus pleasantly. "I'll have to give him my congratulations."

"Apparently the seamstress is beside herself since she was hoping her son would marry a Guardian."

"I did propose to him once, but he turned me down."

Derek paused in his eating to stare at Darus. "This is news to me."

Darus nodded. "I may have been slightly inebriated. Although that doesn't change the fact that he is rather attractive." He sighed dreamily. "Those cheekbones."

"When was this?"

"A few years ago, I can't remember exactly." Darus fixed Derek with a look from across the table. "And do you mind telling me what happened to your hands?"

Derek looked down and saw the yellowing bruises that now decorated the knuckles of both of his hands. He may have hit the training dummy a bit harder than he should have. "I was training," was all he said.

Darus's brow lowered. "You need to take it easy, Derek. You're not even a Guardian yet and you've already injured yourself more times than I can count just from training."

Derek shrugged.

"Really, Derek, what would your parents say?"

"My parents never wanted me to be a Guardian in the first place," Derek said bitterly, spearing a piece of fish with his fork. "I think they'd hardly be thrilled that I'm even living in Ember."

"Still, I'm sure they wouldn't like to see you pushing yourself so much. They—"

"It doesn't matter!" Derek snapped. "It doesn't matter what my parents would say or think if they could see me now. They're—" But he clenched his jaw shut before he could continue.

Across the table, Darus looked startled by Derek's outburst. "Derek," he began in a soft voice one would use to soothe a spooked animal.

But Derek didn't want to hear it. He set down his knife and fork and stood up from his seat. "I'm not hungry anymore. I think I'll just go to bed."

He left before Darus could say another word.

* * *

Half an hour later, Darus eased open the door to Derek's room, stepping inside. The room was small but cosy, with blue painted walls, a single window with a desk, and chair underneath. A wardrobe to the left and a single bed against the wall to the right. The room was immaculate, not a single thing out of place. Darus was hardly surprised, Derek couldn't stand it when his things were a mess, even when he was a child, he always had to make sure all of his things were in order.

The boy in question was currently fast asleep in his bed. Finn curled up at the foot of the bed, raised his head to look up at Darus with half-lidded, green eyes.

Darus was just about to leave when he heard a noise. A whimper. Followed by another.

They were coming from Derek.

Darus was kneeling down beside the bed in an instant. After living with Derek for six years, Darus was all too used to Derek's nightmares. Although they had lessened as Derek got older, he still had them more often than Darus would like. The first time it happened, when Derek was only nine years old, Darus had been at a complete loss at what to do. The boy had been shaking and crying out and Darus had never seen a bad dream cause such a reaction.

Over time, however, Darus had developed the perfect method for helping Derek through his night terrors. With a touch that was feather-light, he moved a hand up to Derek's shoulder and down his arm and up to his shoulder again, in slow movements.

"Hush, Derek," he whispered. "It's all right. You're all right. You're safe. Nothing's going to hurt you. Everything's all right."

Darus continued to whisper soothing words of comfort and rubbing Derek's arm until he felt the trembling lessen and the whimpering cease.

"You're safe . . . I've got you."

Finally, the nightmare seemed to subside. Darus removed his hand and simply gazed at the now serene face, no longer twisted in fear.

Darus wished, not for the first time, that he had the power to take away all the bad memories that crept into Derek's dreams and made him feel such terror. Unfortunately, he did not possess such a power and never would. All he could do was be there for Derek and try to soothe him through the nightmares. Still, Darus would be damned if he said it didn't hurt his heart every time.

He lingered for a moment longer before, silently, Darus made his way out of the room, closing the door behind him with a soft click.

2

After six years at the Academy, it was finally time for the Rookie Examination.

It was an exam that all Academy students must take in their sixth year in order to graduate and become rookie Guardians. They were given a month to study and brush up on their skills and then, on the first day of January, the Examination began.

That morning, as Derek walked through the halls of the Academy, all sixth-year students were abuzz with excitement and nerves. This exam would be the culmination of all the things they had learned over their years at the Academy.

Derek entered the training hall to find that rows of desks and chairs had been set up inside. It was the only room big enough to accommodate all sixth years.

Headmistress Perril took up her position at the head of the hall, behind a large, wooden desk. "Everyone find a seat, please," Her voice echoed throughout the hall in a clear command. "One seat for each student. If you talk during this examination, you fail. If you are caught looking at another student's paper, you fail."

No one dared utter a word as the Headmistress began handing out pencils and sheets of parchment. In the front row, Derek could see Jared bouncing his leg nervously. Two rows in front, he noticed a girl who looked like she was about to weep. He also spotted William Frain, a boy from his History class, sitting as still as a statue and looking as if he were seconds away from being sick.

As Headmistress Perril set down paper and a pencil in front of him, Derek felt his own anxiety begin to rise, but he forced it down. There was no point in stressing. After all the sleepless nights he had spent studying, training until he dropped, he had to believe that he was going to pass this exam.

"I will be reading out questions to you and you shall be given time to answer," explained the Headmistress. "You may ask me to repeat the question if needed but you cannot ask questions regarding the answer."

Headmistress Perril took her time as she made her way back to the front of the hall after handing out the required materials to each student. The room was deathly quiet, except for the clack, clack of the Headmistress's shoes on the bare floorboards. She moved to stand behind her desk and took a moment to survey the array of faces before her.

"Begin."

The written portion of the exam lasted a good three hours and by the time it was over Derek felt as if he never wanted to sit in another chair ever again.

After a break, they moved onto their practical examinations. This exam consisted of everything from how to land properly after jumping from high places to demonstrating their skills with different kinds of weapons.

"Shouldn't be surprised," Derek heard one of the professors mutter to the other after he hit the target four times in a row using throwing knives. He was just preparing to throw the fifth.

"Alexander was always good at this stuff. Makes sense that his son would be too."

"It's a shame he left," the second professor, a burly man with a thick, black beard, replied. "He'd probably still be alive too if he hadn't run off with some elf who—"

The man broke off with a startled yelp when Derek's knife struck the wall only centimetres from his head.

"So sorry," Derek called out. "It must've slipped out of my hand."

He knew he would have a mark taken off for that, but it was well worth it.

The last part of their practical exam was one-on-one, hand-to-hand combat. Derek couldn't stop grinning as Jared was matched against Rosalie Decorus and he definitely couldn't keep himself from laughing when Jared came to sit down next to him after the match, rubbing at a sore shoulder.

"Derek Draco and Elijah Hargrade."

Jared patted him on the shoulder. "Good luck," he said as Derek moved to stand in the centre of the training room, opposite Elijah.

Elijah was a tall, thickset boy with blond hair and a face so handsome that even Derek might have been in danger of falling for if he wasn't such a notorious ass.

Elijah had a pompous look on his face as he regarded Derek from across the floor. Like he believed Derek wasn't any sort of match for him.

"Begin," Professor Ason announced.

Elijah was the first to move. He was surprisingly quick for someone of his build and Derek found himself forced to go on the defensive, only moving to block or avoid Elijah's attacks.

But no matter how quick Elijah was, Derek was still quicker. When Elijah moved to hit him in the chest, Derek ducked under his outstretched arm, hooked his leg around the other boy's ankle, and toppled him over onto his back.

Elijah won the second match, however, when Derek was too slow to avoid a jab to the gut that left him staggering. Elijah had used that momentary distraction to toss Derek onto his back with a one armed shoulder throw.

Not that winning or losing mattered in this exam. They were only being judged on how they fought. How their form was, how quick their reactions were, and if they resorted to any underhanded tactics that would be unsuitable for a Guardian to use.

After winning the third match, Derek held his hand out to Elijah, who was in the middle of pushing himself up off of the floor.

Elijah gave his offered hand a contemptuous look, his upper lip curling as he promptly ignored Derek and stalked back over to where he had been sitting with his friends.

Ass, Derek thought to himself before returning to sit with Jared.

After what felt like a gruellingly long day, the Rookie Examination came to an end and they were all sent home with the news that they should receive their results in a few weeks time.

But as weeks went by and others started receiving their letters while Derek was still left waiting, he couldn't help growing apprehensive. Both Darus and Jared tried telling him not to worry, that he would have passed the exam and he'd be sure to receive his letter any day now.

Still, that didn't stop the pessimistic thoughts from plaguing his mind. Maybe he hadn't passed? Maybe it was because he had thrown that knife at that professor's head? Perhaps Professor Carloth had scored him badly in the History portion of the exam, just out of spite?

Or maybe he had failed because it had been decided that they didn't want a Guardian who was half-elf after all?

That last thought was the one that dogged him for the next couple of days.

Until, one morning, as Derek let Daisy outside, he found a cream coloured envelope lying on the doormat with his name written on it. He snatched it up and brought it inside and into the kitchen. He used a knife to slice open the top of the envelope.

Inside was a letter that read,

To, Derek Alexander Draco,

We are pleased to inform you that you have passed the Rookie Examination.
We offer you our congratulations and we hope that you will carry with you always the
lessons that you have learned at the Academy, as you begin your journey as a Guardian.

Sincerely, Abigail Perril. Academy Headmistress.

Derek read the letter once more, just to help the words sink in. Passed.

He had passed the exam.

He was now, officially, a Guardian.

Finn came scampering into the kitchen, meowing and rubbing against Derek's legs to let him know that he was hungry. Setting the letter down on the table, Derek set about preparing Finn his morning meal. When he was done, Derek set the food bowl down on the floor. While Finn ate, Derek stroked his knuckles lightly down the cat's back.

"I passed, Finn," he said.

Finn raised his head to regard Derek with big green eyes before returning to his food.

Of course, Derek was pleased. It had always been a childhood dream of his, to become a Guardian just like his father had been. Even after the deaths of his family, he had wished to become a Guardian, so that he could learn to become strong. When Darus had found him and brought him back to Ember, there had been no question about it and Derek had been enrolled in the Academy within a fortnight.

Still, he couldn't help feeling a bit melancholy. Perhaps it was because Darus wasn't there, away on another assignment. It would have been nice to have him there to share in Derek's achievement.

And maybe, it was because he was thinking of his parents. What would they think if they could see him now? Would his mother and father be disappointed? Or would they be proud of him despite their feelings towards the Guardians?

Then, inexplicably, Derek wondered what Goldridge would think of him now.

He jerked back as if he had been struck. *No,* Derek thought vehemently. He would not think of that man. Not today. Today was his day. He had passed the Rookie Examination. He had achieved his childhood dream. He had become a Guardian.

Derek would not let thoughts of *him* ruin it.

That afternoon, Derek had been walking past the lounge room window just in time to see a bronze coloured dragon land in the front yard. Jared.

"Mother wants you to come over for dinner tonight," Jared explained when Derek answered the door. "To celebrate our graduating from the Academy."

"How do you know I passed?" asked Derek.

"It's you. Of course, you passed. Now I need to get back before the guards realised I gave them the slip."

That evening Derek made his way to the royal palace.

To get there, he had to walk through the upper part of the city where the wealthy noble families lived. No one in Ember lived in squalor, every single house and street was clean and well built, but there was no denying that the upper part of the city was much more extravagant than where Derek himself lived.

There were the same, black, cobblestone paths that ran through the rest of the city, but the homes that lined the streets were much larger. All double-storey—some were even three storey's tall. The gardens here were wider and much more neatly tended to as well.

There weren't many people still out on the streets at this hour, but Derek still came across a trio of women in extravagant dresses and feathered hats. Two men walking arm in arm with embroidered coats and shoes so polished one could probably see their reflection in them.

Derek's father had been a noble when he had lived in Ember, or so Derek had been told. He'd had a different name too. Instead of Alexander Draco, it had been Alexander Leon Viseric. But when he had gone into exile, his father had given up the name he had been born with and taken on the name, Draco, instead. He had also renounced all of his family's property and wealth. The Viseric name had been struck from the nobility. Their house and their money given over to the crown.

In another life, Derek might have had a different name. He might have grown up living in one of these enormous houses.

The palace was by far the grandest and largest structure in Ember, maybe even in all of Aloseria. The walls and towers looked as if they had been carved from solid gold. The rooftops were a deep, royal blue and gilded with gold. It was all surrounded by expansive and elaborately designed gardens, with fruit trees, hedge mazes and every kind of flower you could imagine and then some. Surrounding it all, was a gilded fence or wrought iron, patrolled by armed guards at all times.

When Derek arrived at the front doors to the palace, he was greeted by the royal footman, Aldred, an amicable man in his late seventies. He led Derek through the palace halls to where Jared and the rest of the royal family would be waiting for him.

The inside of the palace was no less impressive than the outside. High ceilings, marble floors and almost everything was inlaid with gold and there was a crystal chandelier in every room. It reminded Derek of Goldridge's manor house in Windfell. Although it had been nowhere near as large as the royal palace and considerably less gold incorporated into the furniture and ornamentation.

Aldred brought him out to the north side of the royal gardens.

Rose bushes of varying shades of red, flanked a white tiled

pathway on either side. The pathway led to a large gazebo at the very edge of the garden with a domed ceiling. All four members of the royal family sat at a long table that had been set up inside the gazebo. As usual, the Prince and Princess were busy squabbling.

"Mother," he heard Princess Julianna, Jared's older sister and heir to the throne, say. "Jared is being a child, please make him stop."

"I am not," Jared protested. "I resent being called a child, sister. Especially since you're only two years older than I am."

"And yet the difference in our maturity is staggering."

"At least I still know how to have fun and don't always act like a boring, arrogant b—"

"Children," there was a warning note in the Queen's voice.

Aldred cleared his throat. "Pardon me, Master Draco has arrived."

The Queen's three small spaniel dogs, Lucie, Spot and Beth, came racing out from under the table to greet him. Their fluffy white tails wagging madly as Derek bent down to give each of them a pat.

Julianna was the first to reach him. "Derek, it's wonderful to see you," she said brightly and placed a small kiss on his cheek. Julianna and Jared had very little in common in terms of physical appearances. They were both tall, with dark brown eyes and brown skin. But where Jared's hair was wavy and the colour of dark chocolate, Julianna's was straight and red-brown in colour. Her face was also more rounded where Jared's was more angular.

"How come you never seem that happy to see me?" Jared scowled at his sister

"Oh, little brother, you know acting's never been one of my talents."

"Now, now. Don't start you two," said the Queen. Charlotte Regalias looked like an older version of her daughter, only shorter and much more dainty looking. Her red-brown hair fell over her right shoulder in an elegant braid. She beamed at Derek as she drew nearer. "Derek, dear, it's so good to see you."

Derek returned the smile. "And you, Your Majesty."

She pursed her lips. "You know you don't have to call me that. Just Charlotte will do fine."

"Of course."

Charlotte placed one of her hands to Derek's cheek, frowning slightly. "Are you well? You look a tad pale."

"I'm always pale," Derek pointed out with a half-smile. Next to the royal family, who all had soft brown complexions, Derek looked as pale as milk.

The King was the last to come and greet Derek. Jonathan Regalias was a tall, broad-shouldered man. Just as Julianna looked like their mother, Jared bore a striking resemblance to their father; they both had the same brown curls (although Jonathan's were now streaked with grey), the same long legs.

"Derek," said the King, clapping Derek on the shoulder with a firm hand. "It's been too long. I hope you're well?"

"I am, sir. Thank you."

Jonathan nodded in a satisfied manner. "Good. That's good."

Derek couldn't help but take note of the sword sheathed at the King's belt. He wondered why Jonathan saw it fit to bring a weapon to dinner with his family? Still, Derek didn't speak a word of it.

They took their seats at the table. As the sky grew darker, the servants came out to set the table as well as place wooden stands, holding white crystals no bigger than an adult's fist, around the gazebo. When the servants touched the crystals with small, wand-like sticks, they lit up, brightening up their little corner of the gardens. They were called illuminae crystals. Enchanted pieces of stones that some—or those who could afford to buy them anyway—preferred to use in place of candles.

Not long after, the food was brought out. There was roast chicken glistening with butter and sprinkled with herbs. Stuffed eggs, platters of olives and different kinds of cheese, as well as rolls of bread still warm from the oven.

Jonathan and Charlotte both congratulated Jared and Derek on passing their exam. They also expressed how proud they were of the two of them, which made Derek's chest ache strangely. While Derek enjoyed spending time with Jared's family, it made him feel lonely for his own. For the dinners they used to share and the conversations that would be had over them. Even seeing Jared and Julianna bicker made him long for the relationship he could have had with the sibling he had never gotten the chance to know.

"Weren't you going to ask Arabelle to join us tonight, Mother?"

Julianna asked at some point during the dinner.

Arabelle Aloria was Jared and Julianna's cousin. Her father, Victor Aloria was captain of the Crown's Guard as well as the Queen's elder brother.

"I did," Charlotte replied. "And she was going to come but she's leaving for an assignment early in the morning and she wanted to spend tonight preparing."

After a dessert that was just as plentiful as the dinner, Derek announced that it was time for him to head off. Just as Aldred prepared to show Derek out, Jonathan rose from his chair. "Before you go, may I have a word with you, Derek?"

Derek nodded and Jonathan led him, past the rose bushes and over to the cherry blossom tree that stood not too far from the gazebo, but was just far enough that they could have some privacy.

Clearing his throat, Jonathan said, "I . . . I just wanted to say that I think, if your father were here, he'd be proud of you."

Derek looked down at his feet. "I'm not so sure. He was never too happy when I used to babble about wanting to become a Guardian someday."

A pained look crossed the King's face. Jonathan and Alexander had grown up together, they had been the closest of friends until Alexander left. His father hadn't spoken much about his life as a Guardian, but Derek remembered mention of a childhood friend named Jonathan, in those rare moments when he did talk about his life before Derek and Erica.

Derek had never realised that that childhood friend had actually been the King of Aloseria.

"Things were quite different back then and it's understandable that he wasn't thrilled with the idea of his only son becoming a Guardian. Sometimes I think—" Jonathan cut himself off, saying instead, "But despite that, I do believe he'd be proud of you."

Not knowing what else to say, Derek simply nodded.

"And I also know that your father would have wanted you to have this," Jonathan reached for the sword at his side and pulled it from his belt.

He held it out to Derek. It was a shortsword, sheathed in a black scabbard with a pattern of gold stars. The hilt was made from unadorned silver.

"This was your father's sword," Jonathan explained. "He left it in my possession before he left. After you came to Ember, I told myself that I would give it to you on the day you became a Guardian."

Derek reached for the sword but stopped himself. "May I?"

"Of course."

Taking hold of the sword, he pulled it out of its scabbard. Derek never thought he would think of a weapon as beautiful, but if there was one word he had to use to describe this sword, then that would be it. The blade itself was the same length as Derek's arm, from his elbow to his fingertips, and was coloured a vibrant sky blue.

"It's beautiful, Your Majesty," Derek finally said. "But are you sure you want to give it up?"

Jonathan smiled in a way that reminded Derek very much of

Jared. "That sword was your father's most prized possession. There's spell work on the blade so that it's near impossible to break. It was your grandmother's sword before she passed it onto Alexander. That's why I think it's only right that it gets passed down to you as well."

"I . . . Thank you," Derek said. He slid the sword back into its scabbard. "I should really be heading home now."

"Of course," Jonathan said before motioning for Aldred to show Derek out.

Just as Derek began to follow the elderly footman out of the garden, he turned back to the King and said, "Are you ever going to tell me why my father left?"

"I've told you, Derek. He left because—"

"Because he didn't want to be a Guardian anymore, I know. But there's more to it, isn't there?"

The look in Jonathan's green eyes was sad. "I will tell you. But not today . . . I'm sorry."

Derek tried not to let the disappointment and exasperation show on his face. Instead, he offered the King a quick bow before turning around to follow Aldred.

3

Skree was a small harbour town, nestled amongst the giant black rocks that lined Aloseria's northern shores. It was definitely not one of Aloseria's most reputable towns; Skree was well known for its seedy establishments and unsavoury characters. Thieving was common and street brawls happened at least twice a week.

The Guardians had received a tip-off that a boat containing an illegal shipment of enchanted weapons destined for the black market, would be arriving within a week. It was Darus and Derek's job to find and intercept the shipment.

It was Derek's first assignment since graduating from the Academy and becoming a Guardian. It was both exciting and nerve-wracking (not that he would ever admit to that last one). Finally being tasked with his first assignment made the fact that he was now a Guardian feel all the more real.

Rookies, like Derek, were only allowed to take on assignments alongside a fully-fledged Guardian, like Darus. More experienced

Guardians could also make requests to bring rookies along on assignments, which was how Derek ended up in Skree.

Derek's job was simply to listen, observe and follow Darus's orders. He stood mostly on the sidelines as Darus carried out an inspection of each vessel that docked and took note of the way that Darus conducted himself. Darus as Guardian was quite different from the Darus that Derek was used to. Gone was the laid back, rakish young man and in his place was a serious, straight-backed soldier.

Admittedly, it was rather tedious, being forced to stand back and do nothing but watch, although he understood why. At least he was earning some coin by being there. Assignments were also how Guardians earned their living.

The most exciting part of the day, was when the weapons were discovered in the hold of one of the boats. One of the two men on board tried bolting, but Derek was quick to tackle the man to the ground before he even managed to leave the docks. The illegal shipment was seized—but not without some difficulty. A rather temperamental, flying axe would have decapitated Derek had Darus not pulled him out of the way in time—and the two men were arrested and placed in a holding cell. In the morning, Derek and Darus would escort the smugglers to Black Rock prison, only a few miles south of Skree, where they would face a trial before being sentenced.

That evening, when the sun had almost disappeared behind the horizon, Derek and Darus made their way to the local inn. The inside was just as shabby as the outside, thought Derek, as they stepped through the door. The walls of the front room were painted a dreary grey colour and were cracked and peeling in places. It was mostly empty except for a woman in a ratty dress, eating soup at one of the tables beside the cold hearth and an old man at the front desk with scraggly white hair and beard, with a pipe in his mouth.

"Can I help ya?" He asked when he saw them walk in.

"Yes," said Darus. "We'd like to rent a room for the night."

The old innkeeper squinted at them, eyeing their uniforms. He sucked on the end of his pipe before blowing out a cloud of smoke uncaringly in their direction. "Just the one room, then? Only got one available with two beds. Unless you plan on sharin'?"

Derek didn't like the look on the innkeeper's face.

Darus was unfazed. "We'll take the one with two beds," he said, already reaching for his coin purse.

The innkeeper shrugged. "That'll be eight gold."

Darus handed over the coin and the innkeeper picked up a candle and a ring full of keys that jangled noisily when he walked—or hobbled really.

They followed the innkeeper up the stairwell. He brought them all the way up to the third floor and down a rather narrow corridor, with closed doors lining either side. As they passed one of the doors, Derek heard a sound that could either have been someone laughing or crying. He couldn't make out which.

Finally, the innkeeper stopped at the second last door on the left and, after fumbling with his keys for a bit, unlocked it. The room was dark and cramped. Two single beds stood next to each other at the head of the room. There was also a tiny table and two chairs next to the door and a small window that provided a view only to the tall chimney from the building next door.

"Bathroom's just down the hall to your right," said the innkeeper, lighting the lantern on the crooked shelf by one of the beds before leaving.

"This place is a dump," Derek said.

"Welcome to Skree, my boy," said Darus with mock cheer.

Derek set his pack down on top of the moth-eaten covers of the bed closest to the window and took off his uniform vest. While on duty, Guardians were required to wear a special uniform, not only to identify them as Guardians but to offer them protection. This uniform consisted of a brown vest, knee-high boots and arm and leg guards made of the toughest leather in the land that would make it difficult for any blade to pierce through, but was still light and unrestrictive to wear. Derek also wore a blue shirt under his vest, to symbolise his rookie status. Experienced Guardians, like Darus wore gold coloured shirts.

Darus flopped, face down onto the second bed. He had shed his no-nonsense Guardian persona and donned his usual easygoing demeanour once again. "I'm tired," came Darus's muffled pronouncement.

"It's still early," Derek noted.

Darus turned his head to look at Derek, a few strands of golden-brown hair falling over his face. "Why don't you go look around?

Enjoy the sights?"

"What sights? It's a port town."

"It has its charms. Few as they may be," Darus admitted. "Go on, I can tell you're rearing to go and do some exploring."

Derek said nothing. Darus wasn't wrong about his eagerness to take a proper look around. It was his first time visiting a place that was so close to the sea after all.

"I'll be back before dawn," said Derek jokingly.

Darus gave him his best parental scowl. "You'll be back before eight o'clock or I'm coming out there to look for you."

"Well, we wouldn't want that."

He was half way down the corridor when he heard Darus call out to him, "And by the Goddess, stay away from the taverns!"

Skree at night was much quieter than it was during the day. Derek hardly saw a soul as he walked down the lantern-lit streets, past the ramshackle buildings with their slanted rooftops.

The Screaming Siren, however, Skree's largest tavern (they appeared to have about three), was bursting with life when Derek walked past. The sounds of music, laughter and shouted voices could be heard even from halfway down the street. A tattooed man sitting on a chair out the front with a woman in his lap. He leaned in to whisper something in her ear and the woman threw her head back and let out a squealing laugh. A group of men stood on the balcony above, with drinks in their hands as they sang an out of tune sea shanty at the top of their lungs.

Derek kept walking until he reached the docks. The smell of seawater clung to the air of the entire town, but down here the smell was at its strongest. The docks were empty, except for a pair of scrawny dogs fighting over the remains of a fish. He made his way towards the end of one of the wooden walkways and sat himself down, drawing one leg up against his chest while he let the other dangle over the edge.

The ocean at night was just as dark as the sky. The light from the full moon was reflected on the water's surface, like hundreds of tiny, white gems.

Today was the first time that Derek had ever seen the ocean. He had read about it in books and seen it in paintings, but somehow they had all managed to fail at capturing just how incredible it was to see it with one's own eyes. It was just so . . . vast. He couldn't tear his eyes away. He wondered what it would be like to set sail and live on the sea for months on end. He wondered if his parents had ever seen the ocean?

Derek sat there for some time, simply enjoying the sea breeze and the rhythmic sounds of the lapping waves until he finally decided it was time to head back to the inn. Before Darus decided to come looking for him.

He had just stepped off of the docks and back onto the street when he heard a loud *crack* from nearby.

Instinctively, Derek put his hand to the hilt of his father's sword at his side and turned in the direction the sound had come from. In the darkened alleyway to his right, Derek heard a grunt and could just make out something moving.

Tightening his grip on his sword, Derek cautiously drew nearer to the mouth of the alley. What he found was a man, dressed in tattered clothing and slumped against the brick wall to one side. For a split second, Derek thought the man was simply a drunk, but then he noticed the handle of a knife protruding from the man's stomach and the dark stain spreading across his tunic.

Derek knelt at the man's side, a hand on his shoulder. "Sir? Hey, sir?"

There was no response. The man's eyes were closed, his head lolling to the side. There was blood on the corner of his mouth. Derek reached his hand out to search for a pulse at the man's neck when a hand suddenly wrapped around his wrist in a bruising grip.

"Sir—?"

"Who the fuck are you?" The man demanded, gazing up at him with wild eyes. "Where am I?"

"You're in Skree," Derek explained as calmly as he could. "I'm . . . I'm a Guardian."

The man released Derek's wrist as if it were something foul. "A Guardian?" He growled, disdain clear in his voice.

Derek was well aware that not everyone in Aloseria held amicable feelings towards the Guardians, but there was still something disconcerting about seeing such a look of absolute resentment being directed at him. But it didn't matter what this man's feelings towards the Guardians were, he was seriously injured and in desperate need of a healer.

"Sir," Derek began, taking hold of the man's arm. "We need to get you—"

With a snarl, the wounded man jerked out of his grip. "Keep your fuckin' hands off me!"

"You've been stabbed and you're losing a lot of blood. You need help."

"I know . . . that." With some difficulty, the man pushed himself up onto his feet. "But I don't need help from a . . . from a . . . *Guardian*." He said it as if it were the most heinous insult imaginable.

Derek stood up as the man began to stagger out of the alleyway and onto the street. He was prepared to follow the man, even though he had made it clear he did not want Derek's help when the man staggered and collapsed onto his side.

When Derek knelt by his side once again, the man reached out with one bloodied hand to grasp the front of Derek's shirt and pull him down.

"You . . . damn Guardians," he spat. Literally. Flecks of blood flew out of his mouth as he spoke. "It's . . . because of you. You hunted us . . . made the boss desperate." A hacking cough broke him off. More blood from his mouth hit the stone pathway.

Derek tried to pull away. "I—"

But the man only tightened his grip. "Now it's because of you . . . *assholes*, that I'm gonna die here. Bleedin' like a gutted pig."

"You're not going to die," Derek said but his voice didn't hold much conviction.

The man grinned up at him. It was a chilling sight, the man's face was thin and pale, his eyes full of malice and his smile full of crooked teeth stained red with blood. "I just . . . wish that I could have been there . . . could've seen the looks on all your faces when he . . .

when . . ."

But the man was dead before he could finish.

The grip on Derek's shirt relaxed and the man's hand fell limply to the ground. His face had gone completely slack, his eyes wide and vacant. There was blood staining his lips, chin and neck.

Derek had to look away. That the sight of a dead man lying on the ground, covered in blood, reminded him too much of the way his father had looked the night he died.

Derek's eyes were drawn to the man's other hand, lying limply near the knife in his stomach, and for the first time, he noticed that there was something gripped between the man's fingers.

Driven by curiosity, Derek reached out and carefully opened the man's fingers. He pulled out a crumpled piece of paper and when he opened it up, something fell out from inside, landing on the ground with a light '*ding*'. Derek picked up the small object and held it to the lamplight for closer inspection.

It looked like an ordinary coin; small and round. Only it was a dark, dirty bronze colour and there was a small, red stone, no bigger than Derek's fingernail, embedded in the centre on one side.

He turned his attention back to the paper in his right hand. On the inside was an almost illegible scrawl written in black ink.

We have the second piece and we know where you can find the first piece of Milrath's
amulet.
It should be at a shop called Blackwood's in Florinstone. The store is owned by a mage so be on your guard.
Meet us at the Bone Swamp, at Djedric's Tomb a week from now.
- C

Derek read the first sentence of the note twice more, just to make sure he hadn't misread.

Milrath's amulet. Those two words brought him back to that night, nine years ago, sitting in bed, a storm raging outside while his father told him a story about the daemonic amulet that held the power to grant wishes.

Could this be the same amulet? It had to be. Surely there weren't that many amulets out there known as Milrath's amulet?

Derek looked at the strange coin. Then does that mean this is—

"Oi, what's goin' on over there?"

Derek looked up to see that a group people had started to gather on the road up ahead. He knew how this must look, Derek kneeling over the body of a dead man.

Making a quick decision, Derek slipped both the note and the strange coin into his back pocket, before standing up to deal with the situation at hand.

Once Darus arrived, they had quickly been able to identify the dead man as Swift Hand Horace, a well-known thief. Darus had had at least several encounters with the man over the years. According to some of the locals, the man had been staying in Skree for the past few days, although no one had known who he really was.

It was almost midnight by the time the body had been taken away and Derek and Darus finally returned to their room at the inn. Darus was fast asleep in his bed and snoring softly while Derek was wide awake, sitting on top of the blankets and staring down at the coin in his hand.

Derek hadn't mentioned anything to Darus about the piece or the note he'd found on the dead man. There was a part of him that did feel a little guilty about it but Derek knew that if he showed Darus what he had found, he would confiscate them both and right now, Derek did not want to be parted from them.

He turned the coin over with his fingers and rubbed his thumb over the red stone in its centre. This must be the first piece of the amulet that was spoken about in the note. There's something in his gut that tells him

His father's words from all those years ago came rushing back to him. *"It's said that Asmydionn's sons each left something behind before the Aryanna Vir Fortis banished the daemons. Algron created the strains of vampirism and lycanthropy. Zathral placed a curse on the earth elves that turned them into wicked creatures we call grems. And Milrath created an amulet out of three pieces, that when brought together, could grant wishes."*

Derek's mind started racing. He had the first piece to Milrath's amulet and he knew where he could find the second. And if he had all three pieces? If he brought them all together and was able to have anything he wanted come true? Derek thought of his parents. How he still missed them every day and how missing them was constant and excruciating.

He thought of Goldridge. Of those dark days living under his roof. How those memories still intruded on him and left him feeling weak and ill. How he wanted so desperately to just forget it all.

Darus shifted on the bed beside him and Derek was jolted back to reality. Quietly, he reached over the edge of the bed and slipped the amulet piece into his pack on the floor before lying down on his side.

But even after closing his eyes, sleep would not come that easily to him. His mind was still hard at work, thinking. Planning.

Because he knew what he was going to wish for.

Derek Draco was going to change his past.

4

Magic was everywhere. It was in the air, the water and the leaves that fell from their branches and onto the ground.

However, not everyone could interact with it. Only a certain few could see it, communicate with it and use it. Those certain few were known as mages and Aurelia Blackwood was a mage.

There was only one way to become a mage and that was to be born one, something that no one but the Goddess herself had control over. There was no apparent pattern when it came to someone being born with the ability to control magic. Aurelia herself had been born to two magic-less parents. Her grandparents had been magic-less and, as far as she knew, none of her ancestors before her had been mages. It was simply an accident of birth. Along with being a mage, Aurelia also happened to be a wood elf.

Aurelia lived in a town called Florinstone and spent most of her time running her shop, *Blackwood's Spells, Potions and Magical*

Objects, where she sold an array of enchanted items, potions that she had concocted herself and other magical services.

Aurelia had been having a restless sleep that night when she heard the sounds of someone breaking into her shop downstairs. She had only just made it down the stairs when she saw a man standing in front of the large, glass cabinet down the other end of the shop. Somehow, he had managed to open it and was already tucking something away into the inside of his cloak.

Aurelia's shop had very rarely been broken into over the years. The fact that she was a mage was usually enough to deter people from attempting such a thing. Not many people wanted to cross a mage, especially not when that mage could offer you magical favours for a pretty coin.

Aurelia snapped her fingers, lighting the candelabra on the front counter. The thief startled and turned to face her.

"I'm only going to say this once," Aurelia said. "Put back whatever it is you have taken. Walk out the door and we'll forget that this ever happened."

However, the man was not inclined to comply with Aurelia's request. With surprising speed, the thief had a knife in his hand and was already throwing it straight towards Aurelia. She only just had enough time to raise her left hand and stop the knife in mid-air, the tip of the blade just centimetres from her throat.

Before the thief could move to attack again, Aurelia, turned the knife around with a twirl of her little finger and sent it soaring through the air until it embedded itself into the man's stomach.

She watched as the thief staggered and fell back into one of the small tables, knocking over a display of potion bottles to the ground.

Aurelia crossed the room to where the thief now lay sprawled on the floor amongst scattered bottles. The fabric of his tunic turning red where the knife had gone in.

She'd planned on removing the knife, maybe even healing the man, *if* she was feeling that generous; healing magic was strenuous work after all. But not before she'd questioned him and made sure that he knew never to step foot in Aurelia's shop again. She had just come to stand over the thief's body when he produced a small glass vial from his sleeve and, in one swift movement, had smashed it against the floor. A thick cloud of black smoke erupted from the vial, blanketing spot where the thief lay and Aurelia stood within seconds.

By the time she'd dispersed the smoke, by summoning a strong gust of wind, the thief had vanished.

Vanishing Dust, Aurelia thought irritably as she surveyed her now empty shop. Vanishing Dust was a magical concoction, designed to transport the user to whichever location they are thinking of at the moment the dust is spilled.

That was my last vial too. Now she would have to make arrangements to order more ingredients and desert salamander tails weren't cheap.

The first thing Aurelia did was go over to the open cabinet to see what had been stolen. Once she realised what exactly had been taken, her heart sank with dread. The first piece of Milrath's amulet was gone.

Moving with single-minded determination, Aurelia whirled around and strode towards the curtained doorway behind the front counter.

Behind it was the back room where she kept her inventory. There were boxes piled on top of each other containing miscellaneous objects, a table in the corner where she made her potions. A carnivorous plant from Samwea that was currently snoring inside of its locked cage.

She climbed the narrow stairwell with creaking steps that lead to her bedroom, which also acted as a private study, she clicked her fingers and the candles around the room lit up. The room was small and cluttered, most of the wall space was taken up by shelves filled with books, haphazard stacks of papers and jars containing almost everything from dead plants to butterflies' wings to sabre lion eyeballs. There was just enough room to fit her narrow bed, a wardrobe and a desk that was just as equally cluttered as the rest of the room. Above it was an open window and perched on the windowsill was a black raven.

"Ah, Cora," Aurelia said to the raven as she crossed the room to her desk. "Finally back from your hunt? Too bad you just missed out on all the fun."

Cora cawed at her in response before spreading her massive wings and alighting onto her wooden perch across the room.

Animal Familiars were very common among mages. Using

magic took energy, just like any physical activity, and when that energy ran out, it meant that a mage could not use any more magic until they regained their strength. However, by binding an animal to themselves—creating a Familiar—a mage would have an extra reserve of energy to draw upon if need be.

When she was a girl of nine, living in the Great Forest, homeland of the wood elves, Aurelia had come across a raven chick that had fallen from its nest. Aurelia had taken her back home and tended to her. Her parents had told her that the chick was too young to survive without its mother and would not make it. But Aurelia had been determined to keep the chick alive, just as the chick had been determined live. Even before Aurelia made Cora her Familiar, the two had shared a special bond.

Aurelia crossed the room to one of the many shelves and pulled out a round crystal ball, half-hidden by a pile of old spell notes. A Scrying Glass was an enchanted object—usually a mirror or glass orb—that allowed one to see whatever events they wanted to see, so long as it was taking place at that very moment. A Scrying Glass could not be used to see into the past or the future, only the present. They could also be used to help find one's lost set of earrings if that's how one wished to use it.

Aurelia set the Glass down on the desk and placed her left hand on top of it. "Show me what was stolen from me."

The Scrying Glass began to glow an eerie, white light as an image began to form within it. It wasn't long before she saw the piece with the red stone being held in another's hands and when

Aurelia saw who was holding it, she felt as if all the air had been knocked out of her.

For it was not the thief that had been in her shop only minutes ago, but a boy, no older than sixteen if Aurelia had to guess.

All thoughts of the amulet piece were driven from her mind as Aurelia leaned in and was able to get a closer look at the boy's face. His eyes were a rich blue, just like his father's. But the black hair that fell into his eyes, the mouth that formed a perfect bow shape, even the slightly pointed ears, were all *her*.

He was the spitting image of Erianna.

Aurelia felt pressure behind her eyes and a tightening in her chest as if someone had tied a rope around her heart and pulled it taut. It was a feeling Aurelia had not felt for some years and she knew it was the remnants of grief rearing its head.

She noticed that the boy was dressed in the ever familiar uniform of the Guardians and Aurelia felt another twinge of sadness. So after all the effort his parents went through to keep their child away from harm, he had ended up becoming a Guardian after all.

She finally took notice of the familiar figure of the thief from before, lying on the ground in front of the boy. Aurelia only had to take one look at the man's face to know that he was dead. *Serves him right,* she thought.

She watched as the boy turned his head to look at something out of Aurelia's field of vision before he pocketed the piece of the amulet as well as a piece of paper and rose from his crouching position. Having seen enough, Aurelia removed her hand from the Scrying Glass and the image of the boy disappeared and the Glass went blank again.

Aurelia was still for a moment, still trying to process what—*who*—she had just seen. Finally, she leaned back in her chair, tipping her head up towards the ceiling. She gazed up at the shadows that danced along the rafters from the candle's light. Behind her, she could hear Cora busying herself with preening.

I really need a smoke. With that thought, Aurelia summoned a cigar and lit it with a tiny flame from the tip of her finger. There were many who criticized her habit of smoking over the years. Who said it was, *"unladylike"*. She was sure her mother would have had a few things to say about her habit too if she could see her now. Thankfully, Aurelia had never been one to care much for other people's opinions.

She felt at a complete loss. Of all the things she could have expected, she had most certainly not expected to find the stolen amulet piece in the hands of Erianna's son. What would the boy do with it now? Did he even know what it was? What it could do? Aurelia dearly hoped that he didn't.

She took another long inhale from her cigar.

Cora made an anxious clucking sound, sensing her master's unease.

Perhaps she should try getting in contact with the boy? Find some way to get the amulet piece away from him a—

No, she thought. *No, you made a vow that you would not get involved. Erianna would not want you getting involved with her son.*

After a few more moments, Aurelia put out her cigar and pushed herself up from her seat. She snapped her fingers and the candles went out, leaving the room blanketed in darkness once again.

It was late and she felt suddenly very weary, her mind felt clouded and there was an ache building between her temples. She would sleep and she would try to forget about this whole situation.

For years she had done her best to safeguard the first piece of Milrath's amulet, but now it was out of her hands.

You will not get involved.

But sleep did not come easy to Aurelia Blackwood and then when it finally did come, she found her dreams filled with a woman with long, raven black hair and a radiant smile on her face.

5

Derek was lying in bed, staring up at the ceiling. His mind was a tangle of thoughts and his heart felt heavy with emotion.

They had returned home almost eight hours ago and he had barely slept the night before in Skree. He had been distracted throughout their escort of the two weapons smugglers to Black Rock prison, as well as on the journey home. Distracted by the bronze piece that was hidden away in his pack.

All of Derek's thoughts up until now had been about Milrath's amulet and finding the next two pieces. He thought about how he would use the amulet to change his past, for his parents to have never been murdered on that night nine years ago. For him to have never been adopted by the Mayor of Windfell. To just be able to live his life as if neither of those horrors had ever happened to him.

Strangely enough, when Derek actually had managed to find sleep the night before, it had been filled with dreams—no, not a dream, it had been more like a memory, replaying itself through his sleep—of the morning after that horrible night nine years ago. When he had woken up alone in an unfamiliar room. In the Mayor's room in his manor house at Windfell. He had been told that he'd been found lying unconscious on the side of the road just outside of the town gates. The Mayor himself had told him of what had transpired the night before. That his parents were dead and that Derek was the only survivor. Derek remembered how he had refused to believe the Mayor's words at first. He had screamed at the Mayor and called him a liar, much to the shock of everyone else who had been present at the time. But Goldridge had looked completely unbothered by Derek's outburst. He had taken Derek down to the Crypt, where the bodies of those who died in Windfell were kept before they were burned, as was customary in Aloseria.

It had been dark and damp down there as Derek was led through the underground halls. And then he had seen them. Lying on top of a high, stone bench, had been the bodies of his father and mother. Or at least, he had been told that the two, blackened corpses were those of his parents. That it was a miracle they had managed to salvage the bodies at all. Derek had stood there for what seemed like an eternity, just staring at the two bodies—at his parents— burned beyond recognition. He had thought to ask what happened to the baby in his mother's belly, his younger sibling, but as soon as that question had entered his head, it had been replaced by the answer. The baby was gone too. If his mother had died then so had the baby.

He had started to cry then. Noisy, heaving sobs that wracked his whole body. The truth and the enormity of his loss too much for his young self to handle.

The Mayor had placed his arms around Derek's shaking form then, holding his small body close. "There, there, my child," he had said softly, stroking Derek's hair. "It's all right. I am here for you now. I'll take good care of you."

A whining sound tore Derek out of his dark memories. He looked over to where Finn and Daisy were lying on the floor and, what Derek could only describe as, play-fighting. Finn lay on his back, batting his paws at Daisy's muzzle and then snatching them away before she could grab them in her mouth.

Of course, Derek knew that changing his past might also mean undoing everything that had happened to him since he had met Darus. That it might mean losing the life he's made here in Ember. In Ember, Derek had Darus. He had Jared. He was a Guardian just like he'd wanted to be since he was young.

But it still wasn't enough. Not without his mother's melodic laughter and his father's warm arms around him. Not with the memories of bruising fingers on his skin and breath that reeked of whiskey in his face. It was like an open wound that refused to heal; painful and impossible to ignore.

If he had a chance to take that pain away then he was going to take it.

Derek looked up at the portrait that hung on the wall above his bed. It was a family portrait, not of his family—well, not exactly— but of his father's family. The portrait had been given to him by

Jonathan, not long after he came to Ember. It was the only thing left of the Viseric family and Jonathan had said he'd wanted Derek to have it so that he would know even a little bit about the family he'd never gotten to know. In the painting were his grandparents, Arthur and Esmeralda Viseric. His grandfather had been tall and fair-haired with broad shoulders and kind eyes. His grandmother had a much more stern look to her face. Her hair was brown like Alexander's had been, and her eyes were the same sky blue.

Standing between them was Alexander. Looking about fourteen with tousled hair and a lop-sided smile on his freckled face. Beside him was his twin sister, Alana, Derek's aunt. She looked almost like a mirror image of his father, same smile, same freckles, same short, brown hair. Alana had been killed on an assignment when she was only fifteen.

His grandparents had also died before Derek was born, but he had never been told how. Was that why his father had left Ember? To get away from the painful memories of his dead family? Derek supposed he could understand that.

He heard the sound of the front door opening and closing downstairs. Darus was home. He had left some time ago to hand in a report of the assignment to the Mandatrum—a tall, white building where Guardians reported to receive assignments—as all Guardians were required to do after completing an assignment.

Daisy leapt to her feet and bolted out of the room, leaving behind Finn, who looked quite put out at having been abandoned in the middle of their game.

Derek got off the bed and made his way downstairs, Finn trailing after him. He found Darus in the kitchen, already preparing something to eat. Daisy was scratching herself by the table. When Finn saw her, he ran up and tackled her from behind, startling her so badly she knocked her head against the table leg.

"Good morning," Darus said when he saw Derek. "Would you like some breakfast?"

"It's almost one-thirty."

"Would you like some lunch?"

Derek cocked his head to the side. "Wouldn't it be brunch?"

"Don't talk semantics with me, kid. It's been too long a morning."

"Do you want some help?" Derek asked instead.

"Sure. You can take care of the eggs."

They cooked their breakfast / lunch / brunch together mostly in silence.

Derek still hadn't mentioned anything to Darus about the amulet. Or his plan to look for the other two pieces so that he could make his wish. He knew that he needed to, especially if he was hoping to make it to the Bone Swamp a week from now. Derek couldn't help but feel nervous at the thought of telling Darus. He wanted Darus to support him—maybe even join him—on this quest. He wanted him to understand that, even though it was a mad and reckless gambit, this was something Derek *needed* to do.

They plated up their food, soft boiled eggs with sausages on the side, and sat down at the table together. Again, they ate mostly in silence.

When Darus was finished, he stood up from his chair. "All right, I'm off."

"Where are you going?" Derek asked.

"I promised Lila I'd join her for some training exercises," Darus explained. "So I might not be home until later this evening."

Lila Delron was Darus's closest friend since childhood. Derek liked Lila, she was one of the few people who could really get under Darus's skin and she took great pleasure in sharing embarrassing childhood stories of him with Derek.

Darus made to move away when Derek spoke up. "Wait, I, uh, actually there was something I wanted to talk to you about."

Darus paused. "Okay." He sank back down into his chair. "What is it?"

Derek took a deep breath before starting. "Have you ever heard of the story of Milrath's amulet?"

". . . I have. Why?"

"I found this on the bandit that died last night in Skree." Derek dug out the folded note from his pants' pocket and handed it to Darus.

He purposefully didn't show or say anything about having already found the first piece. He'd wait to see Darus's reaction after reading the note before—*if*—he did.

It didn't take long for Darus to read through the note. Derek watched as his brow lowered while he read before his grey eyes flicked up to Derek. "And why are you only telling me now? What's this really about, Derek?"

"I want to find all the pieces of the amulet," he said, cutting straight to the point. "I want to use it to have my wish granted."

"Which is?"

"To change my past. To change it so that my family was never murdered. So that I never had to live with *him*."

Darus's expression changed from hard and impassive to something akin to *pitying* and by the Goddess, Derek hated it. It was the expression people had often worn when they found out both of his parents were dead. There was something just so infuriating about it as if he were some fragile, *broken* thing. He never thought he'd see that expression Darus's face.

"Derek," Darus said softly. "You can't."

Derek frowned. "Why not?"

"Because even if it does really exist—"

"It does exist," Derek cut in adamantly.

"—it's a daemonic object. It's daemonic magic. That's the worst form of magic there is. That makes it highly dangerous and not to be trusted."

"How can you be so sure?" said Derek stubbornly.

Of course, he knew where Darus was coming from. There were three different types of magic in this world. Natural magic; the magic that was all around them. Dark magic; imitation magic that could be used by anyone, mage or not, but only by taking the life of another living creature. And then there was daemonic magic.

Pure chaos and malevolence combined. It was a magic that was unique only to daemons.

"Come on now, Derek," Darus was saying. "When has anyone come across a daemonic artefact and not had something terrible happen to them? Like Dima LaStrosa, that Tybeni historian. He found Asmydionn's sword and as soon as he touched it, his hand was so badly burned his whole arm had to be cut off."

"So what are you saying?" Derek demanded. "That I should just forget all about it? Ignore the chance to have my family back?"

"Yes," Darus said without hesitation.

Derek couldn't believe it. Darus wanted him to forget about it? Just like that? He had been given an opportunity to right the wrongs of his past, to be reunited with his loved ones, something Derek had yearned for, for years, and he was just supposed to *forget* it? Derek felt his nails bite into the skin of his palms. He hadn't even realised that he was clenching his fingers.

Darus had risen from his chair to kneel in front of him. He placed a hand on top of Derek's. "Derek, listen to me, I know you miss your parents. And I know you want to forget about . . ." He trailed off, seemingly unable to continue that part. "But you need to move on. We can't change our pasts, no matter how much we want to and in the end, all any of us can do when misfortune knocks on our door is try to move on with our lives."

Derek pulled his hand out from under Darus's and fixed him with a glare. "Don't speak as if you understand. You may have lost your mother but that doesn't mean you could possibly understand

69

anything else about what I've been through."

The older man looked stunned, and possibly a little hurt, but Derek tried to ignore that. "I know that. But don't forget we've lived under the same roof for six years. I know how your past affects you—"

"Then how can you possibly say that I should give up on this?" He was on his feet now. "If you know, then you'd let me do this."

Darus got to his feet, staring down at Derek. His eyes like steel. "No. I can't allow you to do this, Derek. It's too dangerous."

How could Darus say that? How could he not *get* it? Derek felt the anger and frustration, building within him start to boil over. "So what? You say, 'no', and I'm just supposed to do as you say? Obey your commands like some obedient little pet?"

Darus looked caught off guard by that comment. "It's not just about what I say. You know the laws—"

Derek laughed without any humour. "'Be a good boy, Derek and do as I tell you'. That's what *he* used to say to me. I was always supposed to do as he told me or else. What's going to happen if I don't do as *you* tell me? Are you going to get the cane out and beat me bloody?"

"You know I would never," said Darus, his voice and expression hard as stone. "You know what? That's enough. We're finished speaking about this."

Darus made to turn away but Derek wasn't finished. "Maybe you should lock me up first? To make certain I don't run off."

"I said that's enough, Derek."

"That's what he would've done, you know? Maybe you actually aren't so different from him," Derek sneered.

"Don't you *dare*—"

"Maybe the only difference is that you like them a bit ol—" He was cut off abruptly as his head snapped to the side. A stinging pain blossom in his right cheek.

Darus was standing right in front of him, his chest rising and falling harshly beneath his shirt. His hand still raised from striking Derek.

Darus had hit him.

Darus had *never* hit him before. Derek looked up at him with wide, shocked eyes and was even more shocked to see the look on Darus's face. It was a look of barely suppressed fury. Darus's mouth was pressed into a hard line, his nostrils flaring and his narrowed eyes were fixed firmly on Derek. It was such a foreign look on Darus's face. Derek had seen Darus angry before, but never like this and never directed at him.

In that moment, his eyes seemed to blaze with absolute fury.

Derek felt the bite of tears in his eyes. Ducking his head, he ran straight for the front door and kept running even once he was outside.

He kept running until he reached the giant clock tower in the city's centre. Until his legs felt like they could carry him no longer.

Slumping against the stone steps of the tower, Derek dug the heels of his palms into his eyes. *Stupid, stupid,* he told himself furiously. It was ridiculous to cry over something like this.

But it wasn't the throbbing in his cheek that brought tears to his eyes and a lump in his throat. It wasn't even that he had been hit, but the fact that *Darus* had hit him. That Darus had looked at him like that. Like he couldn't stand the sight of him.

Derek lifted his head and gazed up at the clouds that dotted the sky.

Shame washed over him. It was his fault, he knew it. He had let his anger get the best of him and spoken thoughtlessly and uttered words that he didn't even mean. That he knew weren't true.

Now because Derek had decided to throw a tantrum like a child, Darus probably despised him. Just that thought made something curdle in Derek's stomach. He dropped his head against his knees and just tried to keep his breathing under control.

"Derek?"

He looked up at the sound of his name to see Jared standing before him.

"What are you doing moping around here?" The other boy started to smile until he must have caught the look on Derek's face and his brows drew together in concern. "Is everything all right?"

Derek's eyes flicked to the guard that stood a small distance behind Jared, noticeable by their golden armour, glinting in the sunlight, and blue cape. Members of the royal family were to be escorted by a member of the Crown Guard at all times when they were outside the palace grounds.

With Jared standing before him, Derek felt the sudden need to talk to someone, but he wasn't about to do so here, not with so many people around. So he got to his feet. "Is there somewhere private we can talk?"

* * *

"An amulet of wishes, huh?" said Jared wonderingly.

He and Derek were seated on one of the plush, red sofas in Jared's bedroom. Like many of the rooms in the palace, Jared's room was oversized and opulent. The walls were plain white while the ceiling was painted to look like the sky at sunset. A huge, canopied bed at the front of the room and each of the three arched windows was draped with heavy, red velvet curtains. They were currently pushed aside to allow the midday sunlight to stream into the room.

One of the servants had brought them a plate of small pastries and lemon juice with ice not long after they arrived. Derek had not touched any of the cakes, which Jared couldn't help but find odd; Derek had a fiendish sweet tooth. His friend seemed unusually subdued. Even when Derek started telling him of the night he'd spent in Skree, how he had come across a dying man in an alleyway. How he had found an odd-looking coin that was actually part of some enchanted amulet that could supposedly grant wishes, something about Derek seemed closed off.

"Can I see it?" Jared asked. "The piece you found?"

He watched as Derek reached into his back pocket, pulled out what looked like a bronze coin and handed it to him.

"It doesn't look like much," Jared noted, examining the piece. It looked like any regular coin, except for the dark bronze colour and the red gem in its centre.

"I'm sorry it's not to your liking," said Derek, before taking a sip from his lemon juice.

Jared handed the piece back. "And you know where to find the other pieces?"

"According to the note, one of them is in the Bone Swamp."

"Have you told Darus yet?"

The ice in Derek's glass clinked as his hand twitched. "I told him this morning."

"And?" Jared prompted.

"He's . . . Not thrilled with the idea," Derek said. "He refused to let me go."

Jared stayed quiet. He knew Derek was leaving something out and he knew it had to do with his unusual mood. Had Derek and Darus fought? Jared was a naturally curious person, sometimes to his own detriment, and he wanted so badly to press Derek with more questions. To understand what was going on inside his head.

Above all that, he wanted to comfort Derek. He wanted to reach out and brush his hair behind his ear. Jared wanted to put his arms around him, wanted to press a kiss to the red mark blooming on his cheek. He wanted so badly to be able to do those things because the truth was, Jared was hopelessly infatuated with his best friend.

Instead, he said, "But I'm guessing that's not going to stop you?"

Derek was looking down at the piece in his palm, strands of his dark hair shadowing his eyes. "No."

"So what are you going to do?" Jared repositioned himself so that his legs were tucked under him. "Sneak out of the city in the dead of night and travel all over Aloseria in search of these amulet pieces?"

Jared had said it sarcastically but by the look on Derek's face, he appeared to be seriously thinking it over.

"Wait, you're not seriously considering it are you?" said Jared. "You do realise that, as a Guardian, leaving the city without the crown's permission is a crime, right?"

Now Derek looked at him as if he were being daft. "And you think your father will give me permission to leave for something like this?"

Jared shrugged. "He might if you ask—"

"No," Derek said, shaking his head. "He won't. So there's no point in asking."

Jared chewed on his bottom lip, a habit his mother was constantly trying to nag him out of. "So you'd really be willing to commit a crime just for this?" He nodded at the piece in Derek's hand.

Derek's expression hardened. "I don't expect you to understand," he said. "But I can't just ignore an opportunity like this. I have to have them back. I have to . . . I *need* this."

Silence hung between them, broken only by the sound of birdsong from outside.

Despite being one of his closest friends, Jared didn't actually know a great deal of Derek's past. What he did know, had been told to him by his parents, not Derek himself. He knew that Derek had grown up outside a town called Windfell with his mother and father. That one night they had been murdered and Derek, as the only survivor, had been taken in by Windfell's mayor. He knew that Derek's mother had been pregnant at the time too.

Jared did know, however, at least two things from Derek. One was that Derek held no love for his previous adoptive father. When Jared had asked him, years ago while two of them sat on the rooftop of the palace greenhouse, eating olives and spitting the pips over the side, whether he missed the Mayor, a look so dark had crossed the other boy's face. He had said, "Not in the slightest."

Two was that Derek still missed his parents. Incredibly so. Not that Derek had ever admitted it out loud, but Jared saw it in the way Derek looked when Jonathan put an arm around Jared's shoulders. When his mother pressed a kiss to his cheek and even when he argued with Julianna.

If I lost Mother and Father and Julianna, Jared thought to himself. *Would I be willing to risk everything to get them back?*

The answer to that was an easy one.

"All right," said Jared. "But I'm coming with you."

Derek stared at him in bewilderment. "What?"

"Did I stutter? I said I'm coming with you."

Derek seemed at a loss for words for a good few seconds. He was staring at Jared with those vivid blue eyes as if he were a puzzle he couldn't solve. "Why?" Derek finally asked.

"Well," Jared responded, leaning back against the sofa in a casual manner. "Someone needs to keep an eye on you and make sure you don't get yourself killed."

Derek frowned. "Are you bringing my fighting prowess into question?"

"Maybe just a little bit," Jared said with a teasing grin.

"How dare you." Derek returned the grin and Jared felt his heartbeat stutter at the sight.

Jared had never been a shy person and certainly never when it came to his feelings of attraction for others. When he was eight-years-old, an ambassador from Tybenia had come to the palace to discuss trade negotiations with his father on behalf of the Tybeni queen. During that time, Jared had come to fancy the ambassador's seventeen-year-old son, and at a banquet dinner one night, he had made a grand declaration of love in front of quite a number of people. Poor Pavel had been mortified of course. Jared's parents had both been positively fuming, the ambassador had been speechless and Julianna had burst into a fit of hysterical laughter.

But with Derek, Jared did not feel that confidence. Just the idea of announcing his feelings like that to Derek made him want to crawl under his bed sheets and never come out. Jared wasn't sure why this was, perhaps it was because of the fear he felt at the possibility of Derek not returning his feelings? That if he told Derek the truth about how he felt, then he wouldn't want to be friends with Jared anymore.

Jared forced down such dreary thoughts and tried to ignore the foreboding feeling building in his gut. He knew this wasn't a good idea, running away to look for a supposedly magical amulet that he'd never even heard of up until now, but Jared also knew what this meant to Derek and Derek was his best friend. That was more than enough reason for him to join Derek on this quest. Even if it was an insane one.

"You know this will probably be dangerous, right?" said Derek after a few moments.

Jared made a dismissive sound. "What kind of Guardian would I be if I shied away from danger?"

"And you know we'll get into a lot of trouble? Everyone will panic when they realise that the Prince is missing. The Queen, I'm sure, will be *very* upset when she realises you've run away."

By the Goddess. "I'm . . . I'm the Prince of Aloseria and second in line to the throne. I'm not afraid of my mother."

"Oh, you should be."

Jared and Derek both started at the new voice. Jared turned around and saw that leaning against his now open door frame, was a girl around their age, with golden-blonde hair, tied into a braid and dressed in Guardian uniform with the blue shirt of a rookie.

"Arabelle?" Jared said to his cousin in surprise. "What are you doing here?"

"I just got back from an assignment," Arabelle explained as she sauntered into the room and came to sit on the couch opposite them. "It's been a while since I last dropped by and I thought I'd come around and say hello. Now, what's all this I hear about running away?"

Jared felt Derek tense up beside him and the two of them exchanged hesitant looks. If it was up to Jared, he would tell Arabelle. He and Arabelle had grown up together and been extremely close all of their lives. He trusted her but this wasn't his secret to tell.

"Okay then," said Arabelle when neither of them said anything. "I guess I'll just go find a guard and let them know that the Prince is planning on running away. Or maybe I'll go straight to Aunt Charlotte and Uncle Jonathan?" She stood up and made her way back towards the door. "I think I heard one of the servants mention something about them taking tea in the dining room downstairs—"

"Wait." It was Derek who called out to her. "Come back, we'll tell you."

Arabelle turned around with a smile on her face and resumed her seat across from them.

Jared looked to Derek in surprise. "Are you sure?"

"No," he admitted. "But I'd rather not risk her telling your parents."

"If it helps," said Jared, looking from Derek to Arabelle. "I trust her."

"Thank you, Jared." Arabelle smiled at her cousin.

Derek sighed and rubbed at the bridge of the nose and said to Jared, "I'll let you do the honours."

So he told Arabelle what Derek had told him earlier. About the amulet, how Derek already had the first piece and their plan to sneak out of the city to find the other two pieces.

"An amulet that grants wishes?" Arabelle said when Jared was finished. "Can I have a look at it?"

Derek reached across the small table that stood in between the sofas and gave the first piece to Arabelle. A small line appeared between her golden eyebrows as they drew together in a frown. "It doesn't look like much."

"That's what I said!"

"So now that we've told you, you're not going to say anything to anyone?" Derek asked.

"I won't say anything," Arabelle agreed. "As long as you promise to take me with you."

Jared's mouth fell open. "What? No! Arabelle you are not coming with us."

"And why not?" Arabelle demanded, folding her arms and scowling. "Is this quest for boys only?"

"No," admitted Derek mildly. "But why would you even want to come with us?"

"Maybe I also have a wish I want to have granted."

"Like what?"

"Oh, you know, beauty that never fades. A horde of devoted admirers. That sort of thing."

Having known her his entire life, Jared could read Arabelle just as well as he could read his own name on paper. Therefore he knew she wasn't telling the truth. Arabelle wasn't the type of person to care about looks and she was far too concerned with her duties as a Guardian to want a horde of suitors at her beck and call. It took Jared all of three seconds to realise what Arabelle could possibly want to use the amulet to wish for and he was hit with a wave of sadness. *Oh . . . Arabelle.*

She looked up at the two of them. Her expression was serious and her chin tilted up defiantly. "I've been a Guardian for a year now. I have more experience with what's beyond the city walls than either of you and if you won't let me come with you, I'll go straight to the King and Queen about what you just told me."

Jared's sympathy gave way to annoyance. "You just said you wouldn't tell anyone."

"And I won't. So long as you agree to let me come with you."

Jared opened his mouth to argue further, but decided against it and looked to Derek. In the end, it was his decision.

Derek's eyes were closed, his brow furrowed in thought and he had two fingers pressed to his temple as if trying to ward off a headache. It seemed that both Jared and Arabelle were waiting with bated breath until Derek finally said, "Fine. You can come with us."

A wide grin broke across Arabelle's face. "Wonderful! So, when do we leave?"

6

It was another two days before Derek, Arabelle and Jared were finally ready to leave on their quest.

They couldn't wait too long to leave, not if they wanted to reach the Bone Swamp before the week was up. But before that, they had to make plans, such as what supplies they needed to take and what lies they would tell to their families to keep them from realising (for a day or two at least) that they were gone. They also had to find a way out of the heavily guarded city without being seen. Luckily, Jared had a quick solution to that.

"There's a secret passageway in the kitchens," said Jared one afternoon while the three of them were tucked into a booth at The Gold Rose—a tavern that specifically catered to the youths of the city. "It was made as an emergency exit and it leads you right outside of the city walls. The guards never patrol around there since it can only be opened from the inside."

So it was decided that they would use this secret passageway to sneak out of Ember the very next day. Derek and Arabelle would wait until midnight before sneaking away from their homes and into the palace, where Jared would then lead them into the kitchens and through the secret passageway.

It was a quarter to midnight and Derek was in his room packing some last-minute items into his pack. Finn was perched on the edge of his desk, tracking Derek's movements with those keen eyes of his. His tail twitching back and forth.

Derek didn't want to be slowed down by lugging around a too-heavy bag, so he kept his supplies as practical as he could; a change of clothes, a bedroll, a bit of coin, some food and a water flask. The last item, the piece of Milrath's amulet, Derek wrapped up in an old handkerchief and tucked it into the very bottom of his pack.

Straightening up, Derek glanced over at the clock. Five more minutes until midnight. He grabbed his father's sword, which lay on the bed next to his pack and attached it to his belt. Derek hefted his pack onto one shoulder, gave Finn one last scratch under the chin, before leaving his room.

Downstairs was quiet, except for the rumbling sound of Daisy snoring from her basket in the lounge room. Darus wasn't home so it made it all the more easier for Derek to leave unnoticed.

Following their argument, things had been rather strained between Derek and Darus. When Derek had returned home later that day, he and Darus had apologised to each other, but it had still done little to ease things between them. Meals were eaten in silence if they were even eaten together at all. Darus had spent little time around the house today and Derek could not help but feel as if Darus were avoiding him. Perhaps Darus really did hate him now? Derek felt his throat constrict at the thought.

It was because of this that Derek had decided against telling Jared and Arabelle the full truth of the amulet—in a way, it was lucky that neither of them had ever heard of Milrath's amulet. Not many probably would though, since daemons were a dark part of Aloseria's history. One that many preferred not to discuss unless necessary.

Derek had no idea how Arabelle and Jared would react if he let them know that it was created by a daemon. What if they reacted like Darus had? What if they tried to talk him out of this whole plan? What if they didn't even wait to try and talk him out of it and just went to the King instead?

No, it was best that Derek just kept this secret to himself. Although, that decision didn't come without some guilt.

It was no matter, Derek thought as he made his way, silently, over to the front door. He would be back with his family soon enough and Jared, Arabelle and Darus and everyone in Ember will have never known him.

He was so deep in thought that he jumped when he felt something brush against his leg. He looked down to find Finn. The cat looked up at him, meowed and then continued to make figure eights between Derek's legs. For a moment, Derek had the absurd notion that Finn was trying to stop him from leaving. Kneeling down, Derek picked up the cat and held him close, scratching him under the chin. Finn closed his eyes and leaned into the touch, his purrs growing louder.

"I'm sorry, Finn," Derek whispered against the soft fur. He thought back to a rainy night, almost three years ago when he first found Finn, no more than a few weeks old, alone in the middle of the cold streets and mewling pitifully. At the time, Derek had felt a sort of kinship with the kitten. He had known what it was like to be all alone and afraid.

Derek tightened his hold on the animal who had been a constant companion to him ever since. He hoped that, if he did manage to change his past, Finn wouldn't be left alone in that street gutter. That someone else would find him.

Finally, Derek set the cat back down before he slipped out the front door without a backward glance.

* * *

"Oh, can't you read one more chapter? *Please?*"

Arabelle turned back to face her younger brother from where she stood in front of his bookshelf. She had just been reading another chapter of *Annabeth and the White Wolf,* to him for the past fifteen minutes. She smiled. "Absolutely not. It's almost midnight. That means it's *way* past your bedtime."

Amias Aloria pouted from where he sat in his bed, propped up against the puffy white pillows. "But I want to know what's going to happen next."

"You can read the rest of it tomorrow night," said Arabelle, making her way back over to the bed to tuck Amias in.

"But tomorrow night is *ages* away."

"It's not that long, Amias. Only nineteen hours to be exact."

Arabelle looked up to see her other younger brother, Callum, standing in the now open doorway. He was dressed in his nightclothes, his curly, black hair mussed from his pillow and his slightly oversized glasses sat crookedly on the bridge of his nose. Both Callum and Amias had the same head of black curls and dark, brown skin and dark eyes. With her own straight, blonde hair and paler brown skin, one wouldn't even think that Arabelle was related to them at all.

"Callum, what are you doing out of bed?" Arabelle scowled.

With all the imperiousness a twelve-year-old could muster, Callum crossed the room and sat himself down at the foot of his younger brother's bed. "I couldn't sleep. I think it's because there's a full moon tonight."

She watched as Callum lazily plucked a stuffed rabbit from where it sat near the foot of the bed and began to fiddle with it. Amias sat up immediately. At six-years-old, he was at that stage where he couldn't stand others touching what was his.

"Give it back," he snapped, grabbing for the rabbit.

Callum teasingly held the toy out of reach, grinning down at the younger boy. "What's the magic word?"

Before Amias could start wailing and wake up their parents, Arabelle expertly snatched the rabbit out of Callum's hand and handed it back to her littlest brother.

"Don't tease him just before he's about to go to sleep," she told Callum irritably.

Unperturbed, Callum just rolled onto his stomach and began kicking his legs in the air. "I saw you had a bag all packed on your bed."

Arabelle's scowl deepened and she placed her hands on her hips. "You know you're not allowed in my room without permission."

"The door was open."

"No, it wasn't."

Callum shrugged. "So what are you packing for? Are you heading off somewhere?"

Amias looked up at her with wide, black eyes. His expression was puzzled. "You're leaving?"

Inwardly, she cursed Callum's nosiness. The little imp knew he wasn't supposed to go into Arabelle's room unless he had permission. It was a rule that even their parents strictly enforced, but then again, Callum was never really one for obeying the rules.

"I'm going on an assignment in their morning." The lie fell easily from Arabelle's mouth.

"Didn't you just get back from an assignment?" asked Callum.

"Yes and now I've been given another one. It's not exactly unheard of, little brother."

Now Amias just looked saddened. He was hugging the stuffed rabbit to his chest and it made him look even smaller than usual. "But . . . who's going to read my story to me at night?"

"I'm sure Da will," she said softly, petting his tousled curls. "Or Am— your mother. If you just ask them."

This didn't seem to comfort Amias, who said, "But they don't do the voices like you do."

"I know," Arabelle leaned down to press a kiss to the crown of his head. "But just until I get back, all right?"

Amias nodded glumly and finally lay back against the pillows, allowing his sister to tuck him in.

Once Arabelle had managed to wrangle Callum back into his bed as well, she quietly made her way down the hallway, passing the grand staircase that led down to the first floor. She had just turned the corner when she almost walked right into her step-mother.

Amara Aloria was dressed in a nightgown and a pale blue shawl wrapped around her shoulders. Her glossy, black hair was pinned back, only stray wisps coming loose around her face. Her normally dark skin looked even darker in the nighttime gloom.

She looked down at her step-daughter, startled. "Arabelle? What are you doing up?"

"I was . . . I was just heading back to bed after checking up on Amias."

"Why? Is he unwell?"

"No, he just couldn't sleep so I read to him for a little bit."

"Until now?" Amara frowned disapprovingly. "It's nearly midnight, Arabelle. Next time just send him back to bed, not read to him. Those stories might make him too excited to fall asleep."

Arabelle just nodded. "Right, sorry."

They stood there silently for a moment before Arabelle couldn't help but ask, "So, what are you doing up?"

"Hm?" Amara distractedly tucked some hair back behind her ear. "Oh, I was feeling restless so I thought I'd go and make myself a cup of tea." Amara had been born and raised in Samwea, only coming to Aloseria when she was in her twenties. Even now, in her forties, the rough, guttural edges of her Samweanese accent hung around her Aloserian when she spoke.

Arabelle was just about to say something else when Amara stepped past her. "It's getting late," she said. "You should be off to bed as well." She had already turned the corner before Arabelle could even reply.

Left standing alone in the middle of the hallway, Arabelle felt as if she had just been abandoned. Which was silly, really. *You should be used to this by now,* she told herself sternly.

Ignoring the bitter feeling welling up inside her, Arabelle continued on her way towards her bedroom. The house she lived in had three floors with the second storey, given over to her and her brothers' bedrooms and a bathroom. The third floor was where her parents slept, as well as a study and a playroom for Callum and Amias.

Arabelle's bedroom was all the way down the other end of the second floor. When she reached it, she opened the door and closed it gently behind her. Her room was large, but simple in design. The walls were painted a soft lavender colour and a four-poster bed stood at the opposite end of the room. A large vanity table stood against the right wall right and her wardrobe to the left. A tall, glass door near her bed led out onto a small balcony that overlooked the back garden. The room was lit up by the chandelier, imbedded with illuminae crystals, that hung from the ceiling.

All of her necessary belongings were packed and ready to go on her bed. She had her change of clothes, a plain pair of trousers and a blue, short-sleeved blouse (Derek had suggested it would be better if they didn't dress in their uniform for this journey).

Arabelle stripped out of her nightgown as she crossed the floor to her bed. There was no more time to waste.

She'd been hiding out in the tall bushes outside the palace's kitchen windows now for what felt like an age. The prickly foliage was uncomfortable against her skin and her legs were starting to grow restless from crouching down for so long. Arabelle longed to stand up and stretch them out, but she dared not to move from her position unless she was spotted by one of the guards that patrolled the gardens.

Arabelle lived in the upper part of the city, where the nobles lived, so once she had managed to sneak out of the house, it had been a short trip to the palace. She thought she had been right on time, but it appeared that she was either early or the boys were late.

Where is Jared? Arabelle thought frustratedly, glancing up at the window above her. *Where's—*

She almost jumped when something ducked into the bushes she was hidden behind. Not something, she realised, but someone. Derek Draco was kneeling down in the dirt patch in front of her. His normally unkempt hair was looking especially tousled and his blue eyes looked almost grey in the dark. Arabelle felt her heart begin to beat hard in her chest, as it always did when she was around Derek. As it had done ever since she was twelve-years-old. In a low voice, she said, "What took you so long?"

"Two of the guards decided on a late-night tryst by the west side of the gardens so I had to go around."

Arabelle raised her eyebrows. She could only imagine her father's—the Captain of the Crown Guard— reaction if he found out about *that*.

As they waited, she took the time to discreetly observe Derek. His straight, black hair that always looked in need of a good brush. He had delicate, oddly feminine, features that lent him an almost androgynous look. His face was lovely, she had always thought so. But his looks definitely weren't the only thing she loved about him.

"What's taking Jared so long?" Derek whispered, startling her out of her thoughts. "He should have been here by now."

Just as Arabelle opened her mouth to respond, there was a sound at the window above them. She and Derek both instinctively pressed themselves closer to the wall, but as the window opened and her cousin's face peered down at them, Arabelle felt herself relax. "You sure took your time," she said as Jared helped them up through the window.

"Carla took longer in the kitchens tonight than she usually does," Jared explained, referring to the palace's head cook.

The kitchens were empty but for the three of them. Unlike the rest of the palace, the kitchens were not lavishly decorated. The floor was made of plain, grey flagstones and walls of white brick. A long wooden table stood in the centre of the room and Arabelle remembered running around it as a little girl, playing with her cousins and then being scolded when Julianna accidentally knocked over a couple of dinner plates. There were two pots gently simmering on one of the stovetops and what smelled like cabbage soup wafted through the air.

"We'll have to be quick," said Jared, shutting the window behind them. "Carla will be coming back any minute now."

They followed Jared over a tall cupboard that stood in the corner, between one of the cooking benches and the oven.

Jared opened up the cupboard to reveal rows of shelves stacked with a wide variety of spices, herbs and salt. Kneeling down, Jared reached into the floor of the cupboard, running his hands along the edges. There was the sound of cracking wood and Jared was lifting up the cupboard floor, which, actually, turned out to be a trapdoor.

Arabelle took a step forward and saw that underneath the trap door was a dark, gaping hole, wide enough for one person to fit through.

"I'll go first," said Jared. "There's a ladder just here. Watch your step." He threw his pack down the hole and they heard it land with a faint, thud before he made his own descent.

Arabelle went down next. It wasn't a long climb down and by the time she reached the bottom, Jared had already pulled out and lit a lantern, casting an orangey glow against the walls of a narrow, underground tunnel.

Once Derek had joined them, they set off down the tunnel in single file with Jared leading the way. The walls and floor of the tunnel were rocky and uneven and once or twice one of them would nearly stumble over a dip in the ground or a protruding rock. Whoever had built this passageway apparently did not care if the royal family twisted an ankle while they were trying to flee.

Finally, they reached the end of the tunnel, where a door carved of stone, stood before them.

"Hold this." Jared passed the lantern over to Arabelle before stepping forward and pressing his hand against the door. There was the low sound of stone scraping on stone as the door began to ease open. "The door was enchanted so that only a member of the royal family can open it," Jared explained.

"So how does the door tell if you're a royal or not?" asked Arabelle.

Jared paused, his face screwed up into a look of deliberation before he shrugged in that way that meant, *I haven't got a clue.*

One by one, the three of them stepped out into the cool, night air. The stone door sliding closed behind them.

Arabelle surveyed their surroundings. They were standing on an outcropping of rock, the city walls loomed high above them from behind. The door they had just come out of was conspicuously hidden by tall grass and creepers snaking up the stone walls.

In front of them was the wide-open expanse of the Aloserian landscape; forests, rolling hills, a lake and the dark shapes of mountains in the distance.

They had done it. They had made it out of Ember undetected.

"Are we ready?" asked Derek. A breeze had picked up, whipping strands of his raven hair about his face.

"Of course," Jared answered, blowing out the lantern and dropping it carelessly into the tall grass.

Arabelle took one more look at the city walls behind them. Beyond those walls, were her family, sleeping peacefully unaware in their beds. She couldn't help but feel a twinge of guilt for the worry she was about to cause them. *Would they all worry though?* said a voice in the back of her head. She knew that Callum and Amias would be confused and upset when they realised that their sister had actually run away. She was sure her father would be worried but would Amara really be that concerned? When it came to Amara, Arabelle never really knew where she stood.

Arabelle shook the thoughts away and looked to Derek and Jared, hoping they could see the steely resolve in her eyes and nothing else. "I'm ready."

Derek nodded, pulled out his ring from the chain he wore around his neck. Jared and Arabelle took that as their cue to put on their rings as well. Arabelle wore hers on a golden bracelet around her wrist. The band of her ring was green, inlaid with a tiny, red, ruby. She slid the ring onto her littlest finger and Changed.

Jared and Derek had both Changed as well. For a moment they stood, three young Guardians, breaking a law and about to travel into unknown dangers.

Derek was the first to take flight. He was followed closely by Jared and, finally, Arabelle spread her wings and took off after them.

I'm sorry, Arabelle thought to herself, a silent apology to her family. *But I have to do this. I have to know.*

* * *

Through the Scrying Glass, Aurelia watched the three young Guardians soar across the night sky. Ever since that night three days ago, Aurelia had been keeping a watchful eye on Erianna's son with the use of her Scrying Glass. Since then, she had learned that the boy was intent on finding all three pieces of Milrath's amulet.

Cora was perched comfortably on Aurelia's shoulder and tugging at the short strands of her black hair with her beak.

Without taking her eyes off of the Glass, she brought her free hand up to smooth down the feathers on Cora's chest. "I wonder if he knows, Cora?" Aurelia said quietly. "That using that amulet has consequences."

Aurelia already knew the answer, however; of course, the boy had no idea. Nobody who knew what using the amulet would mean, would willingly use it. Aurelia had thought about seeking the boy out herself and warning him against using the amulet. But she had quickly quashed that notion.

You will not get involved, she told herself over and over again.

Even if she did believe it would be a good idea, Aurelia wasn't sure she was ready to come face to face with Erianna's likeness after all this time.

Maybe he won't find all the pieces, Aurelia told herself. The other two were quite well hidden after all. Still, that thought brought her little comfort.

"*Kra,*" cawed Cora. She flapped her wings once, before lifting off of Aurelia's shoulder.

Aurelia watched as her Familiar flew out of the open window and disappeared into the night. She turned her attention back to the Scrying Glass where the three young Guardians were still flying through the sky, clearly intent on putting as much distance between themselves and Ember as possible. She stayed there watching them until the barest traces of sunlight started to seep into the sky.

7

Darus woke up with the sun in his eyes. The window next to the bed was open, and the curtains were blowing gently in the breeze from outside. He sat up and shivered as the sheets pooled around his waist, leaving his bare torso exposed to the cool morning air.

The person lying on the bed next to him shifted. "Darus?" came the sleepy voice of Augusta Parvo. She blinked up at Darus, squinting in the sunlight. Her fair curls were pleasantly mussed against the pillow.

Darus gave her a soft smile. "I should get going now. Go back to sleep." Just as Darus moved to get up from the bed, a pair of arms wrapped around his waist from behind.

"It's still early," said Augusta. "Stay a bit longer?"

Darus opened his mouth to argue but released an unsteady exhale instead as he felt a soft chest press against his back. Feather-light fingertips swept his long, loose hair over his shoulder and then there was the press of lips against the nape of his neck. The scrape of teeth.

Darus groaned, desire stirring once more and he allowed himself to be pulled back onto the bed.

About half an hour later, Darus was walking down the ever so familiar streets of Ember, towards his own home. Although he would have loved to spend the rest of the morning with Augusta, wrapped up in her arms and their lazy pleasure, Darus knew that he needed to return home. He hadn't spent an entire night out like this since he'd adopted Derek (not including when he was away on assignments of course) and he couldn't help but feel guilty for it.

The atmosphere between himself and Derek had been rather tense ever since their argument that had ended with Darus slapping him and Derek bolting out the door. The memory of it came with a torrent of shame.

Darus still couldn't believe he had *hit* Derek. He hadn't meant to do it, hadn't meant to lose his temper in that way. He knew better than anyone what Derek was like when he was angry or frustrated; that boy couldn't control his temper to save his life. There had been multiple times over the years where Darus had borne the brunt of Derek's explosive temper and each time he had let it go over his head, knowing that there was hardly ever any truth to Derek's words when he was in one of those states.

But this time had been different, hearing Derek insinuate that Darus and *that man* were alike . . . he'd just snapped.

How dare he? Darus had thought in his momentary, blinding rage. *How dare he compare me to* him. *How* dare *he imply that I could do the things that* he *did. How*—And then Darus found himself staring down into those wide, blue eyes. A look of shock and hurt written as clear as day across his adoptive son's face.

The rage had dissipated in an instant and just as he realised what he had done, Derek was already running out the door.

Darus had regretted it immediately. Despite Derek's cruel words, he should not have hit the boy. Even though they had apologised to one another once Derek had returned home, it did little to clear the air between them. Derek was still tense around him, still refused to meet his eyes for more than a second. It was if Derek were *afraid* of him.

The thought that Derek could possibly fear Darus, was like a knife embedded in his gut, slowly twisting. It was why Darus had spent as little time as possible around the house the last couple of days, he thought Derek would prefer it if he were not there so much.

Today, however, Darus decided that he was going to resolve this. He was going to go home, sit down with Derek and talk until all this was settled and then, hopefully, everything would go back to normal.

When he finally returned home, he was greeted by Daisy throwing herself at him ecstatically.

"Derek?" He called out. There was no answer.

Darus slid off his boots and padded further into the house. He peered into the kitchen but found it empty. The same went for the lounge room. And the parlour, the study, the laundry and the backyard.

Darus made his way upstairs, expecting to find Derek still in bed, but instead, he found his bedroom door open and his bed empty, except for Finn, who was curled up on Derek's pillow. Odd, Derek was hardly ever up by eight o'clock.

He's probably with Jared, Darus told himself. Derek had been spending much of his time with Jared lately.

Darus made his way back downstairs and into the kitchen. He would just have to wait until Derek came home to have that talk. Which was fine, he had nowhere better to be today. But as hours passed, and Derek still hadn't returned, Darus couldn't help but grow agitated. Even knitting—his favourite pass time—did little to ease him.

It was late in the afternoon when there was an insistent knocking at his front door. Darus opened it, expecting to find Derek on the other side, instead, he found Lila Delron.

Darus frowned. "Oh, it's just you."

Lila raised an eyebrow at him. "It's wonderful to see you too, Darus. How has your day been? I hope you're well."

"I thought it was Derek."

Lila's brow lowered. She was dressed in uniform, her vest was unbuckled and the thick waves of her auburn hair were pulled into a bun at the back of her head. "He's not here?"

Now it was Darus's turn to raise an eyebrow. "Obviously. Or I wouldn't be thinking he was at the door."

"Do you know where he is?"

"He was gone before I even got home this morning," said Darus. "I can only assume he's with Jared. Why?"

"I came here to speak to him actually, but . . ." There was a deep line between Lila's brows now. She wasn't looking at Darus but down at her feet. He could see the muscle in her jaw working. Signs Darus knew that meant Lila was worried about something.

"But what?" Darus demanded, his own anxiety starting to stir. "What's going on, Lila?"

"It's the Prince. He's missing."

"Missing?" Darus said incredulously.

"He wasn't in his bedroom this morning and no one's been able to find him anywhere within the palace grounds," Lila explained. "Since he and Derek are such good friends I thought I'd try my luck here."

Darus's mind was whirling. Jared was missing. Darus hadn't seen Derek all day. Lila said Jared hadn't been in his room this morning. Derek had been gone since this morning. Darus knew that Derek had been spending most of his time with Jared these past two days.

Ever since he and Derek had had that argument. The argument about how Derek wanted to go off and find some daemonic amulet so that he could—

"Oh . . . *shit*."

* * *

After having flown for half the night and nearly an entire day, with only a couple of short breaks in between, Derek, Arabelle and Jared finally decided to settle down for a proper rest before they all collapsed from exhaustion. With the sun already starting to set, they found a small forest clearing where they set up camp. They ate a small dinner of bread and salted meat from their supplies before, putting out the fire and settling into their bedrolls.

At first, Derek's sleep was peaceful, until his dreams turned dark. He dreamt that he was in the forest clearing, sitting around a small campfire with his parents. He felt calm and content. His father was speaking, but Derek couldn't make out the words he was saying. His mother was smiling and nodding. She held a blanket-wrapped, bundle in her arms, rocking it gently back and forth.

His mother looked up at him, still smiling, even as her hair started to fall away, her skin blackened and withered and her mouth fell open in a silent scream as she transformed into a burned corpse. The bundle that had been in Erica's arms vanished with what sounded like the wailing of a baby. His father was still speaking, even as a long, gaping wound opened up along his throat. Blood poured out from the wound and from his mouth, dripping all the way onto the ground in a never-ending stream.

Derek got up from where he was sitting and began to back away in horror.

He turned around only to find himself face to face with a shadowy figure, bright red eyes staring down at him. Before he

102

could move, Derek felt a pair of arms wrap around him from behind and when he turned his head he saw Goldridge's face leering down at him.

"*My* son." said the Mayor in that deep, rumbling voice.

"*My* Derek."

"*Mine.*"

Derek woke up. His heart was beating a frantic rhythm in his chest. Perspiration dotted his forehead and temples, causing strands of his hair to stick to the skin. He sat up and tried to get his breathing under control. Night had fallen and the clearing was bathed in a moonlit glow. Surrounding him was a cacophony of sounds; crickets, the hooting of an owl and the distant, eerie sound of wolves howling.

Jared was fast asleep in the bedroll beside his. Derek looked around and saw Arabelle only a short distance away, her back facing him. She was in her dragon form and she looked very much like a large cat lounging on a large rock, her tail flicking back and forth lazily. As a dragon, Arabelle's skin was the colour of grass in the sunlight. The paper-thin skin on her wings was a deep, ruby red, as well as on her chest and underbelly.

Knowing that he wasn't going to be going back to sleep any time soon, Derek got up and made his way over to where Arabelle was.

"You can go sleep if you want," Derek said as he climbed up onto the rock and sat down next to her. "I'll take over the watch."

Arabelle looked over at him with large violet eyes. The nostrils at the end of her slender snout flared, like a dog sniffing the air before she Changed. "Can't sleep?" she asked.

Derek nodded. He didn't want to explain why though and, thankfully, Arabelle didn't ask.

"I'm not sure I'd be able to sleep right now, either," she said.

So the two of them sat together in companionable silence. Derek was still feeling rattled from the dream he had just had. He kept seeing the blood on his father's face. Kept hearing Goldridge's voice, *Mine, mine, mine.* He shivered.

"Are you all right?" Arabelle suddenly asked him.

"I'm fine," was his automatic response.

She gave him a sceptical look. "You look . . . pale."

"I'm always pale."

"I suppose that's true. You've got that lily-white skin." She grinned.

Derek rolled his eyes, but as Arabelle spoke, he noticed something. That speaking to her, listening to her voice, had an almost calming effect on him. It helped to drown out the Mayor's voice still whispering in his ears. He didn't know why, but even just looking at her and feeling her presence beside him, made him feel at ease.

It reminded Derek of another time, five years ago, sitting in a dark space, the smell of dirt and damp everywhere. The fear of uncertainty like a vice around his heart. The only bright spot was Arabelle next to him.

In an effort to keep her talking, Derek said, "So why did you really want to come with us? What do you want to wish for?"

The smile slid from Arabelle's face. "I already told you didn't I?"

"What, eternal beauty and an army of suitors?" said Derek, unconvinced. "Somehow you don't strike me as the type to want all that."

Arabelle bowed her head, strands of hair fell into her face and she reached up to tuck it behind her ear. "You may have heard about this already, but you and I have something in common and that's that we were both born outside of Ember."

Derek did, in fact, know this, but instead of pointing that out he simply let Arabelle continue.

"Seventeen years ago, my father was on an assignment and in that time he met a woman and they had me," she explained. "But by the time I was born my father had long since left. He wouldn't have even known I existed. Three years later my mother brought me to Ember and to my father's doorstep. She told him that I was his daughter and he had to look after me now." Arabelle drew her legs up and hugged them to her chest. The look on her face was sad and distant. "I was so young at the time so I don't remember much. I remember that it was at night and I had been sleeping. When I woke up I was in a strange man's arms and when I looked around for my mother she was already walking away. Even though I cried and screamed for her, she . . . just kept walking. That was the last time I saw her."

"So that's what you want to wish for?" Derek questioned. "To find your mother?"

Arabelle nodded. "I just . . . I don't know anything about her. I don't even remember what she looked like, just that she had blonde hair like mine. And my father knows next to nothing about her." Her voice had taken on a bitter edge. "He doesn't even know her name. You think he'd have at least asked for it when he was hopping into her bed. I want to know who she was—is and why she left me. It's hard, growing up without a mother."

"You don't need to tell me that."

He saw Arabelle's eyes widen almost comically. "Oh no, I'm sorry. I didn't mean—"

"It's fine," Derek said, brushing off her attempt at an apology. "What about your step-mother? Don't you get along with her?"

"Amara's—it's not that I don't get on with her," said Arabelle. "She's just . . . distant. I've tried getting close to her but she just doesn't seem interested. I think it's because I'm not her real daughter. Probably all I am to her is her husband's bastard."

Derek didn't know much about Arabelle's step-mother, just that she had come from Samwea some years ago to work in Ember as a healer before eventually marrying the Queen's brother and going on to have two children together. When Derek was twelve he had shattered the bone in his left arm and it had been Amara Aloria who had tended to him. She had been reserved but kind and somehow Derek found it hard to imagine her resenting a child because of something that hadn't even been their fault. But then again, he knew all too well that the face people presented to others wasn't always the one they wore behind closed doors.

"Well for what it's worth," said Derek. "I think there's more to you than the accident of your birth. That you're worth more than that. If anyone ever makes you feel like you aren't, come and see me."

Arabelle's mouth curled derisively. "Why? So you can be my knight in shining armour?" By the tone of her voice, Derek could tell that she was less than impressed by the idea of a man coming to her rescue.

"No, so that I can watch as you beat them to a pulp. Wouldn't want to miss that."

Arabelle's expression changed to one of surprise and then amusement. Her shoulder's started to tremble with laughter and she bowed her head so that her hair fell into her face, shielding it from Derek's view.

"Thanks," she said softly.

"You're welcome."

After a few moments of silence, Arabelle finally slid off the rock and stretched her arms above her head. "I think I might take you up on your earlier offer of going to sleep."

"All right."

She smiled impishly. "Or do you need me to stay in case you get scared being out here all alone?"

Derek made a shooing gesture with his hand. "Be off with you."

With a laugh, Arabelle made her way over to the bedrolls, leaving Derek sitting alone but feeling much calmer than he had just moments ago.

* * *

The throne room was by far one of the largest rooms in the entire palace. The floors were made of spotless, black and white marble. The ceiling was at least forty feet high, with elaborate murals of winged cherubs in the sky and the Goddess Ithulia painted across its length. Arched windows, that nearly reached the ceiling, lined the walls and a long red carpet ran the length of the room, from the double doors all the way to the steps of the dais at the other end.

Two magnificent, marble thrones sat upon the dais, one of which was currently occupied by King Jonathan Regalias. He was dressed in his kingly attire; a red, high-necked tunic with burgundy trousers and polished black boots. The gold medallion of the Guardians hung around his neck. His golden crown, gleaming immaculately from where it rested atop his head.

Two Crown Guards stood before the bottom steps of the dais, facing Darus where he stood, weathering his King's gaze, as well as the gaze of the King's three Advisors, seated in high-backed chairs beside their King. Darus may have been a grown man of twenty-nine, yet standing here under the scrutinizing looks of the King and his Advisors, he couldn't help but feel as if he were merely a boy about to get a scolding from his elders.

"Darus Flynn," the King began, his voice echoing clearly throughout the throne room. "You have been summoned here to discuss the matter of the disappearance of the Prince, my niece and your adopted son. You say you may have answers in regards to where they may be?"

"That's right, Your Majesty," Darus answered, his tone was one of deference.

"Well?" growled Elias Decorus, an old man with wispy, grey hair and a thin face. "Get on with it."

So Darus told the King and his Advisors about how days ago, Derek had expressed a desire to find the daemon, Milrath's, amulet. How Darus had refused him and how he believed that that was where Derek and the Prince had disappeared to.

"What is this, 'Milrath's amulet'?" Elias demanded scowling nastily down at Darus. Elias Decorus was not the most pleasant person in the world and could be quite disagreeable towards anyone he wasn't related to by blood, but he seemed to resent Darus with a passion. Darus was fairly certain that it had something to do with the fact that, years ago, he had had a torrid love affair with Elias's youngest son.

"Hm, Milrath's amulet, eh?" said Albert Thorbone, the second Advisor. He was a man aged in his late fifties with a long, thick beard. "I always thought that was just a myth."
"It is no myth," Vera Avesh, the third Advisor, interjected. She had short, brown hair and wore a pair of large, round spectacles. She was about the same age as Jonathan. When Darus was growing up, King Gerard, Jonathan's father, had had some strange notion that women were not as capable or reliable as men. There had been

109

no women among his Advisors and nor had women been permitted to join the Crown Guard. When Jonathan ascended to the throne, he had made sure to change that as soon as possible. "There have been reports of it existing, but it was said to have gone missing years ago."

"Are you saying," Elias demanded, his voice rising. "That your adoptive son has dragged the Prince off on some foolish venture to find an amulet that was created by one of the most powerful daemons said to have ever existed?"

Albert chuckled. "You make it sound as if the Draco boy stole the Prince away against his will, Elias."

The older man shot his fellow Advisor a withering look. "Well, what other explanation is there?"

Darus scowled. He did not like what Elias was insinuating; that Derek was some out of control hooligan who had somehow coerced Jared into joining him on his mad quest. He felt defensiveness well up within him, but it was the King who spoke up.

"It's because Derek is his friend," said Jonathan. "My son would not sit idly by while his friend rushed into danger by himself. He would want to be there by his side." A sad smile tugged at the corner of his mouth. "Just as I would have done with Alexander."

Darus felt his sympathies go out to his King. He knew that he and Alexander Draco had been close in their youth, up until Alexander's exile and he knew that Jonathan still grieved for his friend.

Darus decided to take this as his chance to speak. "Your Majesty, please, let me be the one to go out and find the missing children."

This earned him four surprised looks.

"You?" said Vera. "Why you?"

Because I can't just sit here and do nothing but wait, Darus wanted to shout in frustration. *I want to go out there and find my boy!* Instead, he said, "Because this situation is in part, because of my negligence. If I had kept a closer eye on Derek, perhaps this never would have happened. Allow me to be the one to set things right and bring the children home."

This was followed by muttered deliberation between the King and his Advisors. Their tones were so low that Darus could not hear what they were saying from where he stood (although it appeared that Elias was doing his best to argue against his request).

Finally, Jonathan held up a hand that swiftly ended the discussion. He turned his impenetrable, green eyes back to Darus. "We will allow you to search for the children," Jonathan announced. "However, if you have not found them by the time autumn is upon us, you will come home and search parties will be sent across the kingdom to find them in your stead. Is that clear?"

Darus felt his shoulders slump with relief. "Yes. Thank you, Your Majesty."

"You will leave in the morning, so take the rest of the day to prepare for your journey."

"Yes, Your Majesty."

The King made a gesture to show that he was dismissed.

With a bow, Darus turned on his heel and made his way out with a new purpose in his step. He was anxious to get home and begin preparations.

He would leave first thing in the morning and morning could not come soon enough.

8

The next morning, Darus descended the stairs, dressed in plain civilian clothes (he thought it would attract less attention than if he wore his Guardian uniform). His pack slung over one shoulder, prepared to depart for his journey. Darus stepped into the lounge room where he found Lila, sitting on the floral armchair by the window, stroking Daisy's head in her lap, while also entertaining Finn with a length of ribbon.

"I'm heading off now," He announced.

Lila stood up from where she was sitting and crossed the room to stand in front of him. She was so small, Darus couldn't help but think, as she looked up at him with concerned light brown eyes. Lila had always been short, always dainty and fragile-looking, like a porcelain doll, but he knew, perhaps better than anyone, that Lila Delron was anything but fragile.

"Are you sure you don't want me to come with you?" she asked.

Darus shook his head. "No, this is your week off. I can't ask you to come with me."

Lila gave him a stern, almost maternal, look and reached out to pull his hand into hers. "You could," she said earnestly. "You know you could."

"I know." Darus smiled. "But I won't. Besides, someone needs to make sure those two don't destroy the house while I'm gone." He nodded over at Finn and Daisy, who were now engaged in a tug-of-war with the ribbon.

Lila huffed out a laugh. "Don't worry, I'll make sure your house stays in one piece."

"Thank you."

She pulled him into a hug and Darus wrapped his arms around her, holding her close and enjoying the way she fit so easily into his embrace.

"Go find your boy," she whispered against his chest. "And bring him home."

Before Darus could leave, however, there was one stop he had to make first.

The Patched Cloak was the only magic shop in all of Ember and could be found in one of the streets west of the city centre.

As he walked through the streets, Darus heard the whispers that were being traded among the people.

"Did you hear?" said the baker's wife to her friend outside their front door. "The Prince is *missing*."

"Apparently so is Captain Aloria's daughter."

114

"I heard they ran away. Right in the middle of the night."

"Why would they do such a thing?"

"Oh, I hope Prince Jared is all right."

"Didn't that Draco boy go with them?"

"*Tsk.* I bet he coerced them into it somehow. I always knew he was a bad egg."

"It's the elf blood I tell you."

Darus did his best to ignore the less than glowing comments about Derek. Deciding instead to, grit his teeth and keep his eyes forward as he continued on his way.

As Darus approached *The Patched Cloak,* a woman and her young son stepped out. The boy looked absolutely ecstatic, grinning ear to ear as he held out a small object to his mother. A ring.

"I got it! I finally got my own ring," the little boy cheered.

"All right, settle down now." The mother cast a nervous glance at Darus, as if he might have some problem with her son shouting loudly in the middle of the street.

"Now Clara can stop teasing me about being the only one in the family without a ring!"

Darus watched as the woman shepherded her son down the pathway. *The Patched Cloak* wasn't *just* a magic store, it was also the place where the Guardians' rings were crafted. Many Guardians had their rings passed down through their families, Darus's own ring had been his father's once, but sometimes there just wasn't

enough rings in the family to be passed down. Or, occasionally, rings were lost during assignments. When that happened, The Patched Cloak was the place to come to.

No one knew exactly where the spell to craft the rings had come from, whether it had been given to them by the Goddess or by an unknown mage. What they did know was that the crafting of rings was a closely guarded secret, only known by the Crafter and the one chosen to be their successor, even the King and Queen did not know how the rings were made.

Seeing that boy with his brand new ring had reminded Darus of when he had brought Derek to collect his very own ring—although Derek hadn't been nearly as outwardly enthusiastic as the boy from before. He had been as quiet and reserved as he always was back then. But still, Darus had noticed the light in his eyes whenever he looked at his ring as if it were the most extraordinary object he had ever seen.

But he didn't want to think too much about when Derek had been a child. Not right now. So with a shake of his head, he pushed open the door of *The Patched Cloak.*

Darus stepped inside and was immediately hit with the smell of eucalyptus and parchment. Inside, the shop was bright from the sunlight that streamed in through the open windows. Dark green carpet covered the floors. Four archways, two on either side of the walkway, led into a different room and each room was contained an array of intriguing magical objects. One was filled stacks of books and vibrantly coloured potion bottles. Another had crystal orbs cauldrons made of bronze, silver and gold.

As Darus passed the room of enchanted household objects—where a rather amorous teakettle was making some very lewd comments about his physique—something darted out in front of him. It was a ferret, with sleek, white fur, standing on its hind legs and peering up at him with beady, red eyes.

"Hello, Cornelius," Darus said to the ferret. "Is Veter around?"

The creature twitched its little pink nose, before turning its tail on him and loping across the floor. He watched as it disappeared behind the front counter and not too long after an elderly man with dark skin a fall of grey hair and a beard emerged from behind the bench. The white ferret was perched comfortably on the man's shoulder.

"Who goes there?" The old man demanded.

"Good morning, Veter," said Darus as he approached the counter. "You're looking sharp today."

"Oh, it's you Darus. Could you come back later? I'm in the middle of a crisis."

"Hm, yes, I've had a few of those myself over the years," Darus said contemplatively. "What is the crisis, if I may ask?"

"I cannot find my slippers and my feet are all but frozen," Veter explained and Darus couldn't help but wonder how one's feet could possibly be frozen in the middle of February. Darus looked across the top of the counter which was in a state of mess. A silver tray with a half-empty cup of tea and a plate half-eaten eggs and toast on it. Rolled up scrolls of paper, three books stacked haphazardly on top of one another and . . . a worn pair of brown slippers.

"Are these it by any chance?" He asked holding the slippers out to the old man.

Veter held out a withered old hand, his face lighting up as it touched the slippers. "Ah! Thank you, my dear boy."

He let Veter take the slippers from his hands and crouch down to put them on. Being as absentminded and peculiar as the old mage was, coupled with the fact that he was as blind as a mole, often caused for incidents such as these. Veter also happened to be the current Crafter of the Guardians' rings.

"Why not just use your magic to find the slippers?" Darus wondered, folding his elbows on top of the counter.

Veter harrumphed. "A mage does not waste their magic on such trivial things as a lost pair of slippers."

"I'd hardly call it wasteful if it saves you hours of searching for them when they're right in front of you."

"Don't patronize me, boy. Or I'll turn you into a goose."

"Now *that* would be a waste of magic. Denying the good people of Aloseria a face like this?"

"I've lived a pleasant enough life without ever seeing your face, I'm sure the rest of the world can too. Now," said Veter, once his feet were appropriately covered. "What can I do for you?"

"I don't know if you've heard, but three young Guardians have run away from the city."

Veter hummed and reached up to pet his Familiar on his shoulder. The loose cuff of his cardigan fell down to reveal a thin, almost bony, wrist braceleted by scars. "I've heard. News spreads fast in this city."

"I've noticed," said Darus. "I'm going to search for them and bring them home but I was wondering if you might have anything that might make it easier to track them with?"

Cornelius scampered from his master's shoulder and down the front of his cardigan. Veter was pulling at his beard with methodical fingers, his milky white eyes stared sightlessly over Darus's shoulder as he thought.

"Aha!" The old man announced. "I have just the spell in mind." He snapped his fingers and a pen appeared in his hand. "Hold out your right arm."

Darus did as instructed and Veter gripped him by the wrist, turning it so his hand was palm up, and pushed up his shirt sleeve, baring the skin of his forearm. Veter set the tip of a pen to his skin. "Give me the name of one of the children you are looking for."

"Derek Draco," Darus said without hesitation.

Veter started moving the pen on the inside of his forearm, leaving black lines on Darus's skin, muttering faintly under his breath as he did so.

Darus winced as he felt a slight sting on his arm where the pen was pressed, then he watched as the black lines of ink began to rearrange themselves on his arm. They formed a tattoo-like marking on the inside of his wrist, shaped like the head of an arrow.

He also felt a new sensation in his arm. The only way he could think to describe it was as if there was something tugging on his arm, trying to pull him along. Trying to get him to follow.

"Do you feel it?" asked Veter. "As if something is trying to guide you?"

"Yes," answered Darus.

"Good. Trust it. Follow it. It will lead you to the missing children."

"I see." Darus looked down at the mark. "Thank you. How much do I owe you?"

Veter waved a hand at him. "Just bring the Prince back home safely."

Darus stared at the old man in surprise. He'd never mentioned anything about Prince Jared being one of the missing children.

"I may be blind," said Veter. "But my ears still work just fine."

That statement was immediately followed by the sound of a loud thump from above them.

Veter sighed. "Damn wardrobe's throwing a tantrum again," he grumbled and turned around to shuffle up the stairwell behind him, muttering something about enchanted wardrobes.

Knowing that it was time for him to go, Darus showed himself out of the shop. He made his way down to the city gates and once he was there, he Changed and finally set out.

* * *

The Bone Swamp was an eerie unnaturally quiet place. There were no birds chirping or squawking to be heard, nor the rustling of the tree leaves in the breeze, none of the usual sounds of the forest that Jared had grown used to over the past three days. Everything was dead still and dead quiet.

The swamp was supposed to be haunted—or it was according to the stories Julianna told him when he was small. Many, many years ago there had been a great battle here, between two tribes who each believed that the swamp belonged to them and them alone. The battle had been so fierce that both tribes had been completely wiped out. However, it was said that the spirits of all those who had died that day, still haunted the Bone Swamp. Still unable to give it up even in death.

Some said that the mage, Djedric, who had lived here over fifty years ago, had been driven mad by the ghosts that haunted this swamp.

Apart from ghosts, the Bone Swamp was also home to a number of nasty creatures, such as aracnas, spider-like creatures that could grow to be just as large as a brown bear, and water imps, fiendish creatures that lurked underwater, waiting to drag unsuspecting victims down to a watery death.

Every now and again, Jared would spot movement in the water down below that alerted him to the presence of water imps and each time, Jared couldn't help but pause and observe them. They looked about the size of a small child, with bloated bodies covered in murky green scales and webbed hands and feet. At one point, when Jared stopped to watch one of them, sitting on a muddy riverbank and biting into a fish, it turned around and looked directly up at him with a disfigured, frog-like face. It blinked its two, bulbous eyes at him before curling its lips back to reveal rows of tiny, needle-sharp teeth and hissed.

Jared never encountered any aracnas (thank the Goddess), but there were a few times when he would happen upon a tree that's branches were covered in a thick tangle of white webbing. He made sure to steer clear of those trees.

Jared leapt from tree branch to branch in the treetops, his keen dragon eyes searching for anything that might point him in the direction of Djedric's Tomb. Upon arriving in the Bone Swamp earlier that morning, Jared, Derek and Arabelle had made the decision to split up to search for the tomb. "This is a large place and the tomb could be anywhere. We'll save more time if we search separately," had been Derek's reasoning.

Although Jared hadn't been fond of the idea of splitting up, he knew that Derek was right. It *would* be quicker.

Jared opened his wings to glide from one branch onto the next and almost missed it when it turned out to be higher up than he had first thought.

A thick mist lay over the swamp, making it difficult to see through at times. The trees that sprouted up from the earth were not like any Jared had ever seen before; the trunks were narrow and twisted and as white as bone, giving the swamp its name.

With the nimbleness of a cat, he navigated his way along the thickly intertwined branches of two separate trees. He almost didn't hear the voices.

"See, Dahlia, I told you we'd catch something eventually."

"Yes," drawled a female voice. "And it only took us two and a half hours."

Jared crouched low on the branch, doing his best to keep out of sight as he peered down at the two figures below him. One was a woman with blonde hair pulled into a topknot and a large battle axe strapped to her back. The other was a tall, lanky man, probably not that much older than Jared by the looks of it, with a head of dirty blond hair. He was dragging something along the ground behind him and it took Jared a moment to realise it was an animal—a large stag—wrapped up in a net. It wasn't moving so Jared could only assume it was dead.

They were both dressed in the ragged, mismatched clothing typically worn by bandits.

"But just look how big it is," said the man with obvious glee. "The meat'll last us for days and I'm sure that hide'll fetch a pretty bit of coin."

"Let's just hurry up and get back to the tomb," the woman, Dahlia, said impatiently. "You know the boss hates to be kept waiting."

Jared's ears pricked up at the word, "tomb". Could they be talking about Djedric's Tomb? They must be because surely there weren't that many tombs around here.

"Speaking of the boss, you think he might give me some sort of reward for finally catchin' us a meal that wasn't fish?" The man asked.

Dahlia made a snorting sound. "I doubt it. You know he's not a generous sort."

Jared wondered just who this "boss" was and exactly how many more bandits were lurking in this swamp.

Their voices faded away as they walked on, dragging their catch behind them. Jared waited until they were a good distance away before he started to follow them.

Sometime later, Jared, now with Arabelle and Derek beside him, was perched high up a branch of one of the trees, overlooking Djedric's Tomb.

The tomb was located in a clearing just below a steep slope in the ground. It was about the same size as a small cottage, with a domed shape roof and built of simple grey stone, covered in moss and creeping vines. From what he remembered from History lessons at the Academy, Djedric had been an incredibly powerful mage, as well as incredibly eccentric. He had dwelled within the Bone Swamp for many solitary years, only emerging to fight in the war between Aloseria and Ishlav eighty years ago. When he died, he used his magic to build a tomb where he laid himself to rest.

The man and the woman that Jared had followed to Djedric's Tomb, had set up a camp just outside the entrance, along with a few others; there was a man with long, fiery red hair and an unkempt beard. Another was seated near the edge of the camp, sharpening a knife, pale and thin with lank, dark hair. The other was rather burly with tattoos painted across his visible skin. While there only appeared to be six of them that they could see, Jared couldn't help but notice that there were seven tents set up around their campsite.

"Who are they?" Arabelle whispered, peering down at the group of bandits.

"They must be the ones who wrote the note to Swift Hand Horace," Derek answered.

"So that would mean they're also here for the amulet," observed Jared.

"It would seem so."

"Wait," said Arabelle suddenly, "I think there's someone coming out of that tent over there."

Indeed, the flap of the largest tent was moving and as they watched, the largest man, Jared had ever seen emerged.

Only, he wasn't exactly a man, but an ogre. And not just any ogre, but the most infamous ogre in all of Aloseria; Durbash.

Beside him, Jared heard Arabelle's quick intake of breath and he knew that he was not the only one who recognised him, his face had been on wanted posters for years now.

Like all ogres, Durbash was much taller and broader than an average human. He had pointed ears, a bare head, a wide, squarish jaw and his oversized canines jutted out from his bottom lip. His skin colour was a pale grey.

"Darus told me that Durbash looked as if he had been carved from a mountain," muttered Derek.

And he was right, Jared thought. Durbash wore only a pair of plain, brown pants and boots, exposing a heavily muscled torso and arms practically as thick as the tree branch Jared and his friends were sitting on.

They watched as the other bandits hopped to attention as their leader strode towards them.

"Good mornin', Boss," greeted the bandit with the red, curly hair. "Hope ya had a good sleep?"

"It was fine," replied Durbash in a deep rumble. He spoke with a thick Samweanese accent. "Has Horace arrived yet?"

It was Dahlia who answered. "Not yet, I'm afraid." She sounded nervous.

Durbash growled in displeasure.

"Don't worry, Boss," said the youngest bandit, who was busy skinning the stag beside the fire pit in the middle of the campsite. "I'm sure Swifty will be here soon. Why don't you come sit down and I'll—"

Before the rest of the sentence had even left the boy's mouth, Durbash had grabbed him by the collar of his animal skin jacket and lifted him almost completely off his feet.

"Are you telling me what to do, Crag?"

"N-No," the boy choked out.

Jared hadn't even realised that he'd moved as if he meant to go straight down there and help when he felt Derek place a restraining hand on his shoulder.

"Because *no one* tells me what to do," Durbash growled.

"Of—of course, Boss. I d-didn't mean—I wasn't trying to—"

Durbash released his grip on Crag and he fell none too gently to the ground. None of the other bandits went to help their younger companion. Dahlia looked at him with a scornful expression on her face and Jared could even see that the red-headed bandit's face was twisted into a gleeful sneer as if it brought him joy to see other people suffer.

"Watch your words carefully next time," warned Durbash, "Or I'll rip your tongue out."

Crag nodded even as a whimpering sound escaped his lips.

"He's horrible," Arabelle murmured in disgust.

"Rall, Dahlia," said Durbash, turning to Dahlia and the red-headed bandit. "Go keep a lookout for Horace. If he isn't back by midnight, we leave here without him."

"But," started Dahlia. "Swift's supposed to have the first piece. How are we going to get it if we leave him behind?"

"You don't think I've thought of that?" Jared saw Dahlia shrink away slightly when the ogre turned his baleful glare on her. "But I'd rather not spend any more time in this bloody swamp full of monsters that are just waiting for their chance to eat us, than necessary. If Swift is smart, he'll meet us at the hideout."

"And if he isn't?" said Rall. "Smart that is?"

"Then I will hunt him down and make him regret the day he was ever born. Now go."

Dahlia and Rall didn't waste any more time, they picked up their respective weapons (Dahlia her axe and Rall a crossbow) and left the clearing.

Jared felt something nudge his right arm. He looked over at Derek, the other boy made a gesture for them to follow him and silently, the three of them withdrew.

"So Durbash is after the amulet too?" said Arabelle once they were a safe distance away from the camp full of bandits. "Well, that's just great."

"So what do we do now?" asked Jared. "It sounds like they've already got the other piece." He looked to Derek, who's eyes were fixed firmly on the ground, his brow furrowed in thought as he rubbed a hand over his chin.

Finally, Derek looked up at them, his hair had fallen into his eyes again—like it always did—and Jared had to fight the urge to reach out and brush it aside. "We'll wait until nightfall," Derek explained. "And then we'll sneak into the camp, find the amulet piece and take it."

"That sounds a lot easier said than done," said Arabelle, a sceptical note in her voice.

Jared couldn't help but silently agree with her. This plan was foolhardy at best and just plain suicidal at worst. Still, Jared understood that it might be the only plan they had that didn't—or at least he hoped it wouldn't—involve a direct confrontation. He wasn't sure how well they'd do if it came to a fight. They were three rookie Guardians against seven bandits, one of whom looked as though he would have no trouble squashing their heads in between his bare hands.

"And what happens if something goes wrong?" Jared couldn't

help but voice his concern. "What happens if it does come down to a fight with, Durbash?"

Derek shrugged in an unconcerned manner. "Then we fight and hopefully one of us will get the chance to run our blades through his heart."

The bewilderment Jared felt must have shown on his face because Derek added, "He's wanted dead or alive anyway."

While Jared understood that, and he certainly did not have any qualms about Durbash dying, he was surprised to hear Derek speak so casually of killing someone, regardless of whether or not they might deserve it. But Derek had always been like that. Had always shown glimpses into a more ruthless nature over the years, such as when Jared had been upset by his father approving of the decision to execute a band of notorious pirates, responsible for murders of innocent merchants among other things, rather than simply imprison them and give them a second chance. Back then, Derek had been completely unconcerned and said, "At least there will be fewer monsters in the world now."

One might simply put it down to having lost his parents at such a young age, but Jared was not so sure.

"All right then," said Arabelle, interrupting his thoughts. "If we've got until nightfall, we might as well work out all the details of this so-called plan."

* * *

Night had finally settled and all of the bandits had retreated into their tents, except for Rall and the dark-haired one. They sat at the edge of the camp keeping watch with their weapons at the ready. Fortunately, they stood with their backs turned to where Derek and Jared crept out of their hiding place in the undergrowth and quietly made their way to Durbash's tent.

They had decided that while Derek and Jared snuck into the camp and stole the amulet piece, Arabelle would keep watch from outside, ready to alert them if something didn't go according to plan (she was surprisingly adept at making bird noises as it turned out).

Derek carefully parted the tent flap and peered inside. Durbash was fast asleep, his huge figure lying down on a bedroll across from them. It really was quite a large tent, with ample room for both Derek and Jared slip into without having to get too close to where Durbash was sleeping. In the dim light cast by the fire outside, Derek spotted a huge broadsword and a hunting knife, laid out on the ground, as well as a large, leather sack in one corner of the tent.

"Keep an eye on him," he whispered to Jared. "I'll start looking for the amulet piece."

"What do I do if he wakes up?"

"Slit his throat?"

"Derek!" Jared hissed, appalled.

"What?"

Jared just shook his head and went over to watch Durbash while Derek crept over to the sack and began rifling through it. Inside he found oversized clothes, knives, a coin purse and finally, a small wooden box, the same length as Derek's hand. It was completely devoid of any details, but for a silver keyhole in its centre. When he tried opening it, he found that perhaps not so unsurprisingly, the lid was locked. But another look through of the sack showed that there was no key to open the box with.

But maybe I don't need one. Derek set down the box and pulled out one of Durbash's knives. He examined the tip of the blade, determined it long and sharp enough and pressed it into the box's lock. It took him a few moments of angling the knife and jimmying the lock before there was a small click and Derek smiled with satisfaction.

"Where did you learn to pick locks?" Jared asked, now looking over Derek's shoulder.

"There are many people with interesting talents in Windfell," Derek said, thinking back to cold winter nights, spent in the company of a retired street performer who had been kind enough to impart a few tricks to Derek before illness struck him down.

"And there aren't any in Ember?" There was a hint of defensiveness to Jared's tone, which Derek found amusing.

He lifted the lid of the box and found it full of odd, and somewhat disturbing, bits and pieces. There were what appeared to be animal claws, tied together with string. A bracelet made of human teeth and, oddly enough, a jagged piece of wood. In amongst it all, however, Derek found just what he was looking for. It was a dark bronze colour, just like the first piece but unadorned by any gems. It was larger than the first piece, and reminded Derek of an oversized ring, with a hole in the middle large enough for Derek to fit two fingers through.

As he slid the piece into his pocket, he suddenly heard Jared yelp from behind him, followed by scuffling sounds.

Derek whirled around, his sword already out of its scabbard, and saw Jared on his knees, with a large hand fisted in his hair and a knife at his throat.

"Drop your weapon," demanded Durbash. "Or I'll cut open your friend's throat."

9

Even on his knees, Durbash made an impressively large figure, his orange eyes narrowed on Derek from where he held Jared from behind.

"I said," the ogre growled. "Drop your sword, or I'll bleed out your little friend here."

Without hesitation, Derek released his grip on his sword and let it fall to the ground.

"Good boy," said Durbash. He kept his knife to Jared's throat as he called out, "Rall! Crane!"

It wasn't long before there was a shadow at the tent's flap and the wild, red-headed bandit peered inside. A lopsided grin appeared on his face as he took in the scene before him. "Well, what d'ya know? Looks like Crane was right. We did have some company."

"Get this one outside." Durbash nodded to Derek.

"Right." Rall held a loaded crossbow aimed straight at Derek's face. "Come out nice and slowly, lad."

Derek looked from the bandit to Jared and back again before doing as he was told. Perhaps if Jared didn't have a knife pressed to his throat, Derek would have tried fighting back. But it hadn't worked out that way and he wasn't about to risk his best friend's life.

Rall prodded Derek none too gently in the back with his crossbow as Derek walked past him. "Don't look at me like that," said the bandit when Derek shot him a glare. "S'your own fault for tryin' to rob the boss."

Stepping back outside, Derek found that the rest of the bandits were already awake and out of their tents. It was as if they had been expecting this.

Derek gritted his teeth. They were foolish to think that they could outsmart a seasoned band of criminals so easily.

He was marched over to the fire pit, before being forced to his knees. Jared fell beside him a moment later. Rall kept his crossbow pointed at Derek's head while the youngest bandit, Crag, took up a place next to Jared with a knife to the back of his neck.

"Don't forget to search them," Derek heard Durbash order from somewhere behind them. "One of them stole something."

The woman, Dahlia, sauntered up to them. She searched Jared first and then, when she found nothing, moved onto Derek. He clenched his jaw as the woman's unfamiliar hands moved over him, fighting down a shiver of disgust and the urge to lash out when she came to the amulet piece in the pocket of his pants. He doubted he'd do little more than wind up with a crossbow bolt through his head if he tried anything.

"I found this, Boss," Dahlia announced, holding up the amulet piece.

Durbash's heavy boots crunched on the dirt and dried leaves that were strewn along the ground as he came to stand in front of Dahlia. She handed the piece back to him.

He had the broadsword, strapped to his hip now and was carrying Derek's own sword in his hand. Derek hated it. Seeing his sword, his *father's* sword, in Durbash's hands.

Durbash tucked the piece into a small, black pouch that hung on a string around his neck, before turning his glowering gaze onto Derek and Jared. A small, ruby piercing in his right eyebrow winked at them in the firelight.

"Who are you?" Durbash demanded in a low, surprisingly calm voice. "And why do you want this?" He asked, pointing to the pouch hanging from his neck.

Neither Derek nor Jared said a word.

A smirk curled Durbash's mouth as he knelt in front of them. "Now, now. There's no need to be afraid, boys. Just answer my questions and I might even let you go."

Doubtful. Derek had no illusions that they would allow Jared and himself to simply walk away from this, no matter what they said.

When he didn't get the answers he wanted, Durbash let out a tired sigh.

The next thing he did was he backhand Jared across the face.

He moved with a speed that was surprising for one of his size and the blow was hard enough that it had Jared falling onto his side with a grunt of pain and surprise.

"Hey!" Derek shouted, rising on instinct to defend his friend.

Before he could even get to his feet, Durbash caught Derek's jaw in a bruising grip. Those large fingers pressed in so hard Derek was sure his bones were about to crack.

"Don't touch him!" He heard Jared say angrily. Out of the corner of his eye, he saw Crag pin Jared back to the ground.

Durbash leaned in so close that Derek could feel the bandit leader's breath on his face and see the tiny red flecks in his orange eyes. "I wonder what sort of price you boys would fetch me on the market?" He wondered idly. "What do you think, Crane?"

"I'd say three hundred each," replied the dark-haired bandit.

Rall scoffed. "Three hundred? I'd reckon more than that. Take a look at that one's ears."

Durbash tilted Derek's head to the side. "Oh? Looks like this one has a bit of elf blood in him."

"I can certainly think of a few people who would pay a hefty price for that one," Dahlia sneered and it turned Derek's stomach to be talked about as if he were livestock.

"Hold on," Rall said suddenly. "This one here. He kind of looks like—" The rest of his sentence was drowned out by Crag's surprised screams as a large shape swooped down from the shadows and snatched the boy bandit off of his feet.

Arabelle threw the still screaming Crag, against one of the stone pillars of Djedric's tomb, where he fell limply to the ground.

"Guardians!" shouted Durbash, releasing his hold on Derek and leaping to his feet.

Thank the Goddess for Arabelle, thought Derek before taking advantage of the distraction to lunge forward and snatch his sword out of Durbash's lax grip.

With Crag no longer holding him down, Jared had scooped up the bandit's fallen knife and used it to deflect a bolt that was shot at Derek by Rall. Meanwhile, Arabelle was in the midst of battling against both Dahlia and Crane.

One of the other bandits rushed at Derek. He was quick to duck out of the way of the sword that was swung at his neck. While he was crouched down, he lashed out his sword, slashing at the backs of the bandit's feet.

The bandit howled and went to his knees. Derek sent him sprawling to the ground with a kick to the jaw.

He was just about to go and aid Jared and Arabelle, who were fighting back to back against the rest of the bandits when Durbash stepped in front of him.

The smug confidence and twisted smile from moments ago was gone, instead, Durbash glared at Derek with a hard fury as he unsheathed his broadsword. "You Guardians dare to attack us?" He growled, hatred coating his voice as he pointed his sword at Derek.

"Hand over the piece of the amulet and we'll leave," Derek said, holding his own sword aloft.

"Oh, none of you are leaving here. Not while you still draw breath." And then he was charging towards Derek.

Like a dancer, Derek spun to the side to avoid the strike of Durbash's sword. He brought his own sword up just in time to parry another one of Durbash's attacks. As their swords clashed, again and again, Durbash fought with all the quickness of a snake and the ferocity of a sabre lion.

While Derek may not have been a match for Durbash's strength, they were equal in speed, making it easy for Derek as he was forced to go on the defensive; hardly doing more than ducking and dodging Durbash's attacks.

They had moved to the outer edges of the clearing and Derek was already breathing hard by the time he finally managed to wound Durbash.

As Durbash thrust his sword forward, Derek ducked, getting underneath the ogre's guard. He struck out with his own sword and managed to open up a long line of red on Durbash's bare abdomen.

With a yell that was more anger than pain, Durbash aimed a kick at Derek's chest that sent him falling onto his back. He got to his knees just in time to block Durbash's next sword strike with his own blade.

With their blades locked, Derek's arms quivered as he tried to keep the weight of Durbash's sword from bearing down on him. A sneer twisted the ogre's features as he pressed down harder. The edge of the broadsword just barely touched the skin of Derek's forehead. Summoning all of his strength, Derek pushed Durbash's sword to the side and in that brief moment, where Durbash had let down his guard, he leapt forward, intending to drive the point of his sword through Durbash's stomach.

A hand shot out and grabbed him by the throat, halting his attack. He lost his grip on his sword as Durbash lifted him off of his feet. Derek tried in vain to pry Durbash's fingers from his throat, but they only squeezed tighter.

"Idiot boy," Durbash snarled. "You really think you can best me? Don't make me laugh!" And as if Derek weighed as little as a pebble, Durbash *threw* him.

He hit the ground with a bone-jarring thud. Rolling until he came to lie in front of the low burning fire in the pit. His head was spinning and his shoulder throbbed where he had landed on it. Distantly, he heard someone shout his name, but he couldn't be sure who.

"You should never have come here, Guardians," said Durbash as he made his way over. He was brandishing Derek's sword now, along with his own. "I was just going to sell you off on the slave market to the highest bidder, but that would be too good a fate for a bunch of Guardian brats."

Derek struggled up onto his elbows and found himself looking into the bright, leaping flames in the pit. One of the burning pieces of wood shifted as part of it crumbled to ash, embers jumping and scattering.

"No, what you deserve," Durbash went on. "Is death. A slow, painful death. It's what all you *damn* Guardians deserve."

An idea formed in his head and Derek looked over his shoulder to see that Durbash was only a few feet away from him.

"Please," Derek whimpered. "Stay away from me."

Durbash barked out a dark laugh. "Not so tough now are we? But it's too late to beg for mercy. I will not spare your life. I'm going to cut you open like a fish with your own blade," a manic edge had entered Durbash's voice. "I'll watch as your blood bathes the ground beneath you. Then, I will do the same to your friends and I'll hang your carcasses up for the ravens to peck at."

He's crazy, Derek thought. He dragged himself along the ground, pulling himself closer to the fire. "No. Please, *no*."

Durbash came to stand above Derek. "Go on and beg," he chuckled. "I actually enjoy the sound of your pitiful whimpering." He held the sword, point down over Derek's back—

Derek plunged his hand into the fire. Grasping a handful of embers and burning bits of wood, he hurled it over his shoulder and straight into Durbash's face.

An agonized yell tore from Durbash's throat, as he staggered back onto his knees, dropping his sword and Derek's, his hands flying to his face. "My eyes! *My eyes!*"

Derek didn't waste a second. Ignoring the burning in his palm, he snatched his sword up off the ground and drove it into Durbash's shoulder. The ogre released another cry as Derek forced him onto his back.

Dark blood welled around the wound as Derek's blade inched deeper into muscle and sinew.

Durbash's face was twisted into an ugly grimace of pain. His eyes were squeezed shut, but tears and blood leaked from them in rivulets. The surrounding skin was already turning red and blistering.

Derek reached for the pouch around Durbash's neck and yanked on it hard enough for the string to snap. "Go on and scream," he hissed close to Durbash's ear. "I like the sound of your pitiful whimpering." And he pulled his sword from Durbash's shoulder.

Durbash loosed another cry but did little to get back to his feet. Derek swayed as he stumbled back from the fallen ogre.

For what felt like the hundredth time that night, his sword fell from his grip. His right hand was *burning.* The skin was already turning an angry red and there were patches of shiny white skin where blisters were already starting to form.

He heard a scream from somewhere behind him, followed by the loud snapping of tree branches above them and monstrous clicking sounds.

* * *

Arabelle hissed as blood poured into her eye. She'd been only a second too slow and moved out of the way in time to avoid the sharpened edge of the battleaxe.

The female bandit, Dahlia, was smirking, clearly proud of herself for managing to wound Arabelle.

Fortunately, it was not a serious wound, just a scratch really, above her left eye. Still, it twinged painfully and the blood flowing freely into her eye was more than a little bit distracting.

Not much further away, Jared was holding his own against Rall and Crane. He tried reaching for his ring and was nearly disembowelled for it.

"What's the matter?" Dahlia asked gleefully, drawing Arabelle's attention away from her cousin. "All the other Guardians I've fought have been a lot tougher than this. But then again, I guess you are just a little whelping."

With a snarl, Arabelle lunged for the older woman, her shortsword clashing with Dahlia's axe. Their weapons rang against each other a few more times before Arabelle managed to land a spinning kick to Dahlia's middle, sending the woman stumbling back.

Before Arabelle could even think of her next attack, something slammed into her side with enough force to knock her off her feet and sent her sprawling into the base of a nearby tree.

Arabelle pushed herself up onto her hands and knees. There was a throbbing pain in her shoulder and ribs.

Someone came to stand over her and a heavy foot planted itself on her back, forcing her flat onto the ground.

Turning her head to the side, Arabelle saw the tattooed bandit standing above her. He held a shield in one hand and in the other was a long blade. The bandit grinned unpleasantly at her. "Too bad, sweetheart. But this is the end for you."

Just before the man could plunge his blade between her

shoulders, or before Arabelle could make any attempt at throwing him off and freeing herself, a shadow fell over them.

A huge, dark shape that Arabelle couldn't quite make out at first, fell from the tree branches above them and onto the bandit, knocking him off of Arabelle and allowing her to scramble away and to her feet.

She rushed over to pick up her fallen sword as she heard the tattooed bandit let out a horrified scream, followed by deep chittering sounds.

Dahlia screamed from somewhere nearby as more dark shapes descended into the clearing.

One of them landed behind Arabelle with a thud. She spun around just in time to face a creature with eight, hairy legs and dripping fangs, lunging towards her.

* * *

When Derek looked over his shoulder, he spotted at least three large shapes dropping down from the trees and into the clearing. Shapes with huge round bodies and eight legs.

"Aracnas!" Someone cried out.

The giant spider-like creatures scrabbled across the clearing, their bodies covered in course, brown hair, their long legs knocked over the tents in their haste to get to the prey that was on offer to them. With the arrival of the aracnas, the camp was plunged into even more chaos.

He saw Jared, now in his dragon form, breathe a gout of flame at an aracna racing towards him. It let out a high-pitched, whining sound as it caught alight.

Another aracna pinned Rall to the ground but before it could sink its fangs into him, however, Dahlia was there, driving her axe into its round, hairy body.

Further away, Arabelle dropped to the ground and slid underneath an oncoming aracna, driving her sword through the unprotected flesh of its underbelly. He spotted another dragging away the limp body of tattooed bandit, while the bandit who's ankles Derek had wounded was knocked to the ground by two others.

One of the smaller aracnas sped towards Derek, it's huge, black fangs dripping with clear fluid and he knew that if even a drop of that fluid touched him, he'd be paralysed.

Derek snatched up his sword in both hands and when the aracna was close enough, he sliced cleanly through one of its front legs.

Blood gushed out and spattered the ground. The aracna let out a high-pitched squealing sound as it lost its balance and toppled over.

Derek used this as his chance to drive his sword down through the beast's head, right between its many eyes. There was a sickening squelching sound as his sword buried deep into the aracna's flesh. Its body shuddered and its mandibles clicked together once, twice before the creatures went completely still, blood oozing from the wound in its head and its severed limb.

It took some effort for Derek to yank his sword back out.

"Derek!" He heard Arabelle cry out his name. "Look *out*!"

He spun around, expecting to see another aracna coming his way, but instead, it was Crag rushing towards him, a sword in his hands and a wild look on his face.

Before Derek could even think to move, Jared, appearing as if from out of nowhere, leapt at the attacking bandit.

It was a blur of flailing limbs and claws and teeth as Jared tackled Crag to the ground. Crag let out a harsh scream and Derek heard Jared growl loud and guttural, almost drowning out the bandit's screams.

Crag's cries quickly died away and Derek watched, frozen, as Jared stayed crouched over the still body before finally stepping away.

Derek now had a clear view of the bloody, mangled mess of Crag's throat. He looked to Jared who stood there, almost as still as a statue. He was panting slow, deep breaths. Blood stained almost the entirety of his snout and dripped from the points of his teeth. His pupils had narrowed to slits and Derek couldn't help but think that he looked like a mindless, wild animal.

Suddenly, Derek was grabbed from behind and lifted off the ground.

It didn't take long for him to realise who it was. "Arabelle!"

But instead of acknowledging him, Arabelle turned her attention to where Jared was still standing by the dead bandit and let out a loud, hissing roar that appeared to wake Jared from whatever reverie he had been in. He looked up at them, his eyes no longer vacant, but glimmering with human intelligence, and leapt from the ground just in time to avoid an attack from behind from Dahlia.

"*Damn you!*" She screamed at them.

They paused only to collect their packs, which they had stored safely in one of the nearby trees before Derek, Arabelle and Jared were putting as much distance between themselves and the Bone Swamp as possible.

10

Aurelia Blackwood had led quite an eventful life up until these last few years.

Many moments in her life had been pleasant, she had to admit. Such as running and laughing through the tall green grass with the other elf children. Falling asleep in the sun on one of the giant toadstools that grew only in the Great Forest. Her father lifting her up into a sweeping hug. Her mother singing her to sleep.

Erianna laughing and pulling on her hand.

However, there had been just as many awful moments. Her father's death. The war. The cold expression on her mother's face on the day she was cast out of the Great Forest. The last time she had ever seen Erianna. The look of shock and betrayal and *fury* on her face.

Over the years Aurelia had done her best to suppress those memories, the good and the bad. But there were times when, no matter how hard she tried, the memories managed to worm their way in. So when that happened, Aurelia went drinking.

The Ivory Horse was probably the nicest tavern Aurelia had ever visited. The staff clearly went to great lengths to make sure the place was cleaned spotless before it opened every evening (even though it would all succumb to mess in a matter of minutes).

The staff were always polite and friendly, even when the customers were not. The food was good and the drinks were even better.

Aurelia sat in a more secluded corner of the tavern, nursing her third mug of ale. All around her, the tavern was filled with people talking, laughing, singing and even dancing. She could hear the sound of pipes and a lute being played but it was near impossible to see where it was coming from past the throng of people around her.

On the table in front of her, Cora stood pecking at a scattering of seeds that Aurelia had brought in for her. Animals weren't usually allowed in here, but the owners made an exception for Familiars. The fact that she had been a regular paying customer at the Ivory Horse for the past four years didn't hurt either.

The music took on a more upbeat tune and Aurelia watched from over the rim of her mug as two clearly intoxicated men, hopped up onto one of the centre tables and started to perform a sort of jig. A few of the surrounding patrons began to cheer and clap.

By now Aurelia was feeling pleasantly tipsy. She felt calmer, lighter, less weighed down by the memories of her past.

So Aurelia kept drinking. She ate some food and then drank some more. She talked with a few of the other patrons and charmed them into buying drinks for her.

"What's with the gloves?" asked a handsome young traveller at one point. "It's a bit warm for them isn't it?" It was probably the alcohol that made him brazen enough to simply reach out for her gloved right hand. She snatched her arm away before he could touch her and walked away without another word.

It was close to two o'clock in the morning when Aurelia left the Ivory Horse. Cora had flown on ahead, clearly not interested in hitching a ride on her shoulder when Aurelia could hardly walk in a straight line.

The air outside was pleasantly warm as she walked through the streets back to her shop. Hardly anyone was still around at this time of night. She did pass two patrolling Town Guards, both clad in silver armour and yellow capes. She quirked a cheeky smile at them as she went by (something she probably wouldn't have done had she been completely sober).

One of the guards was polite enough to incline their head to her, while the other just fixed her with a suspicious glare. Most folk here in Florinstone were friendly enough toward wood elves, but there were still some who clung to their prejudices. Aurelia imagined that if she were not a mage, some may have felt more confident to give her a hard time for it.

As she walked up the empty, narrow street that she lived in,

Aurelia was brought up short by the sight of someone crouched down in front of the door to her shop.

They didn't stay crouched for very long. As Aurelia drew nearer, the person stood up and began to back away from the door. However, she still couldn't get a good look at them as their face and body was concealed by a long, hooded cloak.

"Hey, you," Aurelia called out.

The cloaked figure obviously hadn't expected to be caught. They startled and turned in Aurelia's direction, only long enough for her to catch a glimpse of a pale jawline, before turning and fleeing up the street.

"Wait!" She considered using magic to try and stop the cloaked figure but wasn't sure whether that was a good idea since she really had no idea whether the person had even been doing anything wrong. And it was never a good idea to use magic while intoxicated. Using magic required a clear head and in the state she was in she might end up accidentally shooting the person with a bolt of lightning.

Instead, Aurelia made for her front door, where the cloaked figure had been only moments ago. It was only as she drew closer that she noticed something had been left there on her doorstep. Something long and wrapped in thick, brown cloth and string.

Aurelia lifted up the object and began undoing the string and unwrapping the cloth.

At first, she thought it was some kind of jagged blade, but no, it was made of glass, not steel, a glass that clearly reflected, Aurelia's green-eyed gaze. It was a mirror. Or at least, part of a mirror.

Why would someone leave a mirror shard at my doorstep? Aurelia frowned and reached out to run her fingers along the glass.

A burning sensation shot up her arm from where her fingertips touched the glass.

Images flashed before her eyes, as quick as a lightning strike; a dead landscape, a blood-red sky. Indiscernible shapes, skulking about in the shadows, a snarling mouth full of jagged teeth.

A pair of burning, red eyes.

A voice—or rather many different voices mingled into one— speaking in a hissing language that she'd never heard before.

Aurelia staggered back, her breaths leaving her in sharp gasps. She felt as if she had just been pulled from a much too vivid nightmare.

The glass shard had fallen from her hand at some point, the cloth and string lay in a haphazard mess against the ground. The glass was undamaged.

What in Ithulia's name was that?

She could still hear that voice ringing in her ears. It made a shiver run down her spine and there weren't many things in the world that gave Aurelia Blackwood the shivers.

Aurelia had half a mind to toss the blasted thing down the street and run inside. But something in the back of her mind warned her against the idea.

There was something about the glass shard—something dark. Something *wrong*—and Aurelia didn't like the idea of leaving it lying in the street for just anyone to find.

So she stooped over to pick up the glass—being mindful to touch only the cloth and not the glass—and carried it in through the front door.

Once inside, Aurelia put the shard in one of the spare boxes in the backroom, placed a locking spell on it for good measure and covered it up with an old blanket.

She would figure out what exactly to do with the shard in the morning. For now, she had nearly a whole night's worth of drinking to sleep off.

11

Derek, Jared and Arabelle landed on a high outcropping of rock. They didn't bother with making a fire or even with setting out their bedrolls, as all three of them were still too full of adrenaline to even contemplate falling asleep.

Derek sat with his back against a boulder as Arabelle rubbed a salve into his burnt right hand. "Couldn't you have used something else to throw at him?" she asked, her head bowed over his hand. "Something that would have only injured him and not you?"

"Somehow I don't think throwing dirt at him would have done the trick," was Derek's response.

Arabelle gave him an unimpressed look and turned his palm over so she could apply the salve to the back of his hand. The burns weren't quite as bad there. "Why didn't you just Change?"

He leaned his head back against the rock, revelling in the cool sensation that spread across his burnt skin thanks to the salve. "He would have been expecting that," he said. "If Durbash had seen me going for my ring, he wouldn't have even given me the chance to put it on."

"You're just very fortunate that I decided to bring this salve along with me," said Arabelle after a moment.

"I am," Derek said honestly. He watched as Arabelle started to wrap clean strips of gauze around his hand with practised ease. It made him wonder if she had learned this from her step-mother. Had Amara Aloria actually taught her step-daughter any healing techniques or had Arabelle just quietly observed from a distance?

"The burns are pretty bad," Arabelle said. "The salve should ease the pain for now, but you'll definitely have scars."

Derek didn't care about that. "What about you?" He asked, referring to the gash that ran horizontally above her left eyebrow. Trails of dried blood ran down her eyelid and cheekbone.

"It's fine." Her tone was dismissive as she started tying the ends of the bandage into a knot.

On an impulse, Derek lifted his free hand and brushed aside the strands of hair that hung in front of the cut. "Are you sure? It looks like it bled a lot."

Arabelle went completely still at the touch. She looked up at him with a startled expression and Derek quickly dropped his hand. Had he made her feel uncomfortable?

"Yes," she said, resuming her work. "Head wounds always tend to bleed a lot. It's not that big of a deal."

For a moment, he wondered if that was a flush that had risen in Arabelle's cheeks? It was hard to tell in the dark. Then again, it was a warm night so if Arabelle was feeling a little hot in the face, that was probably why. Maybe he should remind her to drink some water?

Once she finished binding his hand, Arabelle began packing away her meagre medical supplies. Derek had pushed himself up to his feet to stretch when he noticed something, or rather *someone* was amiss.

"Where's Jared?"

Arabelle, who was crouched down in front of her pack, tilted her head to the side and Derek saw, sitting huddled on the edge of the rock outcropping, a little ways away from them, was Jared. His figure illuminated by the silvery glow of the moonlight.

"He killed a man for the first time tonight," said Arabelle, her voice soft enough that Jared probably wouldn't hear them. "I remember once when we were children, we were playing in the palace gardens and Jared kicked the ball so high, it knocked down a bird's nest from one of the tree branches. There were two baby birds in the nest. They hadn't even grown their feathers yet and they must have died as soon as they hit the ground. Jared was beside himself for days." There was a faraway look on Arabelle's face. "He's always been surprisingly sensitive and I always wondered how he would cope when the time came for him to take a life."

Derek remembered when he first met Jared, as a lively ten-year-old, all smiles and easy confidence, in stark contrast to Derek's, more reserved and sullen nine-year-old self. It was almost hard to imagine him as being such a sensitive soul. But Derek also knew that underneath the confidence and princely charm was a boy who had locked himself in his room and cried when he heard his old nursemaid had died from a winter chill. Who fretted over his best friend when he broke his arm. Who knew each member of the palace staff by name and always inquired after their wellbeing and the wellbeing of their families.

"You should talk to him."

Derek gave Arabelle a surprised look. "Me? Why not you?"

"You're his best friend. I think your words would bring him more comfort than mine right now."

Derek sighed. He wasn't known for his ability to comfort others. He lacked the soothing mannerisms and was oftentimes too blunt with his words. But when he looked at Jared now, looking small and alone—and the look on Arabelle's face that suggested if he didn't go over there right now he was in for a stern talking to—he picked his way across the rocky plateau.

Jared did not move or even acknowledge his presence, even as Derek eased himself down to sit beside him, his legs dangling over the rock's edge. Neither of them spoke, instead, Derek looked out at the view laid out before him; the grassy plains and hilltops. The river snaking between them turned silver under the moonlight. The mountains in the distance, against the background of a dark sky, dotted all over with shining, white stars.

"That's a great view," Derek said at last and was rewarded by a muffled sound of agreement.

Jared had his legs pulled up against his chest, his arms folded over his knees and his head rested on top of them. The light breeze toyed with the strands of his wavy brown hair.

"Are you all right?" Derek asked because that was what everyone seemed to say first when they were trying to comfort someone. Although why that was, he didn't know. Surely, if a person was truly, all right, then they wouldn't need comforting.

Again, Jared just responded with a noncommittal grunt.

Derek noticed that there was a dark stain on the back of Jared's left hand, a stain that he quickly recognised as blood. "Your hand. It's bleeding."

Jared glanced at his hand and closed his eyes, letting out a long, shaky sigh. "It's fine. I'm not hurt. I used my hand to- to wipe away the . . . the blood."

Oh. Derek remembered the blood that had coated Jared's mouth back in the Bone Swamp.

"But I can still . . . *taste* it. By the Goddess. Derek, I *tore* his *throat* out."

"You did," Derek agreed. "But I doubt anyone will miss a person like him though."

"That's not the point!" Jared snapped. "I *killed* a man. I- *I* killed him." He ran shaky hands through his hair and Derek noticed a shine in his eyes that looked suspiciously like tears.

This was why Derek should not be allowed to try and comfort others. He had barely said anything and already Jared was on the verge of tears.

For a while, neither of them said anything. Jared had his face buried in his arms, his shoulders trembling and occasionally making little hiccupping sounds. Derek sat there feeling awkward and helpless all at once. His friend was, to a certain degree, suffering and he hadn't the slightest clue how to make it better. What words should he say? Should he try patting Jared comfortingly on the shoulder?

I really am hopeless at this, he thought frustratedly.

He was just considering going to ask Arabelle to take over when Jared finally spoke. "W-Was it like this for you? The first time you killed someone?"

Taken aback, Derek stared at Jared, who looked back at him with sad, but curious, eyes. "H-How did you—?"

"I just assumed. The way you'd sometimes talk about killing like you were . . . familiar with it. It just made me wonder."

Derek felt as if he had just been picked up and spun around. There were many details about his past that he had never told anyone, including Jared. That he had made his first kill at the age of nine was one of them.

"I'm not asking you to tell me the whole story," said Jared. "I just want to know how it felt . . . if—" He closed his eyes. "Does the shaking ever stop?"

He wants reassurance, Derek realised. Not just about whether he'll ever get over it, but if he did the right thing. Derek cast his thoughts back to a memory he tried never to, consciously, revisit; the dimly lit room, the smell of expensive Aloserian wine. A lifeless body underneath him, the knife in his hands and the red stain spreading across the white sheets.

Derek swallowed. "The first time I killed a person, I couldn't stop crying."

Jared managed to push out an amused breath. "I don't think I've ever seen you cry before. You didn't even shed a tear that time you fell off my balcony and broke your arm. It's kind of hard to imagine."

"I'm not made of stone you know," Derek huffed, feigning indignance. For a brief moment, he allowed his thoughts to stray to that cold, winter's day, four years ago. He had been walking along the railing of Jared's balcony and failed to notice the bit of ice that still clung to the stone. Derek had fallen four stories and by the time Jared, the Queen and the Guards reached him, they had been almost certain he had been killed. Instead, all he had suffered was a minor concussion and a broken arm.

Now, he said, "The shaking does stop. It may take some time, though. Just ask yourself, did I do the right thing? Would I do it all over again? If the answer is yes, then you'll be fine."

"I think," Jared said after a hesitant pause. "That my answer is yes."

"Well, there you go."

"If it was to save you, I'd do it all over again."

Derek blinked in surprise. When he looked at Jared again, he found that his friend was gazing back at him with unwavering brown eyes.

Derek felt an odd tightening in his chest and found that he had to look away. "Thank you," he said, suddenly feeling awkward. "I appreciate the sentiment."

"I'm the one who should be thanking you," said Jared with a weak, but genuine, smile.

Getting up to his feet, Derek held out his unbandaged hand to Jared. "Are you finished moping now? If so, let's go get some sleep."

Jared took hold of his hand and allowed Derek to pull him to his feet. As they made their way towards where Arabelle was now setting out her own bedroll, Jared asked him, "What was your answer? The first time you killed someone?"

Derek didn't hesitate when he replied, "Yes."

"So . . . how does this work?"

It was midmorning and after eating breakfast from their now dwindling supply of food, Derek, Arabelle and Jared, now sat together in a small circle. The two pieces of the amulet lay on the ground in the middle.

"I guess you just fit the pieces together?" Arabelle suggested.

"But is that all?" said Jared.

"What do you mean?"

Jared shrugged. "The amulet's magic. Maybe it needs magic for it to be brought together? Maybe you need to wait until a certain time of day? Or maybe you need to sacrifice a pint of blood?"

"That sounds a little farfetched, don't you think?" Arabelle frowned.

"I guess there's only one way to find out." Derek reached for the two pieces.

He looked down at them in his hand and wondered for a moment if perhaps Jared was right? What if they did have to make a blood sacrifice first? Who knew what was farfetched and what wasn't when it came to daemonic magic.

Here goes. They all watched with bated breath as Derek fitted the two pieces together. The first piece slid easily into the second, larger, one.

A strong gust of wind blew over the trio. The source of it seemed to be from the amulet. Derek shielded his eyes with his free hand, Arabelle's hair whipped about her face and the water flask that had been propped up beside Jared, tipped over, spilling water onto the rocky ground.

The sun, which had been shining brightly only moments ago, seemed to have disappeared, the sky growing darker as though preparing for an oncoming storm. Along with the wind followed the sounds of whispering voices, their words indiscernible, but Derek could have sworn he heard the faint sound of a woman screaming. Followed by a deep, rasping chuckle.

And just as suddenly as it had all come, the wind and the whispers dissipated. The sky cleared and the sun was shining down on them once again.

A stunned silence fell over the three of them.

Jared was the first to break the silence. "What the hell was that?"

"I guess that's what happens when you put the pieces together?" Derek said, looking down at the now nearly complete amulet in his hand.

"That was . . . not at all what I was expecting," said Arabelle, still with a bewildered look on her face. Her normally straight hair looked a little bit dishevelled. "I wasn't the only one who heard those voices was I?"

Jared shook his head. "No. But I couldn't understand what they were saying."

"Neither could I."

"It was very . . . unsettling, to be honest," said Jared.

"At least we didn't need to perform any blood sacrifices," said Derek after a moment.

This earned a small smile from Jared. "Boring," he said.

Arabelle, however, still looked troubled. She was gazing at the amulet in Derek's hand with a worried frown.

"It's fine," Derek assured her. "We're all still in one piece aren't we?"

Arabelle's expression was still dubious. "I guess." She didn't say anything more on the matter.

Using the tip of his fingernail, Derek tried to pry the first piece away from the second but found that it was actually quite impossible. It was as if the two pieces were now melded together. As if they had always been one piece.

"So we've found two out of the three pieces," said Jared. "Any ideas on where we're going to find the third?"

He and Arabelle both looked to Derek.

"I'm not sure," he said, a little self-consciously. "The note only mentioned where to find the second piece, not the third."

The disappointment on both their faces could not have been any plainer and Derek couldn't help but feel that it was his fault.

"So now what do we do?" asked Jared. "The next piece could be anywhere."

They sat in contemplative silence. Derek thought about travelling to the nearest town and trying to find a library. He had come across books about daemons before, rare as they were, so surely there must be one about Milrath's amulet? One that would perhaps offer them some kind of clue as to where to find the third piece? But Derek quickly quashed that idea, as it would mean risking Jared and Arabelle finding out about the amulet's true origins.

"Why don't we ask around?" suggested Arabelle.

"Ask who?" said Jared, spreading his arms in a gesture that summed up just how far away from other people to ask.

Arabelle reached over to whack him in the shoulder. "I mean we could find a nearby town ask there," she said. "There must be someone who knows about this amulet and where we can find the next piece."

"If there are," said Jared."Don't you think they might've taken the piece for themselves then?"

"If they have, then we do what we did before and take it," Arabelle said, unconcerned.

"I'm pretty sure it would be frowned upon for *Guardians* to just steal from anyone they please."

"We've already done plenty of things that would be frowned upon," said Derek. "What's one more?"

"Exactly." Arabelle flashed him a grin.

Jared pointed an accusing finger at them both. "Scoundrels! The both of you!"

Derek swatted Jared's finger away from his face. "So where's the nearest town?"

It was Arabelle who went to retrieve the map they had brought along with them. When she returned, she unrolled the map of Aloseria, spreading it out on the ground in the middle of them.

Arabelle ran a slender finger over the map's surface until it landed just outside a spot labelled, *The Bone Swamp*. "I don't think we travelled *that* far last night, so it's safe to say that we're still somewhere around the Bone Swamp. So the nearest town from the swamp is . . . Florinstone."

Derek remembered the note he had found on Swift Hand Horace back in Skree. How in it had been written that the first piece of the amulet could be found in Florinstone. What were the chances?

"We go there," he said. If the first piece really had come from Florinstone, then that's probably where they were likely to get some answers on the third.

"Right," said Jared, practically leaping to his feet. "Then let's get going."

* * *

Darus woke up feeling sore and not at all refreshed from the previous night's sleep. Although he supposed he could hardly call what he did last night, sleeping. It had mostly just been tossing and turning on a mattress full of lumps that poked uncomfortably into his spine.

He rubbed the back of his neck and blinked blearily around the tiny, sparsely furnished room, now lit up with morning light streaming in from the single, small window. As Darus stood up and moved around the room getting dressed, he supposed that he couldn't entirely blame the bed for his restless night. He hadn't been getting much sleep since he set out on this secret mission. Since he learned that Derek was missing. He could only imagine it was due to all the stress of the situation.

"You're making my hair turn grey, Darus," his mother used to say to him when he was younger and did something to cause her to worry (which had been a lot).

He wondered if this was his punishment for causing his mother trouble so many times over the years? *If it is, I'm so sorry, Mother,* he thought. *Please don't let my hair turn grey prematurely.*

Dressed and with the rest of his things packed, Darus made his way downstairs to the main room of the inn to have some breakfast.

The common room was small and homely. An open hearth in the middle of the floor and set up around it were only a few tables and chairs. The room was empty except for the innkeeper sweeping in one corner.

When Darus took a seat at one of the tables closest to the empty hearth, the innkeeper set down her broom and shuffled over to him.

"What can I get you, dear?" she asked, tucking a strand of silver hair beneath her white cap.

"Just the porridge will do, thanks," said Darus with a smile.

With a decisive nod of her head, the innkeeper shuffled off into the backroom.

He looked down at the tracking rune on the inside of his wrist that was just visible above the cuff of his shirt sleeve. It had been irritating at first, but he was finally starting to grow used to the sensation of having his arm pulled on. He could feel the rune was now drawing him in a north-easterly direction.

"Well, well. If it isn't Darus Flynn."

Darus's head snapped up at the sound of his name. He looked over his shoulder to see a pair of familiar faces. One was a woman, short but stocky with braided dark hair. The other was a young man, Darus's age, tall, handsome and with a sweep of thick, brown hair. They were both dressed in the uniform of a Guardian.

"Cassandra," he said, nodding to the woman with the braided hair. Then to the man, he said, "Charles. Fancy meeting the two of you here."

"That should be our line," said Charles Decorus, son of Elias

Decorus, with a wry smile. Both he and Cassandra sat down at the table opposite him.

"It's been a while since I last saw you both," Darus mused. "What brings you here?"

"What do you think?" Cassandra said gruffly. She had her arms folded against her chest. "Work as usual."

"What kind of work?"

"Apparently some former members of Durbash's gang were spotted in these parts just over a week ago," Charles explained. "The chances that they're still around are low but we've been sent to see if we can at least find any clues as to where they might be."

Just then, the innkeeper approached their table with Darus's bowl of warm porridge.

"Thank you." He offered the old woman a smile.

"I think we're here more to provide the townspeople some peace of mind as well," added Cassandra once the innkeeper had left.

Darus hummed solemnly around a spoonful of porridge. He could understand why the people of this town might feel fretful at the notion of bandits lurking close by. Nockfield was a small hamlet with a population of no more than fifty or sixty. Hardly more than a year ago, Durbash and what was left of his crew had razed Nockfield to the ground in what they all suspected was nothing more than a hate-fuelled attack. Thankfully, many of the townspeople had managed to escape into the surrounding hills unharmed, but all of their homes and most of their belongings had been lost. For what felt like a long time, Nockfield had been nothing more than a town of tents. While they rebuilt, the King had decided to send Guardians to watch over the people and ward off any trouble.

Charles and Cassandra weren't even the first Guardians he had come across since he came to Nockfield, yesterday afternoon.

"And what about you?" asked Charles. His keen hazel eyes were looking Darus up and down, taking in his plain white shirt. "Judging from your attire, I'm guessing that you're not here on official business?"

"Your guess is correct," said Darus. "I'm just here in passing. I'll be leaving once my stomach is full."

Cassandra cocked a thick eyebrow. "That's it?" she said after a moment's pause. "You're not going to tell us anything else about why you're here?"

Darus just shook his head, swallowing another spoonful of porridge. Before leaving Ember, Darus had been given instructions to try and avoid revealing any details of his assignment to anyone unless absolutely necessary. The King didn't want news that the Prince of Aloseria was missing to reach the wrong ears.

"Are you on some sort of secret assignment?" said Charles, half-jokingly.

"Well if I was, I wouldn't tell you, now would I?"

This question seemed to catch both Cassandra and Charles off guard like they had only expected Darus to dismiss the suggestion of a secret assignment. They exchanged perplexed looks.

Having finished his breakfast, Darus pushed back and out of his chair. "Anyway, I have to get going," he said before they could start asking him more questions. "It was lovely seeing you both. When we're all back in Ember we really should catch up some more over dinner or a few drinks maybe?"

He gathered up his pack, handed a few gold coins over to the innkeeper and, with a final wave to Charles and Cassandra, he left the inn.

12

It took them another day's journey before they finally arrived at Florinstone.

The town sat on the very edge of a cliff face and Derek, Jared and Arabelle had to cross over a wide stone bridge to reach the town gates.

Despite the heat of the day, Jared had opted to wear a woollen cap over his head, hiding his brown curls from sight. He'd taken to wearing it whenever they stopped off at a town, he said it was to keep people from recognising him as the Prince.

Derek had always believed that there couldn't possibly be any town in Aloseria as colourful or as lively as Ember. As it turned out, he had been wrong.

The streets of Florinstone were lined with buildings made of brightly coloured brick and mortar.

The pathways were crowded with people. Children played games in the streets and store owners stood outside their shops, hawking their wares. A trio of women, dressed in extravagant dresses walked out of a clothing shop, their arms ladened with paper bags. Further up the street, a greengrocer was making a delivery to one of the houses in his horse-drawn cart. When a woman opened the front door, two small children ran past her and down the front steps so that they could pat the horse.

As they walked through the crowded pathways, one of a pair of women accidentally knocked into Derek's shoulder.

"Sorry," he said to the woman.

She gave him a half-smile and moved on.

Before she moved out of earshot, however, he heard the woman say to her companion, "Oh, did you see his *ears*?"

Derek's mood darkened instantly.

Not that he wasn't used to this sort of thing—the cold glares, the snide remarks, the way people whispered as if he were some sort of exotic creature that had escaped from its cage. Derek even liked to think he had become quite good at ignoring it over the years. At letting all of the looks and comments go straight over his head.

But there were times—like now—when they didn't quite go over his head. Times where they struck and left him feeling tired and bitter at the world.

Jared must have heard the woman and the noticed Derek's sour mood because he sidled up to him and said, "Don't worry about what stuck up shits like them think. It's not worth your time."

"Mm."

"Do you want to wear my cap?" Jared asked after a moment.

"Cover your ears?"

It was Arabelle who answered for him. "He doesn't need to hide his ears," she snapped. "You only hide something when you're ashamed of it and Derek has no reason to be ashamed of who he is." Arabelle looked at him with a hard-eyed expression. "Don't you dare let anyone make you feel ashamed of who you are."

It wasn't long before they came to what seemed to be the town square where an open-air market, that was very similar to the ones back in Ember, appeared to be taking place. The smell of fresh food permeated the air and made Derek's mouth water. It felt like forever since he had eaten something that wasn't fruit or dried meat.

"Excuse me," Derek heard Arabelle ask as they moved through the crowd of people. She was speaking to a woman—a Tybeni, judging by the pale skin, dark hair and monolid eyes—who tended a nearby fish stall. "Are there any magic shops in this town?"

"Magic shops, eh?" The woman said. She spoke in halting Aloserian. "There's Blackwood's, which is just further up the street, opposite the blacksmith's. You could also try the Magic Menagerie which is two streets down. Big, pink building, you can't miss it."

"I see. Thank you so much."

"You two go check the Magic Menagerie," Derek said while they were gathered by the ornate fountain in the middle of the town square. "And I'll go to this Blackwood's."

"Are you sure?" said Arabelle, as if splitting up in a place like this was a cause for concern.

"It'll be quicker this way." He slid his hands into his pockets. "Besides, I can take care of myself."

And so it was agreed; Arabelle and Jared would go to the Menagerie to see if they could find any information on the amulet or where to find the third piece, while Derek would go to Blackwood's and afterwards they would meet back up at the fountain.

It wasn't long before he turned onto a narrower street. This one was empty of people and had a much seedier look to it than the rest of the town. The buildings on this street looked slightly dilapidated and not quite as well maintained.

He continued up the street until he came to a stop in front of a small building opposite a blacksmith's. It was made up of plain, grey brick and mortar. A sign hung above the door that read, *Blackwood's Spells, Potions and Magical Objects.*

A bell chimed above his head as Derek walked through the door. The inside of the store was empty of other people and quite dark, with dark, wooden floorboards and black painted walls. Heavy, black curtains covered the windows, letting in only the barest slivers of daylight. There was an impressive collection of strange and fascinating items on display all over the place; in the centre of the room was a table stacked with glass bottles of all different shapes, sizes and colours. All were filled with some type of liquid. Potions, Derek guessed. In one of the corners was a rack of enchanted weapons. Mirrors of all different shapes and sizes were hung up on the left wall. A large, glass, cabinet filled with an assortment of miscellaneous objects stood against the far right wall.

He wandered over to look at a large, metallic, black box that was sitting on a pedestal beside the glass cabinet. Something about the box drew Derek's curiosity and he was just reaching out to lift the lid when a sharp, cawing noise startled him. Snatching his hand back, Derek looked up to see a black raven, perched on top of the cabinet, staring down at him with light coloured eyes.

"I wouldn't open that if I were you," came a new voice. Derek looked over to the other end of the store to find there was now a woman standing behind the front counter. She smiled at him. "You never know what might just pop out."

"I was just looking," said Derek.

"In an ordinary shop, there would be no harm in, *'just looking'.*" The woman stepped around the counter and walked towards him. "But that's not always the case in a magic shop. Especially one like mine."

Derek looked from the box to the woman. "Is it dangerous?" he asked.

"Maybe," said the woman. "I'm honestly not quite sure. I only got it in the other day."

The raven alighted from the cabinet and onto the woman's shoulder. She was tall and willowy. Her black hair was cut unusually so that one side fell down just below her jaw, while the other fell halfway down her pointed ears—

"You're a wood elf," Derek said before he could even think to stop himself.

The woman's green eyes gleamed. "I am." She tilted her head slightly. "And so are you. Or at least, partly anyway."

"Mother's side," said Derek, bringing a hand up to touch one of his ears self-consciously.

He could have sworn he saw a strange look pass over the woman's face, but it was gone so quickly he wondered if he had even seen it at all.

She looked as if she were only in her late twenties, but Derek knew that when it came to wood elves, appearances were no indicator of age. Wood elves had incredibly long life spans and could live up to be up to three hundred years old and never look a day over twenty. For all Derek knew, this elf could really be a hundred years old.

Aside from his mother, Derek had never met another wood elf before. There were so many questions he wanted to ask her. He was even curious to know what she was doing here, as all wood elves resided in the Great Forest to Aloseria's east. Only those that were outcasts could be found living outside the Forest. Like his mother.

Stop it, Derek. he told himself. *You came here to find out about the amulet. Not to bond with the store owner over our shared heritage.* "So I presume you're Blackwood?"

"You presume correctly," said the woman. With a mock little bow, she added, "Aurelia Blackwood, at your service."

175

Derek tried not to let his surprise show too plainly on his face. Another thing he knew about wood elves, was that they didn't have last names. Although, his mother had taken his father's last name and even changed her first. Perhaps it was normal for wood elves that had been cast out to change their names? Derek had never gotten the chance to learn what his mother's true name was. But it was no matter now, he told himself.

"And my apologies if my Familiar startled you," Aurelia said. "We've been on high alert here lately."

Derek raised his eyebrows. "How come?"

"There was a break in a couple of weeks ago and unfortunately some of my merchandise was stolen."

Derek thought of the half-complete amulet, tucked away in his pack and fought the urge to reach for it.

"Ah . . . That's terrible."

"Indeed." Aurelia lifted a hand to pet the plumage of her raven Familiar. "I would so like to have it returned to me."

Derek cleared his throat. "There's something I was wondering if you could—"

"What did you do to your hand?" She cut him off rather sharply.

Derek blinked. "Excuse me?"

"Your hand. The right one."

He looked down at his bandaged hand and frowned. "I . . . injured it." Odd. What did it matter to this woman what had happened to his hand? They were strangers after all.

Aurelia Blackwood held out one of her own gloved hands.

"Give it to me. Come on now, I haven't got all day," she added when Derek hesitated.

Feeling even more confused, he held out his bandaged right hand and tried not to flinch as Aurelia took hold of it and began undoing the bandages. The skin of his hand was covered in raw, pinkish-red burns. Thanks to Arabelle's salve, however, the burns looked worse than what they actually felt.

Aurelia's dark eyebrows drew together as she examined his hand. "What did you do, boy?" She clucked. "Stick your hand into some fire?"

"Something like that," Derek said wryly.

Aurelia Blackwood made an exasperated sound that reminded Derek very much of the Queen whenever Julianna and Jared did something to vex her. The raven on her shoulder made a clucking sound as if it too were exasperated by the state of Derek's hand.

With her left hand, Aurelia pressed the fingertips of her middle and index fingers, to the back of Derek's hand.

Before his very eyes, the puckered, burned flesh on his hand and fingers began to close up and heal. Aurelia didn't release her hold on his hand until all the burns had disappeared and only pale, unblemished skin remained.

"There," she said once she was finished. There was a slight flush of exertion on her cheeks.

Derek held his hand up to his face, turning it from side to side. It was completely healed. All traces of injury had vanished. When he flexed his fingers, he felt no pain or stiffness. It was as if he had

177

never been hurt at all.

"Thank you," said Derek, still barely able to comprehend it. "How much—?"

Aurelia held up her hand. "No payment necessary."

"You're sure?"

"Yes," Aurelia said in a tone that brooked no further argument. "Now, was there anything else you needed?"

"Yes," said Derek, getting back to business. "I was wondering if you know of any magical objects that have the ability to grant wishes?"

The Familiar ruffled it's feathers as if in response to a chill breeze, while Aurelia simply cocked an eyebrow. "My that is an odd thing to ask."

"It's for a school report," Derek lied. "I'm researching strange magical artefacts and I'm sure I heard somewhere once that there was something that could grant wishes. A necklace maybe?"

Aurelia made a considering noise before saying, "No, I am afraid I've never heard of such a thing."

Derek fought the urge not to furrow his brow. How could she never have heard of such a thing? According to the note, he'd found on Swift Hand Horace, this was where the first piece had come from after all. Unless there was another shop called Blackwood's that was owned by a mage in Florinstone?

What if she never knew what it really was? The thought occurred to Derek. If that was the case . . .

"Then do you have anything that I could use to help me find it?"

The words were all barely out of his mouth before Aurelia replied, "Sorry, but I am afraid I sold the last Search Stone yesterday. Now, I run a shop here, not a library so if you are not going to purchase anything then I am going off for my lunch break."

Without even waiting for a response, Aurelia Blackwood turned on her heel and strode across the room, disappearing through the curtained doorway behind the counter.

Derek just stood there for a moment or two, feeling confused and a bit irritated.

That was probably one of the oddest encounters I've ever had in my life.

As he made his way towards the door, Derek paused by the potion display, two bottles, in particular, catching his eye. He hesitated, glancing up at the doorway where Aurelia Blackwood had disappeared through, before making his decision.

He found Jared and Arabelle standing by the fountain in the town square.

"Did you really have to buy all those cakes?" He heard Arabelle saying as he drew nearer.

"I've been living off of nothing but stale bread and nuts for almost a week," said Jared as he pulled out a jam tart from the paper bag he was holding. "So pardon me if I want to indulge myself."

"I hope some of those are for me?" said Derek.

"Derek!" Jared said happily around a mouthful of jam tart (the

Queen would be horrified). Using his mouth to hold onto his tart, Jared dug around in the bag and produced a round pastry topped with white icing and offered it to Derek.

Derek reached for it with his right hand, only for Arabelle to grab hold of it. "What happened to your hand?" She asked, astounded.

The moment, Arabelle grabbed his wrist, Derek flinched and instinctively jerked his hand out of her hold.

They stared at each other; Arabelle looking at him with startled violet eyes. "I'm sorry," she said after a moment.

"No, I—" Derek started. He rubbed his other hand over his wrist, in an effort to rid himself of the memory of another's hand touching him. "Sorry. It's—the mage at Blackwood's healed it for me."

"You asked them to?"

"She was a wood elf," he explained. "She knew I had elf blood in me and must have felt she owed me because of it, I think."

"Huh," was all Arabelle said.

Jared passed him the pastry and Derek accepted it gratefully. As he bit into it, he savoured the sweet, cinnamon taste."So how did your trip to the Magic Menagerie go?"

Arabelle scowled. "The woman there was so annoying." She huffed. "She didn't know anything about an amulet that can grant wishes and she barely even let us ask any questions. She was too busy trying to sell us things."

"Arabelle's just upset because the lady tried offering her a spell that would make her nose look smaller," Jared explained.

Arabelle's cheeks flushed red. "My nose isn't even that large!"

"Of course it isn't."

Arabelle's scowl deepened. "You're going to get fat if you eat all those cakes."

"Hold your tongue," said Jared as he started on his second pastry. "And I didn't buy them just for me. Do you want one? I think there's one with chocolate in it."

Arabelle wrinkled her nose. "No thanks. I hate sweets."

Both Derek and Jared stared at her twin expressions of incredulity.

"And to think we share blood," Jared sighed mournfully.

Arabelle just rolled her eyes. "Anyway, we couldn't find out anything about the amulet, but we did get this." She reached into the front pocket of her pack, pulling out something and holding it out for Derek to see.

It was a compass. Completely ordinary looking and made of brass metal. Derek noticed that the needle hung down limply behind its glass casing.

"Apparently it's some enchanted compass that points you in the direction of whatever you really want to find while you're holding it," she explained.

"And it definitely works," said Jared, answering Derek's unspoken question. "Before I really wanted to find some sweets and it led us to a little bakery where I found these." He happily patted his bag of pastries.

Derek held out his hand and Arabelle passed him the compass, the metal cool against his palm.

He looked at it a little sceptically, despite Jared's assurances. But what else were they supposed to do? Blackwood's had turned out to be a complete waste of time—well, not exactly a *complete* waste—and this was probably the best chance they had of finding the last piece.

I want to find the third piece of Milrath's amulet, Derek thought, gazing down at the compass, it's needle still dangling uselessly. Just when he was beginning to think that this wouldn't work, the needle began to move. Derek watched as it swung around wildly a couple of times before slowing down, pointing from east to west and then finally coming to a halt and pointing north.

* * *

Aurelia stood by the open window and released a breath of smoke. She watched as a couple walked up the street below. Cora stood on the windowsill next to her, occasionally twisting her head to preen at her back feathers.

She kept thinking back to that unexpected encounter in her shop just minutes ago. To the sight of Erianna's son standing inside of her shop, of him looking up at her with that face that was near identical to his mother's, it had had a very strange effect on her, to say the least. It had muddled her mind, surfaced old memories and old wounds, while she had done her best to act like the perfect stranger to the boy.

Aurelia took another long, deep inhale from her cigar.

And then he had started asking questions, questions about a "necklace" that could grant wishes, whether she could offer him something that would help him find it.

She hadn't wanted to give him answers or any sort of assistance in finding the pieces of the amulet, but she hadn't been sure how to do that without giving away that she knew exactly what he was looking for. So she had come up with that excuse about needing to go on her lunch break and retreated upstairs as quickly as she could.

As Aurelia watched the transparent tendrils of smoke from her cigar drift up into the air, she wondered how far along the boy was in his search. Had he found the second piece yet? He obviously hadn't found all of them or he wouldn't have asked her for something he could use to find it.

And then, she thought, just because Aurelia hadn't helped him didn't mean his search had been hindered. She wasn't the only owner of a magic shop in these parts after all. Certainly, if the boy went to the Magic Menagerie, that irritating woman, Gretchen, would sell him something that he could use to find the rest of the amulet.

Do not worry about it, she tried telling herself. *Do not worry and do not get involved. Remember that you always said you would never get involved.*

She felt like she told herself this a lot lately.

But then, a thought occurred to her. Not just a thought, but an idea.

Would she truly be getting herself involved if she were to inform others of this situation? If she were to let them put a stop to it for her? Aurelia thought of the one person who could possibly be of help. A person she had not had any contact with in years. A person she was loathe to ask help from now. But if it meant helping Erianna's son . . .

Deciding to put personal feelings aside, Aurelia pushed herself away from the window and strode over to her desk. She pulled out a pen and a sheet of paper and began writing. When she was finished, she rolled up the paper and tied it together with some string.

"Cora," she called out to her Familiar. "I have a job for you."

13

The room was shrouded mostly in darkness. The curtains had been drawn shut, but the window was still open, allowing a gentle breeze to drift in, bringing the salty, ocean scent along with it.

Durbash lay on his back in the bed that stood in the centre of the room. The cool press of another's hands on his shoulder soothed him as healing magic poured into the wound there (although he did wish the foolish girl would stop trembling. It was very distracting).

A dark elf, no older than fourteen (probably), sat on a small stool by his bedside. The girl was a mage. He had picked her up about three years ago while he and some of his men had made port in Tybenia. She had been the poor daughter of a poor fisherman if he remembered correctly. Durbash had never intended to take her, he would have passed her by without a second glance if he hadn't seen her pick up a crate of ice cod that she had just dropped with only a wave of her hand and he knew that she was one worth taking. Mages always fetched the highest price on the slave market.

Durbash had meant to sell her off with the others they had collected that month, but he had never gotten the chance. It wasn't long after that that the Guardians raided his hideout in the eastern mountains, where he, and most of his crew, had been staying. The Guardians had either captured or killed more than half of his men and robbed him of his merchandise. But the elf girl had not been so lucky, she had been the only one he had managed to take with him when he went on the run. And it was a good thing too, having a mage around had proven to be incredibly useful. It had actually been thanks to the girl's magic, that they had been able to find out where the first two pieces of Milrath's amulet were hidden.

Around both of the girl's dark grey wrists were a pair of silver cuffs, with runes carved into them. They were called Magic Mufflers; they blocked a mage's magical capabilities. When worn, a mage could only use their magic when ordered to do so by the one who had put the Mufflers on them in the first place. Magic Mufflers were illegal in three of the four lands and incredibly difficult to find outside of the black market.

The girl's hands fell away from his shoulder once it was sufficiently healed. "I-I've done all I can for your shoulder," she muttered and if Durbash had been in his usual state, he would have snapped at her to speak louder. He despised the meekness that often came with these slaves. "It shouldn't be long before it's completely healed on its own now. I . . . I'm going to check your eye now."

Durbash only grunted.

It wasn't that Durbash hated slaves, he had been one himself once. Although, he had not been the type of slave that cooked or cleaned or warmed their master's bed. No, Durbash had been a gladiator; a warrior that fought purely for the entertainment of others.

The old king of Samwea had been quite fond of watching his slaves tear each other to pieces in the arena and Durbash had been one of the best. In fact, he had been an undefeated champion for years, until the old king died and the sport, along with slavery, had been abolished. Until then, his strength and brutality had been unmatched.

Durbash didn't resent his time as a slave, actually, for him, they were fond memories. His time as the old king's gladiator had instilled him with the strength and the will to do whatever it takes to survive in this world. With the knowledge that to survive one had to be more than just strong, one had to be *powerful*. Ruthless. Feared.

The girl began undoing the bandages around his right eye and Durbash held himself still. He thought about the burning, blinding pain that had hit him when the boy had thrown hot embers and wood into his face. How he had cried out and how he had done so again when the boy forced his sword through Durbash's shoulder.

He felt the familiar heat of anger build up inside him, his fingers curling into fists where they lay at his sides.

So as the bandages came undone, Durbash braced himself. This time, he would not cry out. This time, he would not show weakness

The girl laid one feather-light hand over his injured eye and he felt the healing magic begin to seep in.

But instead of the cool, soothing sensation that engulfed him when she had healed his shoulder, he felt a burning pain that intensified with each passing second. It felt like he was being burned all over again. Behind his closed eyelids, he kept seeing the boy, lying on the ground in front of the fire before he threw burning, embers into Durbash's face.

Anger started to stir inside of him. Dark and primal and ever closer to boiling over.

"You're supposed to be healing me," he growled through gritted teeth. "Not making it hurt more than it already does."

"I'm sorry. Your eye," the girl started saying. "I-It's too—I can't—"

The last threads of Durbash's endurance snapped and the all-consuming, black rage stole over him. "*Get out!*" He roared."Leave! *Now!*" His hand struck out, catching the girl in the face with enough force to knock her off her stool.

Cradling a sore and bleeding mouth, the girl scrambled to her feet, sobbing and rushed over to the door before pulling it open.

The door had just closed behind her when Durbash decided to pick up the fallen stool and hurl it at the door.

It hit with such force that one of the legs fell off and a sizable dent on the door was left behind.

It wasn't long before the door was thrust open once again. This time by Dahlia, who stood in the doorway, her face set into a mask of frantic worry.

"Boss?" She said. "I heard you shout. What is it? What's wrong? Are you—?"

"Leave me!" Durbash shouted.

"But—"

"I said, *leave,* or I will kill you where you stand."

Fear and hurt flickered across Dahlia's face before she did as she was told and left, shutting the door again as she did so.

The room was now quiet, save for the sound of Durbash's heavy breathing. He stayed there, sitting on the edge of his bed with his head in his hands.

How had it come to this? Three years ago, Durbash had been one of the most powerful men in all four lands. He had been the leader of a booming slave-trading business. He had been a king among thieves and murderers and all matter of criminals. He had been feared and revered in equal measure. He had been in possession of the only two things he ever could have wanted; power and wealth.

And now? Now he was forced to hide in a hole like a rat. His business was in ruins, his riches gone. His gang, which had boasted some hundreds of members, was now down to a mere handful. Everything that he had worked so hard for, everything that he had lied and cheated, stolen and killed for, was crumbling down around him. And it was all because of those Guardians. *Those miserable,*

bloody Guardians.

Why couldn't they have just let him be? Why did they have to be so relentless in hunting him and bringing his budding empire down? Just because he stole people? Because he sold and bought them as if they were trinkets? Because the Guardians deemed his actions too cruel? Life was cruel enough anyway, what did it matter if he was as well?

Durbash rose from his bed and made his way across the room to the water basin on top of the rickety, wooden table by the wall. He was a bit wobbly at first, walking was quite disorientating when one only had the use of one eye, but he got his bearings soon enough. He picked up the basin, which was filled with clear water, and tipped it over his head. There was a brief shock of cold as the water cascaded over him, washing away all of the perspiration that had built up along his skin and soaking the floorboards beneath his feet.

When he had first heard about Milrath's amulet, an amulet that could grant you any wish that you desired, Durbash thought that he had found the answer to his problems. The amulet was to be the key to regaining everything he had lost and then some.

The amulet would be his redemption. His salvation. And it was to be the ruination of the Guardians.

The only problem now was that one piece, along with his most skilled thief, was missing and the other was in the hands of a bunch of snot-nosed children. *Guardian* children, no less. Just the thought made the familiar rage that was always churning inside of him, begin to boil. Not to mention there was still the third and final piece that needed to be found, but only the Goddess knew where it could be.

But it was no matter, he thought, trying to get a hold on his temper before it spilled over again. He'd find those brats, even if it meant tracking them all over Aloseria, he would find them. He would take back the amulet piece and he would make them suffer for daring to humiliate him the way they did.

Sometime later, once he had covered up his injured eye with fresh bandages, Durbash finally emerged from his bedroom. He entered the common room, where he found Crane reading by the unlit hearth on the floor and Dahlia carving the tabletop with her knife.

The rest of his crew were probably loitering around outside. The house was only big enough to house four people, so the remaining members were forced to sleep in tents outside.

Of all the hideouts he'd had scattered across Aloseria, this one at Serpent's Cove was the smallest and dingiest, nothing more than an oversized hut hidden inside of a cove by the shoreline. But it was the only one they had left.

It was located along Aloseria's western shores and was a good distance from the nearest town. When the Guardians started raiding their hideouts, Durbash hired a mage to cast as many protective enchantments on this one as possible. At first, he had worried that it wouldn't work. That the enchantments wouldn't be enough to keep the Guardians from sniffing them out here. But it had been a year since the Guardians had taken their last hideout and there was still no sign that they were close to finding out this one.

"Boss!" Dahlia leapt from her seat when she noticed Durbash enter the room and came to stand in front of him. "Are you okay? How are you feeling?"

"I'm fine," Durbash said gruffly, his irritation rising. He had very little patience for Dahlia and the way she clung to him like a besotted school girl. There were even times where he regretted ever having offered her a place in his gang all those years ago when he first met her as the daughter of a drunkard and his miserable wife.

"Are you sure?" Dahlia asked. There was a long, half-healed gash running along the left side of her face. A remnant from their fight in the Bone Swamp. "Do you want me to get something for you?"

Durbash pushed past her to take a seat at the table. "Just go fetch me a drink."

"Of course. I'll be right back," she said before disappearing through the doorway he had just entered from.

This place wasn't much to look at, even Durbash had to admit. The floor was made of plain, grey flagstones and the walls from colourless brick. The common room was scarcely furnished, only with a long table and some chairs and an empty dish cabinet. There were cobwebs in the corners of the ceiling and around the stuffed, sabre lion head that he had mounted above the mantelpiece on the east wall. The curtains on the two windows by the front door were always closed so the space was always illuminated either by candlelight or by the open hearth.

Although it didn't look it, the front door was probably the only thing of real value in this entire room. It was no ordinary door and was imbued with powerful magic that would take the user anywhere they desired, even if it was a great distance away. One could also make a return trip just as easily, so long as they carried a piece of the door with them. Durbash and all the members of his remaining crew carried a piece with them. It was thanks to this, that they had managed to evade capture from the Guardians for so long. And, more recently, how they managed to escape the Bone Swamp before they could become meals for some ravenous aracnas.

It wasn't much longer before Dahlia returned with a bottle of mead in her hands. "Here you go, Boss."

Wordlessly, Durbash took the bottle from her, uncapped it and took a swig. The drink went down his throat, sweet and thick. When he was done, he wiped the back of his hand across his chin, where some of it had dribbled down from his mouth. He looked around the room.

"Where's Rall?"

"He went into town," said Crane without looking up from his book. He had his right leg propped up on a worn footrest. The cuff of his trousers rolled up just enough to reveal the white of bandaging. He'd been bitten by an aracna back at the Bone Swamp, leaving his entire right leg paralysed and with two nasty looking, fang marks. Fortunately, the paralysis had almost completely worn off, though he still complained of pain from the bite wound.

Durbash scowled. "What? Why?"

Crane simply shrugged. He turned a page in his book.

Durbash's scowl deepened. He'd made it clear that he didn't want any of them leaving the cove without his say so. All he needed was for one of them to be recognised and bring the Guardians swarming here.

As if summoned by their words, the front door swung open and in stepped, Rall. He was dressed in a pair of ragged trousers and a worn grey, travelling cloak. His wild mass of red hair stood out even more against the drab colours of his clothing.

"And just where the hell have you been?" Dahlia demanded, hands on her hips.

"Went to town," said Rall unconcerned.

He stepped further into the room, pulled out a chair and sat himself down. He leaned back just far enough that he could place both of his dirt-encrusted boots on top of the table.

"You went whoring I bet?"

Rall shrugged. "Gotta keep myself occupied somehow. I'd go crazy otherwise just being cooped up in here."

"You know we're not supposed to leave here without the boss's say so," said Dahlia. "What if a Guardian had spotted you? What if you'd led them right to us?"

"Don't get your knickers in a twist. I'm not that stupid that I'd go out without keepin' a low profile. That's why I wore the cloak." An ugly grin spread across his face. "If ya don't want me goin' out so bad then maybe you could invite me into your bed sometimes, Dahls?"

Dahlia's glare was murderous. "If you even think about setting foot in my room, I'll open up your skull with my axe."

"That's too bad. But I guess the boss is the only one you'd ever let into your bed anyway. Not sure I'd want his seconds anyway."

Dahlia's face was flushed with both anger and embarrassment. "You piece of—!"

"That's enough," Durbash ordered and Dahlia immediately fell silent.

He took another long drink of his mead before he rose from his chair, setting the bottle down on the table. "But Dahlia is right, Rall." He walked around until he came to stand in front of where the man was seated and towered over him. "I believe I made it explicitly clear that none of you are allowed to leave this hideout without my permission. So if you ever leave here again without checking with me first, I'll have your head mounted on the wall above my bed. Understood?"

Rall at least had the good sense to look afraid. All the colour drained from his face as he nodded, his throat clicking as he gulped. "Yes, Boss. I understand, Boss."

Durbash couldn't deny that it gave him a certain thrill to see the fear in another's eyes when they looked at him. Ever since he was a boy, Durbash had always wanted to be someone that people looked on with fear. His father had always said to him that one wasn't truly powerful unless they were feared.

"But, I didn't just go out whorin', ya know?" said Rall.

"Oh? What else did you disobey my orders for?"

Rall swallowed again and sat up a little straighter. "Those Guardian brats that attacked us, I recognised one of 'em."

"Which one?" asked Crane.

"The one with the brown hair. I couldn't figure it out at first, so I thought I'd go into town and see if any of the blokes in the back alleys could help me out."

"And?" Dahlia prompted impatiently when Rall decided to pause, most likely for the dramatic effect. "Did you figure out who he was?"

A self-satisfied grin slid onto Rall's face. "I did. Turns out the boy was, Jared Regalias."

Jared Regalias. Durbash knew that name. Anyone who lived in Aloseria knew that name.

"The Prince?" said Dahlia, astonished. "You're saying the Prince was one of those little shits who attacked and robbed us?"

"How can you be so sure?" Crane asked, sounding a little dubious.

"He's the spittin' image of his old man," Rall explained. "Who,

I've had the displeasure of meetin' once before."

"What the bloody hell would the Prince be doing running around and hassling us for?" demanded Dahlia.

Rall shrugged and scratched his nose. "Does it matter? What What matters now is that we know who one of those brats are now." He looked up at Durbash, his eyes brimming with excitement. "We can track 'em down now. Get the slave girl to whip us up a tracking spell and Crane, Dahls and me will go after 'em and we'll take back the amulet piece they stole from you. We'll even teach 'em a little lesson for ya. What do ya say, Boss?"

It took a moment of silent deliberation on Durbash's part. He was, admittedly, hesitant, but when he thought of those brats being hunted down and taken just as unawares as they were. When he thought of the looks on their faces when Rall and the others exacted their revenge and, most importantly, when he thought of the amulet piece being returned to him, it dispelled any and all of Durbash's reservations.

"Fine," he said. "Go after them. Get the amulet piece back and make them suffer for daring to target us. But, I have one other request."

"What's that, Boss?"

"The boy with black hair, the one with the elf blood in him, bring him back here. You can kill the other two but I want that boy brought back to me alive. I want to be the one to make him pay for what he did to me."

Rall nodded, an ugly grin twisting his face. "Sure thing, Boss."

"And if any of you kill that boy before I can get my hands on him," Durbash added. "I'll do to you what I would have done to him. Tenfold."

Durbash left that threat hang in the air before he gathered up his bottle of mead and retreated to his room.

Nursing his mead, he let himself wallow in the pleasant thoughts about that half-breed boy, lying bleeding and broken at his feet, pleading for mercy that Durbash would be sure not to deliver.

Once he finished his drink, Durbash drifted off into slumber with a smile on his face.

14

It was nearing midnight when a large, yellow dragon touched down on a grassy hillside, sending a group of nearby rabbits scattering.

Changing back, Darus gathered up his pack and set off towards the copse of trees further up the hill. There he found a shallow cave and after checking it for any bears, sabre cats, or nefarious humans, Darus laid out his bedroll and settled himself down for the night.

He ate a meal of bread and dried meat and after he had finished he rolled down the sleeve of his shirt on his right arm, revealing the tracking rune on his wrist. It was still very prominent against his skin, even after nearly two weeks of travel. He could still feel the pull of the rune, a sensation that had now grown familiar to him. Guiding him towards Derek.

If Darus had not been feeling so fatigued, he would have gotten up and continued on his way. But he had been on the move since dawn and his body was in desperate need of rest. *Besides,* Darus thought to himself, *there's no chance of me catching up to them tonight.*

Still, it didn't stop the worrying thoughts that had been plaguing his mind for the past few days. It conjured up images of Derek's throat being slit by a faceless stranger while he slept. Derek being shot out of the sky by an arrow to the heart. He even imagined Derek and the others running into Durbash and being shipped off to another country to be sold as slaves.

There was really no end to the morbid scenarios his mind kept coming up with. But there was one thing that Darus was certain of and that was, if any harm came to Derek, then he wouldn't be able to live with himself. Nor did he think he would even be able to live without that boy. Life without Derek and his snarky remarks and childish refusal to eat most vegetables was simply unimaginable for Darus.

Lying back on his bedroll, Darus sighed and folded his arms behind his head.

When exactly had that boy come to mean so much to him?

Darus had never met his father. He died before Darus had even been born. His father hadn't been killed, however, while in the line of duty like most Guardians. No, his father had taken his own life. His mother, Rosemary Flynn, had always told him that his father had had the gentlest of souls. That he had been too kind and too compassionate and ill-suited to the life of a Guardian. That one day all the things that he had seen and done had just become too much for him to bear.

Despite his mother's words, Darus had thought his father weak and a coward and had resented him for a long time. Now that he looked back, it was possible that he had also resented his father for the fact that he had chosen to kill himself rather than live with his wife and son.

Then, when Darus was fifteen and finally a rookie Guardian, he had seen a boy, who he had used to sit next to in Mathematics class at the Academy, a boy who used to help Darus out with his homework, stabbed through the throat.

Darus had always thought he knew just how harsh the life of a Guardian could be and that he was prepared for it, but nothing, *nothing,* could have prepared him for that. He didn't remember much after that, just that he had been sick in some bushes later on. The days following he had been wracked by a guilt that demanded to know why Darus hadn't tried harder to save his comrade. That told him he wasn't good enough, that he didn't deserve to be alive while the other boy was now nothing but ashes in the wind. It had been then that Darus started to realise that maybe his father hadn't really been a coward after all. That maybe he could understand why his father had ended his own life rather than live with those kinds of horrific memories.

Then, when he was nineteen, his mother died. Killed while trying to rescue children from a cave-in while she was on an assignment. His mother, with her warm smiles and infinite kindness. His mother, the only parent he had ever known, was gone.

Darus still remembered that all-consuming grief and how it had turned into bitterness and self-destructiveness that lasted for a few years after. He would drink himself into a stupor almost every night. At first, he did it to drown out the grief, but after a while, he started doing it just because he didn't know how not to. Darus would stay out late and fall into the bed of any willing man or woman and shirk all of his responsibilities. He had managed to push away all of the people who had cared for him up until then. All, except for Lila.

"This can't go on, Darus," Lila said to him the day before his twenty-first birthday. He had just woken up from another night full of drinking and sex with someone whose name he couldn't even remember, to find Lila storming into his bedroom. "Do you think your mother would be happy to see you the way you are now? Coming home drunk every night? Isolating yourself? Something has to change."

And something did. That something was a nine-year-old boy named Derek Goldridge.

Darus had been sent on an assignment to the town of Windfell to deal with a band of lycanthropes causing trouble in the area. While there, they had been introduced to the Mayor and his son. Darus's first impression of Derek had been that he reminded him of the stray cats that sometimes wandered the streets back at Ember, with his glowering looks and surly attitude. Despite the boy's sullenness, there was something about him that had endeared him to Darus. Especially when he found out that Derek had lost his real parents three years prior.

Over the course of his stay in Windfell, Darus had noticed some things between Derek and the Mayor; the way Derek's mood darkened whenever he was around Goldridge. The way he would flinch whenever the Mayor touched him or stood too close. The bruises on the boy's pale skin.

"He has a fondness for picking fights with the other children around town," Goldridge had explained. "It happens you know, children acting out when they've been through a traumatic experience."

Although Goldridge had sounded as sincere and concerned as any parent might it had still done little to assuage Darus's apprehension.

After asking around town, Darus had discovered that Derek Goldridge was really Derek Draco, son of the exiled Guardian, Alexander Viseric.

Then, one night, Darus stumbled upon one of the most horrific scenes he had ever seen in all his twenty-one years of living.

Even now, it turned Darus's stomach to think about that night. The Mayor of Windfell, lying sprawled out on his bed, his blood soaking into the sheets, and Derek—small and wide-eyed—kneeling next to the body of his adoptive father, clutching a bloodied knife in his trembling hands.

Darus remembered lifting the boy's small body into his arms, holding him close as the sobs and the trembling wracked him. He remembered feeling such a fierce protectiveness towards Derek at that moment that it almost startled him. As did the hatred and revulsion he had felt for the dead Goldridge.

And so, after that night, it was decided that he would bring Derek back to Ember with him and within the week, Darus had adopted the boy.

It seemed that becoming responsible for a child was just the thing that Darus needed to kick him back into shape. He quit drinking and taken up knitting instead. His nights were spent at home with Derek and he took on more assignments so that he could earn enough coin to support Derek. In his spare time, he taught himself how to become a better cook (also for Derek) and suffered many burnt hands and cut fingers in the process.

Some months after taking Derek in, Darus had been trying to bake a bread and butter pudding for the first time while Derek watched. It had been going well until he'd pulled it out of the oven, burned his finger on the hot pan and subsequently dropped it onto the floor.

The pudding that he had so lovingly tried to prepare lay as a scattered mess on the floor and Darus fell to his knees with a heartbroken, "My pudding."

That's when Derek had started to laugh.

Not a chuckle or a derisive snort, but genuine laughter that had him clutching his stomach and wiping away tears.

It was the first time Darus had ever seen Derek laugh like that.

The sound of Derek's laughter and the sight of his bright, boyish smile, made a warmth bloom in the middle of his chest and his anguish over his ruined dessert had been quickly forgotten.

Before long, Darus would find himself watching Derek while he slept, while he trained. While he read a book by the fire and while he ran around with the dog in the backyard, he found himself wondering if this feeling in his chest was what all parents felt when they looked at their children?

The sound of snapping twigs brought Darus back to the present. Quick as a whip, he was up on his knees, sword in hand and body tensed for action. But he quickly found that the source of the noise was just a fox with a dead rabbit in its mouth. The fox stared at him with wide, glowing eyes before darting into the nearby bush. Darus allowed himself to relax and set his sword back down.

As he settled himself back down onto his bedroll, Darus closed his eyes and listened to the first drops of rain begin to fall outside of the cave. *I'll get him back,* he promised himself as he drifted off to sleep. *I will.*

* * *

"By the Goddess, why won't it stop raining? My clothes are soaked!"

"We're all soaked, Jared," Arabelle pointed out. "No need to whine about it."

Jared huffed. "I'm a prince," he said sulkily, ringing out his shirt. "I'm not used to spending more than a minute or two in wet clothing. Of course, I'm going to whine."

Arabelle only shook her head and pushed the wet strands of her hair behind her ear.

It had been raining off and on for the past four days, which was how long they had been travelling for. After flying through the pelting rain for the better part of the day, Arabelle, Jared and Derek had taken cover under a thickly clustered, group of trees on top of a hill. It didn't keep them completely dry, but the trees provided enough cover from most of the rain at least.

Arabelle sat on top of a moss-covered log, her knees drawn up to her chest. Even through the dense mist of rain, she could see the towering shapes of giant trees in the distance. The Great Forest, home of the wood elves. She looked down at the enchanted compass in her hand, the needle was pointing north. Towards the Great Forest.

Arabelle just hoped that the last piece of the amulet wasn't *in* the Great Forest, otherwise things were going to become a lot trickier for the three of them.

Standing next to her, Jared had packed away his wet shirt and was slipping a new one over his head. Movement to her right drew Arabelle's gaze and was just in time to see Derek, stripping out of his own wet shirt.

It felt highly illicit for her to be watching Derek while he was in a half state of undress. Still, Arabelle could not tear her eyes away from the sight of the pale, lightly muscled back. When he turned so that Arabelle could see his flat stomach, she, ridiculously, felt her face warm up.

At the same time, she heard Jared make a choked sound

followed by the soft thump of him dropping his water flask onto the ground. Arabelle watched as he fumbled to pick it up, looking oddly flustered. When she looked back over at Derek, he had already changed into a clean shirt. Arabelle mourned the loss of the sight of his bare chest.

"Is the compass still pointing north?" Jared asked as Derek came over to join them.

"Did you think it was going to change?" Arabelle said archly.

Jared just shrugged as if to suggest that was a possibility.

"Just because it's pointing in the direction of the Great Forest, doesn't necessarily mean that the next piece is there," Derek pointed out.

I hope you're right, thought Arabelle.

The Guardians and the wood elves had endured a rocky relationship for years now, ever since the war man years ago. She didn't think that they would be allowed to just waltz through the Forest in search of this amulet piece.

They wouldn't be able to rely on Derek being half wood elf to help them out either. Having romantic or sexual relations with anyone who was not of their own kind was considered to be extremely taboo among the wood elves. Any elf that broke this law was to be shunned and cast out of the Great Forest. Therefore Arabelle wasn't too sure how the elves would react to someone like Derek, the product of a union between a human—a Guardian no less—and a wood elf.

They waited in silence under the cover of the trees for a little while longer. Arabelle fiddled with the compass, absently opening and closing the cover. They were getting close now, she could feel it. The anticipation was like a live thing thrumming through her bones.

It shouldn't be much longer now, she thought to herself. *Soon, I'll be able to meet her. I'll be able to meet my real mother.*

That thought brought with it a mix of emotions. On the one hand, she was excited; after so many years of wondering and yearning, she would finally be able to meet the woman who gave birth to her, who raised her for the first three years of her life. She would finally know what her mother's face looked like. Finally, get to talk to her and be close to her.

On the other, she was nervous, because what if her mother wasn't at all like what she hoped she would be like? What if she was left nothing but disappointed?

In her fantasies, Arabelle imagined her mother being so filled with happiness to see her again after all these years. She imagined her crying with joy and holding Arabelle in her arms, explaining that she had had no choice but to leave Arabelle that night. That she had never wanted to leave her and that she would never let Arabelle go again.

But there was a doubtful voice in the back of her head that whispered, *what if that's not the way it goes? What if she isn't happy to see you?*

Now, she imagined a faceless woman with blonde hair, saying to her in a cold voice that the reason she abandoned Arabelle all those years ago was simply because *she didn't want her.*

Arabelle snapped the compass close and put it in her pocket with shaky fingers. She felt on edge all of a sudden. When Arabelle went to take a drink from her water flask to try and calm herself, she found that it was empty.

"I'm out of water," she announced, rising from her seat on the log. "I think I saw a stream not too far from here. I'll be back soon."

"Do you want me to come with you?" Jared asked, frowning up at her from where he sat beside Derek on the thick, protruding root of a tree. His hair had gotten longer since they'd left Ember and was starting to fall into his eyes.

Arabelle smiled and ruffled his hair. "Don't worry about me, little cousin," she said, handing him the compass. "I'll be back before you know it."

Indeed, it didn't take long for her to arrive at the stream, but by the time she made it there, the rain had lightened to a drizzle.

The stream was flanked on both sides by tall, overreaching trees. Pebbles and mossy rocks littered the banks on either side. The stream was shallow and the water was clear. Still, she'd have to make sure to boil the water before drinking it, just to be safe.

Arabelle picked her way carefully over the slippery, rocks before crouching by the edge of the stream.

She was in the middle of filling her flask, then she heard what sounded like pebbles shifting underfoot. She looked up, expecting to see an animal, a deer perhaps, looking for something to drink, but instead, she saw the female bandit from the Bone Swamp, Dahlia.

She was standing on the opposite side of the stream from her. There was a look of malicious glee on her face.

Two other bandits that she didn't recognise stepped out of the underbrush to stand beside Dahlia.

Before Arabelle could even react, something, or someone rather, grabbed her from behind. Two strong arms wound themselves under her own and hoisted her to her feet and trapped her in place.

How had she not heard anyone come up behind her? How could she have been so careless? They were the last thoughts Arabelle had before a cloth was pressed into her face, a sickly sweet stench filled her nostrils and everything went dark.

* * *

"She's been gone for a while now," said Jared fretfully.

"Maybe the stream was further away than she realised?" Derek suggested.

They'd been waiting for Arabelle to return for longer than they had expected and he could tell by the way that Jared was fidgeting like a man about to face a criminal trial, that he was getting worried.

Jared shook his head. "No. No, I don't think that's it." For a moment, Jared didn't say a word and Derek watched as his friend sat motionless before getting to his feet. "I'm going to look for her."

"Are you sure? Arabelle could be on her way back right now."

"If she is, then you can tease me for being a worrywart as much as you want. But I'd still feel better going to look for her."

"All right," said Derek. "Just try not to get into any trouble on the way. It'd be bothersome if I had to come and rescue you."

"I guess it's a good thing that I'm a fully capable fighter then and not some damsel in distress."

"Now now, you can always be both."

Jared made a rude hand gesture that his mother certainly wouldn't have been proud of before he put on his ring and Changed. He whipped around and took off in the direction Arabelle had gone, leaving Derek alone.

He leaned back against the tree trunk of the root he was sitting on and gazed out at the Great Forest beyond. Even from this distance, the trees were massive, towering over the surrounding forest like a castle towered over smaller buildings.

Derek reached into his pack and pulled out the amulet, unwrapping the handkerchief from around it. The red gem in the centre winking up at him in the sliver of noonday sun that managed to peek out through the clouds. He imagined what it would be like once the amulet was complete. How he would feel when he finally held all three pieces in the palm of his hand.

They were so close now. Just one more piece. Just one more piece and he would finally be able to undo his past.

In his mind's eye, he saw his parents. They were standing in front of their cottage in the Valley, both smiling and holding their arms out as if to welcome him back home.

He would finally be able to have his family back.

Out of the corner of his eye, Derek saw something coming towards him.

He expected it to be either Jared or Arabelle, but instead, it was a familiar man dressed in ratty clothing and a wild head of red curls and a matching beard.

Rall. One of Durbash's bandits. The one who had held a loaded crossbow to his head back at the Bone Swamp.

Derek was on his feet in an instant. His hand went to the hilt of his sword at his side and drew it out of its sheath.

He noticed that Rall wasn't alone. Following him, a few paces behind were three other bandits. One was the woman, Dahlia. The other two were men that Derek didn't remember seeing at the Bone Swamp. One of the men was carrying something. Something with a fall of golden hair.

Arabelle. His heart slammed in his chest. For a few eternal seconds, all he could think about was Arabelle. That was Arabelle in the bandit's arms.

Arabelle with her head tipped back and her eyes closed.

Arabelle *not moving*.

"'Lo there, Guardian!" Rall called out once they were only a few feet apart. "How go's it?"

"What do you want?" Derek demanded in response.

Rall made a 'tsk' noise. "Rude thing, isn't he?" he grumbled.

"I ask him how he is and he just says, 'what do you want?'"

"Children these days," said Dahlia. "No manners."

"I mean really. The least ya could do is ask how we've been doin' since ya left us to deal with aracnas all by ourselves back at the Bone Swamp. Bloody beasts almost killed us."

"And that would have been a bad thing?" asked Derek.

Rall glared at him. "I don't like you."

"The feeling's mutual. I'll ask you again, what do you want?"

Rall chuckled and ran a hand through his curls. "Actually we're here to strike a deal with ya."

"A deal?"

"It's quite straightforward really," said Dahlia. As she spoke, the bandit holding Arabelle changed his grip on her and produced a knife, holding it up so the blade caressed Arabelle's exposed throat.

"You hand over the amulet piece you've got there in your hand," she continued. "And we won't slit your little friend's throat."

After a beat, Derek said, "And how do I know you won't just try to kill her once I hand it over?"

"You don't." said the bandit holding Arabelle. "But do you really want to risk it?"

Derek gritted his teeth. His mind was racing, trying to figure a way out of this situation. He could try attacking, but that might just lead to them cutting Arabelle's throat as soon as he made a move. Running was out of the question.

The last thing he wanted to do was give them the amulet but he wasn't willing to trade Arabelle's life for it.

"I'm getting tired of waiting," sighed Rall. "Maybe we should just slit the girl's throat now and—"

"No wait," Derek said in a rush. "Wait, I'll . . . I'll give it to you. Just don't hurt her."

"Well hurry it up! We don't got all day."

"Fine." He sheathed his sword and brought the amulet over to Rall.

The bandit smirked as he practically snatched the amulet out of Derek's hand.

A quizzical frown appeared on Rall's face as he looked down at the amulet. "Hang on," he said. "It looks different. It—"

"That must be the first piece," said Dahlia incredulously, peering over Rall's shoulder.

"Where the hell did *he* get it?" demanded the other bandit, the one not currently holding Arabelle.

"I took it off of some dead bandit in Skree," Derek admitted bluntly.

All four bandits looked at him in disbelief. A grim smile spread across Rall's face. "Ah, so that's what happened to Swifty. Well, it's no matter now," he slipped the amulet into the inside of his jacket. "Now, Dahlia—"

"Wait," said one of the bandits. "Where's the oth—"

Bursting from out of the tree branches, a massive, bronze blur, descended upon them with a furious, animalistic cry.

Derek launched himself backwards and out of the way as he heard the bandits cry out in alarm.

Jared went for Dahlia first. He didn't give her any time to react and before she could even reach for her battleaxe, Jared sent Dahlia flying a small distance into one of the nearby trees. Her body struck it with a force that left her lying motionless on the ground.

In the commotion, Arabelle had been released and was now lying forgotten in the wet grass.

The two other bandits were coming at Derek, with their weapons drawn.

He kicked out at the ankles of one, causing them to stumble, before drawing his sword and stabbing it into the other bandit's— the one that had held a knife to Arabelle's throat—thigh.

The man fell to his knees with an anguished shout and Derek finished him off by slashing his blade across his throat. Blood spattered onto the ground and the bandit's body toppled face-first into the grass.

Derek spun around, looking for Rall and was just in time to see a flash of red hair disappearing down the hill.

He heard someone yell out from behind him and turned around to see Jared standing over the now unconscious form of the bandit Derek had kicked to the ground.

"Take Arabelle and go," ordered Derek. "Get her somewhere safe. I'll catch up." And he took off after Rall.

As he ran down the hill, Derek pulled out his ring, slipping it onto his finger. He Changed and launched himself into the sky.

Raindrops fell into his eyes, but Derek ignored them in favour of searching for the red-headed bandit.

It didn't take long for him to spot Rall. That wild red hair was like a beacon, even partially obscured by the rain and the treetops. With his target in sight, Derek closed his wings, diving towards the ground.

He broke through the treetops, landing badly on one of the lower branches and hissing at the jarring pain that shot up his foreleg.

Rall whirled around and his eyes widened at the sight of him.

Derek growled, baring his teeth in a snarl. He would have liked nothing better than to incinerate the man before him with a gout of flame, but it Guardians were forbidden from using their fire to harm another living creature. It was only to be used as a last resort.

Rall whipped out a dagger from his belt and threw it at him.

He ducked the blade at the same time he leapt from the branch. He was on the other man in seconds, knocking him onto his back and sinking his teeth into his shoulder.

Rall yelled out as his teeth tore through the fabric of his clothes and into his skin. The wet, metallic taste of blood exploded in Derek's mouth. He bit down harder. Rall's screams grew louder. He could feel the strength leaving the bandit's body from underneath his paws.

Blood was dripping from his mouth when Derek finally tore his jaws away from the man's shoulder. He Changed so that he could pin Rall's arms to the ground with his foot and right hand while he searched with his left hand through the inside of Rall's jacket, before finally retrieving the amulet from one of the pockets.

With a quick sigh of relief, Derek slipped the amulet into his own pocket and lifted himself off of the bleeding bandit.

He was just turning to leave when he heard Rall chuckling.

"What's so funny?" he demanded.

Rall still lay on the wet grass with both his arms now spread out on either side of him. The wound at his shoulder bled sluggishly, staining the shoulder of his jacket. His wild mess of hair was fanned out around his head, the strands wet with rain and dirtied with mud and grass in some places. Still, he looked to Derek with a fiendish grin. "Ya know what my pa used to tell me when I was a boy?" He said.

"I don't really care."

"He said, 'don't charge into a battle until you've counted every blade.'"

What's that supposed to mean? Derek opened his mouth to say but didn't get the chance. At that same moment, a loud cry tore through the air. A pained cry. A dragon's cry. *Jared.*

Rall chuckled again. "Ya didn't count all the blades."

Derek had Changed and was in the air in seconds, flying in the direction that he had heard Jared's cry.

He scanned the ground anxiously for any signs of Jared or Arabelle. Finally, he spotted them and his heart thudded painfully in his chest.

Derek made his descent, Changing as soon as he touched the

ground. He rushed over to where Jared and Arabelle lay, sprawled in the grass, only a few meters away from the Great Forest. Their packs were scattered around them, two had even fallen open, spilling their contents onto the ground.

Derek fell to his knees beside where Jared lay, his arms still wrapped around his cousin, as if he had been trying to shield her. Both had their eyes closed. There was mud on Arabelle's cheek and clothing and a leaf in her hair but she looked otherwise unharmed.

The relief Derek felt quickly dissipated when he saw the long shaft of an arrow sticking out of Jared's side.

It had struck him just above the hip and appeared to be embedded deep into his flesh. The surrounding material of his shirt was already growing red with blood. Derek also recognised the type of arrow that was sticking out of his friend's body. It was the kind that the Valley dwellers near Windfell had used to hunt animals. The tips were long and broad, perfect for piercing through even the toughest hide but were oftentimes difficult to extract.

Without even thinking, Derek found himself reaching over to press unsteady fingers to Jared's neck. He felt the flutter of a pulse beneath his fingertips and almost sagged under the weight of his relief.

Jared was still alive.

But he won't be for much longer if you don't find him any help, said a voice in his head. The arrow needed to be taken out and then the wound needed to be cleaned and stitched up. But first, he had to get Arabelle and Jared somewhere safe.

Before he could do any of that, Derek felt the cold press of steel against the side of his neck. "Hand over the amulet."

Derek turned his head just enough so that out of the corner of his eye, he could see the pale, dark-haired bandit, Crane, standing behind him. Holding the hilt of the sword that was now pressed to Derek's neck.

There were three other bandits with him, moving in to surround Derek and his fallen friends, all sneering down at him.

Derek spotted a quiver of arrows and the tip of a bow behind Crane's back. So he was the one who shot Jared down. Derek felt a surge of hate and anger pulse through him. A desire to turn around tear the man to shreds. The only thing holding him back was the razor-sharp edge of the blade pressed against his skin.

"Do as you're told boy," Crane growled. "Or I'll cut your head clean off your shoulders before I do the same to your friends over there."

"Just kill him, Crane," said one of the other bandits impatiently.

"What are you waitin' for?" another one demanded.

"Now, now, let's not be too hasty. Let's at least give the lad a chance to do the right thing."

Derek looked at the unmoving forms of Jared and Arabelle. At the arrow sticking out of Jared's side. He felt a wave of frustrated helplessness that made him sick. Even if he did hand over the amulet, there was no guarantee that their lives would be spared.

The word of a bandit was worth as much as the dirt beneath their shoes.

Derek felt the edge of the sword bite into his skin and a warm trickle of blood slide down the side of his neck.

"If you won't give it to me," Crane began. "Then I'll just have to—"

He never got to find out what Crane was going to have to do. The bandit had stopped mid-sentence and it was then that Derek realised that they weren't alone.

To his left, standing just a few feet away from them, was a woman, dressed in a green half-cloak, leggings and brown boots. Her brown skin stood out in stark contrast to her snow-white hair, pulled into a long braid. She held a loaded bow in her hands with the arrow pointed directly at Crane.

"Drop your weapon," she said, her voice somehow soft and commanding all at once. With a familiar lilting accent.

The woman was a wood elf.

"This is no business of yours, *she-elf*," Crane hissed.

The elf didn't waver. "So close to our borders, we shall decide what business is ours and what is not."

All of a sudden, Derek became aware of more green-clad figures descending from the tree-tops and moving to surround them. Elves. There were fifteen of them at least and every single one of them had their bows out and arrows trained on the four bandits. Derek felt the sword against his neck begin to waver.

"I'll sever the boy's head before any of you even loose your arrows," hissed Crane.

"You doubt our speed, *human*." the female elf said.

Before Derek could even blink an arrow cut through the air, taking one of the bandits in the chest, directly through the heart. He fell to the ground just as two more arrows were fired in rapid succession. One bandit went down with an arrow through the head, the other with an arrow through his throat.

Within seconds, Crane was the only one left standing.

"If you draw another drop of that boy's blood, you will end up just like your friends. Do you really want to make that sacrifice?"

No one moved for the longest time, the tense stillness broken only by the rainfall. Finally, Derek felt the sword draw away from his neck and he let out a quiet, but shaky, exhale.

Crane begrudgingly sheathed his sword, holding his hands above his head in a show of surrender, he turned to face the female elf.

Without lowering her bow, she ordered, "Leave. *Now*."

Crane bowed his head in a gesture that was more mocking than respectful. "So kind," was all he said before he loped out of the small clearing and out of sight.

The female elf switched to elvish as she addressed the two elves closest to her. *"Dilnych if a gwendch cad sol durefin,"* she said. "Follow him and make sure he does not come back."

Then, she turned her attention to Derek and stepped forward. She had put away her bow and arrow but that still did little to put

221

him at ease. How did he know she hadn't just saved them only to take them prisoner?

She stared down at him with an impenetrable brown-eyed gaze. "Boy, what is going on here?"

15

Aurelia snapped shut book she was reading, the old spine making crackling noises as she does so, and tossed it over her shoulder.

Instead of falling to the floor with a heavy thud, the book went to join four others, which were floating lazily in the air in the centre of the room.

Clenching her cigar hard between her teeth, Aurelia pushed herself up from her desk and stepped over to the floating books. All were thick leather-bound tomes that she had borrowed from the town library. On the cover of one was the title, *Magical Artefacts Throughout the Years.* Another was titled, *The Dark History of Dark Magic.*

All five books revolved around the same subject; magical objects.

She had scoured through them nearly all afternoon and none of them had provided her with any answers. There was no mention of a mirror, or at least a mirror shard, that showed one strange visions when they touched it, in any of these books.

The mirror shard, which she had found a week ago now, lying on her doorstep was still sitting in an unused crate in the back room and she couldn't stop thinking about it. She couldn't ignore it's presence, as much as she tried. Even though Aurelia had not touched or even looked at it since that first night, she could still clearly see the visions of a grey landscape. Could still hear that strange voice speaking in a strange language.

They had even started creeping into her dreams at night, twisting them into something dark and frightening that had Aurelia waking up trembling and covered in sweat.

She wanted to rid herself of the blasted thing but didn't know how. Perhaps if she knew what it *was,* then maybe she could figure out what to do with it.

So she had gathered all of the books she could find on dark magical objects—natural and dark magic alike—but not one of them had helped her out in the slightest.

Aurelia looked at the floating books arrayed before her for a moment longer before, with a frustrated click of her tongue, she made a sharp motion with her fingers. The books went flying across the room to lay themselves one on top of the other in a neat pile at the foot of her bed.

Aurelia ran a gloved hand through her hair, upsetting the strands there. *Well, this was a bloody waste of time,* she thought.

She gazed down at the fraying edges of the carpet, the threads coming loose, her mind wandering to the mirror shard lying tucked away just below these floorboards. Like an unwanted guest.

What are you?

* * *

The cool, evening air made gooseflesh rise up on Derek's skin. Still, he refused to go inside just yet.

The wood elves had brought Derek, Jared and Arabelle to their village deep in the Great Forest. It was a village, unlike any Derek, had ever seen before. All around him there was a network of trees as wide as houses and much, much taller. Rounded doors and windows dotted the trunks of the giant trees at intervals. Branches as wide as the cobblestoned streets back in Ember, acted as bridges for the elves to walk along from one tree to another.

This was where my mother lived, Derek thought, as he watched a couple of youths leap from tree branch to tree branch, as nimble and sure-footed as possums.

But any feelings Derek might have had from seeing his mother's homeland for the first time were dulled by the worry and guilt churning inside of him.

Sylvina, the female elf and captain of the elven guard, had brought Derek and the others back to her home. Her wife, Aravanea, was a healer and as soon they walked through the door with an unconscious Arabelle and an injured Jared, she dropped what she was doing and went to work, no questions asked.

As Jared was the most seriously injured, Aravanea turned her attention to him first. She'd ordered them to lay Jared down on the bed and cut him out of his shirt. The arrow had lodged deep into his side, but according to Aravanea, it had not hit anything vital. Both Derek, Sylvina and two other elves held Jared down while Aravanea pulled the arrow out. Once she had started, Jared had awoken, thrashing and grunting and biting down on the wad of cloth they had stuck into his mouth. Even as he pressed Jared's hands onto the mattress, Derek had felt like a bystander, watching as tears leaked out of his friend's eyes. As his body convulsed once the arrow was removed and as blood leaked from the wound, staining the white sheets.

Aravanea had worked as quickly as she could to get the wound cleaned and stitched up before bandaging it. Then she had given Jared, pale and weak and covered in sweat, some kind of drink, that smelt strongly of peppermint, that had him falling asleep within seconds.

Derek had then stood by numbly as Aravanea moved to check over Arabelle who still had yet to open her eyes. She had pronounced that there was nothing seriously wrong with Arabelle and that she should regain consciousness within a few minutes. Hearing those words brought some relief, but when Aravanea came to him and asked to see the wound on his neck, Derek felt as if he were moments away from being ill and he turned on his heel and rushed out the door for some much needed fresh air. He had been sitting on the edge of the tree branch that led to Sylvina and Aravanea's front door since then.

He couldn't stop thinking about Jared with the arrow sticking out of his side. Or about Arabelle, unconscious and fragile-looking. The guilt was like a live thing, eating him from the inside out.

Jared and Arabelle could have died today.

This whole quest had been Derek's idea and even though Arabelle and Jared had both joined him of their own volition, Derek couldn't help but feel responsible for their current conditions.

If I told them the full truth about the amulet, they might never have agreed to come with me and they might never have ended up in this situation.

Derek thought of the King and the Queen and Julianna. What would they say if they could see Jared now? Would they be angry at Derek? Would they blame him for putting Jared in this position? He wouldn't be surprised if they did.

The door creaked open behind him and Aravanea stepped out. When she saw Derek she smiled. Aravanea had a pretty, youthful face, framed by a curtain of long, brown hair. Her feet were bare beneath her simple, purple dress.

"Sut ti mae ed?" Derek asked in elvish as she came to stand next to him. "How is he?"

"Still sleeping," she responded in Aloserian. "But with enough rest and medicine, he should recover in no time."

Derek released a breath he hadn't even known he was holding. "I . . . Thank you."

"There is blood on your neck. We should clean that up."

Derek nodded noncommittally.

Aravanea offered him another smile. "I also came to tell you that your other friend is awake now if you wanted to see her?"

He followed Aravanea inside.

Sylvina and Aravanea's home was made up of one, large circular room that looked like the hollowed out inside of a tree (which it was of course). Four circular windows lined the walls. A small, round table with a vase of freshly picked flowers in the middle and two chairs stood in the very centre of the room, a woven green rug laid out underneath it. A winding staircase at the other end of the room, led up to a loft and near the stairs was a bed where Jared lay sleeping.

Next to the bed, Arabelle was sitting up on her bedroll, looking more than a little dazed. Sylvina knelt beside her, offering her a cup, which she took and drank from gratefully.

Derek crossed the room to kneel at her side. "Arabelle, how are you feeling?"

"I feel . . . strange." she frowned. Her voice sounded slightly slurred.

"Strange how?" Sylvina asked.

Arabelle passed the cup back and placed a hand to her forehead. "I don't know. Kind of dizzy, I guess."

"It is probably a side effect of the drug you inhaled," Aravanea explained. "It should pass soon, but you must be sure to drink plenty of water."

"I see," said Arabelle. "And not to sound rude or anything, but,

228

who are you?" She looked from Aravanea to Sylvina. "And where are we?"

"This is Sylvina," said Derek. "And her wife, Aravanea."

"And you are in our home in the Great Forest," Sylvina added.

Arabelle blinked in surprise. "How—?"

"We had a run-in with Durbash's bandits," Derek explained. "Sylvina and a few other elves saved us and then brought us back here."

Arabelle started looking around the room. "And where's Ja—" before she could finish her question, her eyes landed on the bed and who was lying on it.

With a gasp, she leapt to her feet and scrambled over to the side of the bed. Her eyes were wide with horror as she looked down at the bandages wrapped around Jared's middle, already spotted with blood. "Wh-What *happened*?"

"He was shot by an arrow. But he'll be all right." Derek hastened to add as Arabelle's expression grew more alarmed.

"Shot by an arrow?!"

"But he'll be all right," Derek repeated.

"Your friend is right," said Sylvina in a placating tone. "His life is in no danger."

"Yes," Aravanea chimed in. "He bled a bit once the arrow was extracted, but I managed to clean and stitch the wound. He should also be safe from any risk of . . . oh, how do you say— infestation?"

"I think you mean, 'infection', *nygaria fi*," Sylvina said to her wife with a fond look.

"Yes! Infection is what I meant."

Arabelle groaned and rubbed at her temples with her fingers.

"Perhaps some food will make you feel better?" Aravanea suggested. "I will go and fetch you something to eat."

She and Sylvina moved to one of the wooden benches across the room, leaving Derek and Arabelle with some semblance of privacy.

"What happened to you?" Derek asked after a moment. "How did the bandits get you?"

"They snuck up on me while I was at the stream," Arabelle explained. "I was grabbed from behind and they shoved a funny-smelling cloth in my face that made me blackout." She made a frustrated sound. "It shouldn't have happened. I should have heard them coming but I was careless. Maybe if I hadn't been knocked out then Jared wouldn't be . . ."

"What happened to Jared wasn't your fault. You can't—you *shouldn't* blame yourself."

But Arabelle still looked as if she was doing just that. Finally, she tore her eyes away from Jared's prone form and looked up at Derek. "But how did they even find us?" she asked. "The last we saw of them was at the Bone Swamp and surely if they had been following us since then, we would have noticed much sooner."

"I don't know," Derek admitted shaking his head. He was at just as much of a loss as Arabelle was as to how the bandits had managed to track them down after all this time. The only explanation he could think of was if they had some sort of magical assistance. It wasn't too outlandish to think that maybe they had gone to a mage for some help in hunting them down.

Aravanea brought them a tray with two cups of plum juice, a sprig of grapes, strawberries, a wedge of cheese and rolls of soft herb bread. At the sight of the food, Derek's stomach growled, as if only now realising just how in need of food it was. The last time he had eaten had been that morning, which now felt like a week ago.

"Thank you," he said, accepting the tray so that he and Arabelle could dig in eagerly.

"Once you have finished," Sylvina said. "I will take you down to the lake so that you may clean yourselves and your clothes."

"Oh— I . . ." Arabelle cast a hesitant look at Jared.

"And I will stay here and watch over your friend," Aravanea added gently, noticing Arabelle's uncertainty.

So it was decided. Once Derek and Arabelle were finished with their meal, they followed Sylvina outside while Aravanea stayed behind to keep an eye on Jared.

They made their way onto the ground, the way all wood elves did, by jumping from branch to branch. Sylvina did it with grace and surefootedness, never once stumbling or hesitating before a leap. Derek and Arabelle had a bit of a harder time, making their descent. It appeared that Derek's elf blood did not provide him with the ability to leap across tree branches with perfect elegance.

Once on the ground, Sylvina led them through the village. Lush, green grass stretched as far as the eye could see, dotted here and there with bunches of flowers and bright red toadstools that were much larger than any toadstools Derek had ever seen before. They were almost big enough for one to sit upon.

Doing just that, Derek spotted three small girls, sitting in a circle upon a single toadstool and weaving yellow flowers into each other's hair. Two older women sat in wooden chairs nearby, sewing pieces of colourful cloth.

The air was filled with the sound of laughter and elves calling out to one another in loud, boisterous voices. He could even hear the faint sound of music, a pipe, being played but couldn't determine where it was coming from.

Still, despite the cheerful ambience of the elf village, Derek couldn't help but notice the way some stopped to stare at them, specifically Derek and Arabelle, as they walked past. While some watched them with nothing more than open curiosity, he also took note that other's gazes were less than welcoming.

An elf called out a greeting to Sylvina from where he was tending to his small vegetable garden. When he caught sight of Derek and Arabelle, his face crumpled into a mean frown. A small child peered out at them from a half-opened door before an older woman, most likely the mother pulled them away and shut the door with a bang.

"It has been quite some time since humans set foot in the Great Forest," Sylvina explained, taking notice of some of the unfriendly reactions they were garnering. "Much less a pair of Guardians."

"I see that some aren't all that thrilled about our presence here,"

Arabelle remarked. Two women carrying woven baskets of clothing openly scowled at them as they walked past.

"You will have to forgive them," Sylvina said, slightly apologetic. "Ever since the war, sentiment towards your kind has not been very affable."

"Even towards those that are only half-elf?" Derek asked and he was surprised to find that his tone held a hint of bitterness to it.

Sylvina stopped and Derek and Arabelle came to a halt behind her, gazing at her taut back with confusion. Had Derek's words offended her? "It is one of our oldest laws that wood elves do not cavort with anyone but our own kind." she sounded as if she were reciting a line she heard a thousand times. "Any elf who breaks this law is to be cast out and any half-breed children that they may have are to be shunned and never recognised as one of our own."

Derek heard Arabelle make an affronted sound. That . . . stung. A half-breed. Is that what Sylvina thought of him? Is that what every elf here thought of him? He suddenly had the urge to cover the ears that were the only indicator of his 'half-breed' status.

Before Derek could feel any more offended, Sylvina turned to face them and there was a sadness in her dark eyes. Derek wasn't quite sure whether it was sympathy or guilt or maybe even a mixture of the two.

"I am sorry," she said and her voice was soft and sincere. "Our people are an old one, Derek Draco. Even I will admit that we are too set in our ways and traditions sometimes, but there is nothing that can be done about it."

Derek was taken aback and could do no more than blink for a moment or two. "I . . . I understand."

Sylvina offered him a half-smile before she turned back and started walking again. "But do not worry. Not all of us hold ill feelings towards humans and Guardians. Some of us even find them to be quite . . . intriguing."

Derek looked up to see a trio of young elves, probably about the same age as Arabelle and himself, gazing down at them from one of the branches up above with open fascination.

Derek and Arabelle exchanged a look before they both waved.

The faces of the young elves lit up as they waved back with great enthusiasm.

It wasn't long before they came to a tree that looked quite different from the rest. With a trunk of white bark, it stood just a little apart from the rest of the trees. While just as tall, it was the widest by far and had a grander air about it. There was a set of tall, double doors at its base and was manned by two armed guards.

Arabelle let out a low whistle. "Who lives here?" she asked.

"This is the residence of our Fair Lady. The Queen of the wood elves." Sylvina explained, pausing so that she could allow them the chance to look.

"Only the Queen lives here?" asked Derek. "Doesn't she have any family? Any heirs?" He knew that he probably sounded nosy, but he was curious. Not much was known about the royal family of the wood elves. At the Academy, they had only been told that the elves were ruled by a Queen known as the Fair Lady and that she had helped to cement a truce between the Guardians and the wood elves. All of the books Derek had combed through over the years about wood elves, were scarce on information as well.

Sylvina was quiet for perhaps a moment longer than she should have been and when he looked at her, she would not meet his eyes.

"It is . . . a topic that none of us elves like to discuss," was all she said before leading them on.

They came to a large meadow with a sea of grass that reached up to their knees and swayed gently in the breeze. Dragonflies droned lazily and not too far away, a young elf lad tended to a herd of deer that grazed contentedly on the green grass. When the elf spotted them, he raised a hand in greeting and Sylvina returned the gesture.

They crested a rise in the earth and below was a large stretch of crystal, clear water, the surface was glimmering in the late afternoon sun. An old willow tree stood on the edge of the lake, its leaves hovering just above the water.

"It's beautiful." Derek heard Arabelle say under her breath.

The water was cool and refreshing. It felt wonderful to be able to wash away all the dirt and sweat that had accumulated on his skin in the past four hours.

Arabelle stood in the water only a short distance from him. Although he and Arabelle had both decided to leave their small clothes on, since neither of them were exactly comfortable with the idea of bathing naked in front of each other, Derek still felt awkward. He tried to avoid looking at her as much as possible since it felt far too indecent to even glance at her while she was so underdressed. But it seemed that the more he tried to keep his eyes off of her, the more he ended up looking at her.

At one point, he glanced over his shoulder to see Arabelle standing with the water up to her waist with her hands combing through her wet hair. For a moment, Derek was lost to the sight of her lightly muscled arms and stomach. The way the water and the light from the setting sun cast a dusky, golden hue against her light brown skin.

"Can I help you?" Arabelle asked, looking over at him.

Derek started and turned away. "N-Nothing," he muttered. He could feel his face turning warmer by the second.

Behind him, he heard Arabelle giggling and his mortification grew.

Derek submerged himself beneath the water, wondering if it would be considered overdramatic if he were to drown himself?

The next time he looked over at Arabelle, he caught sight of a large, purple bruise on her right shoulder and felt that stirring of guilt. How long had she had it for? Had she gotten it back in the Bone Swamp? When the bandits ambushed her? Or when she and Jared had fallen from the sky after he had been shot?

"I'm sorry," he said. The words were out of his mouth before he could stop them.

Arabelle looked over at him, her golden brows furrowing slightly. "What are you sorry for?"

"This quest was all my idea and today you and Jared could have been killed."

"You make it sound as if you coerced us into this. I don't know if you've forgotten, but I'm here so that I can find my birth mother," Arabelle said with an air of nonchalance. "And I can't really speak for Jared, but, knowing my cousin, I'd say he would have rather chopped off all of his hair than let you come on this journey alone. And that's saying something."

"But I bet neither of you expected that we'd be facing the likes of Durbash," Derek pointed out.

"That's true," she conceded. "But my point still stands, Jared and I made our own decisions. Sure, we might not have been expecting to fight against Durbash of all people, but it's not as if we thought this journey was going to be completely without danger. So it's not your fault if we end up getting hurt along the way. We're not getting into anything that you didn't already tell us."

She smiled and Derek tried to return it, despite the guilt that continued to roil through him. *Oh, if only you knew.*

"But what about the elves?"

Derek frowned at the question. "What about them?"

"Well, I know they came to our aid and of course we should be grateful, but why do you think they've brought us here and treated us like invited guests?"

Derek turned to look over his shoulder where he could see Sylvina leaning against the willow tree, sharpening her curved blade with a whetstone. Far enough away to give him and Arabelle some privacy but also close enough that she could still keep an eye on them.

"You're suspicious of them?"

"Aren't you?" Arabelle retorted. "We don't know them and wood elves and Guardians haven't shared the friendliest of relationships over the years. I'm not saying for certain that they have some ulterior motive for bringing us here, but I just don't want us to be caught off guard if they do."

Arabelle turned and waded her way back to the edge of the lake, leaving Derek to absorb her words.

Despite everything, it had never occurred to him to be suspicious of the elves. Perhaps he had just been too swept up in the fact that these were his mother's people? *His* people. Why should he have any reason to fear the people his kind and gentle mother had lived amongst for most of her life?

But then he remembered that these were also the people who had cast her out for falling in love with his father, a human. He remembered there were times when a glumness would steal over Erica and there had been one such time when his father had lifted Derek into his lap and said to him, "Your mother just misses her home from time to time."

"But isn't this her home?" Derek had asked with all the innocence and naivety of any child.

"Yes, it is, but there will always be a part of her that yearns for the Great Forest and its people and will see that as her true home."

Derek hadn't quite understood his father's words back then, but now he did and it made him angry to think that his mother had been caused such heartache by her own people who she had clearly loved despite everything.

Derek's father had chosen to live his life in exile, but his mother had been forced out.

Arabelle did have a point, he thought, in a pragmatic way. It probably was for the best that they stay on their guard in case it turned out that this really was all part of some sort of scheme to get revenge on the Guardians.

Derek moved to join Arabelle and Sylvina by the lake's edge. Once they were dried and dressed, they made their way back to the village.

When they reached the door to Sylvina and Aravanea's dwelling, Derek was surprised to find two elves, standing on either side of the door. He knew right away that they weren't members of Sylvina's guard because, unlike Sylvina and her guard, they wore long, green capes with gold trimming draped over their shoulders. Their armour was the colour of bronzed tree bark and the matching steel helmets upon their heads obscured all but the lower halves of their faces. Both had swords sheathed at their sides.

Derek exchanged an uncertain glance with Arabelle.

Sylvina did not seem surprised to see the other two armed elves. But then again, nothing about her posture or expression gave any indication to what she was feeling.

"Ti fwyt," said Sylvina.

"Ti et fwyt," the two other elves responded in unison.

This was a customary greeting amongst wood elves, with no clear translation. It could mean anything from hello to good morning or how are you?

Without another word, Sylvina stepped towards the door, placing her hand on the handle. The other elves did not stop her. She glanced back at Derek and Arabelle. "Come," she told them and opened the door.

Derek stepped forward first, Arabelle following close behind him. The elves did not look at them as they walked past. They were as still as statues.

As he and Arabelle stepped through the threshold, Sylvina closed the door behind them and Derek tried not to feel like they had just walked into a trap.

But then, he noticed two things. One was that Jared was awake and sitting up in the bed.

And second was the woman with long, golden hair, sitting elegantly in a chair next to Jared's bedside. Aravanea was offering her a cup of some drink, her head bowed in a deferential gesture.

Sylvina fell to one knee.

"*Ti fwyt nyaf, Claned Madis fi,*" she said. "Greetings, my Fair Lady."

16

The Fair Lady was quite possibly the most beautiful woman, Derek had ever seen in his life. Even amongst wood elves, who were all uncommonly beautiful, the Fair Lady had a face that could leave any man or woman breathless. Her hair was like spun gold and when she rose from her seat, Derek saw that it fell all the way down to her knees. She wore a green dress made of silk, that fell loose around her pale shoulders.

"Sylvina, fyn syfich," said the Fair Lady in a soft voice. "Rise, Sylvina."

Sylvina did as she was bid.

"Jared!" cried Arabelle, bolting across the space that separated them, inadvertently ignoring everyone else as she threw her arms around her cousin.

Derek noticed that Sylvina looked displeased by the lack of deference shown to her queen, but the Fair Lady looked completely unbothered by this. In fact, all of her attention seemed to be solely focused on Derek.

She stared at him with a calm, but unreadable look on her face and he fought the urge not to fidget under her unrelenting, green-eyed gaze. He felt as if he were being studied. Did she already know that he was half-elf? Was she judging him for it?

"Are you all right?" Arabelle was asking Jared. "How do you feel?"

Jared still looked pale and there were dark rings under his eyes, but still managed to quirk a smile. "I'm all right, really," he said, placing his hand over the one Arabelle had on his cheek. "I'm just a little sore."

That's an understatement, Derek thought. With a wound like that, he had to be more than 'just a little sore'.

"I am sorry I could not wait until you were all more rested," the Fair Lady said, switching to flawless Aloserian. "But I am afraid this matter cannot wait."

"I am sorry if we kept you waiting," said Sylvina. "I did not realise that you would come so soon. If I had known otherwise—"

The Fair Lady held up a pale, elegant hand. "There is nothing to apologise for, Sylvina. It is not a crime to keep the Queen waiting for a few short moments." The smile that had been on her face slid away for a more serious expression to take its place. "But I am afraid I must ask if you and your wife could please allow me some time alone with our . . . guests."

"Of course, Your Majesty."

With one last bow, Sylvina and Aravanea left, leaving Derek, Jared and Arabelle alone with the queen of the wood elves.

No one moved or said a word for a few tense seconds. It was the Fair Lady who broke the silence. She looked back over at Derek with bright green eyes and an ethereal smile. There was something about those eyes that were vaguely familiar to Derek. "Please take a seat."

She held out a hand to gesture to where Jared and Arabelle were sitting on the bed. Seeing no reason to deny her request, Derek strode over to sit at the foot of the bed next to Arabelle.

The Fair Lady seated herself once again on the chair, facing all three of them directly. Derek noted that she wore a silver crown upon her head. Well, not a crown really, more like an intricately designed circlet that looked as if it had been woven out of metallic sticks and leaves. She smoothed out the creases in her dress. "As I am sure you have already gathered, I am Nyalra, Queen of the wood elves and Fair Lady of the Great Forest."

Arabelle spoke first, "My name is Arabelle Aloria. And this is Derek Draco and Jared . . ." she hesitated, unsure of whether it was wise or not to speak Jared's last name.

The Fair Lady smiled. "And Jared Regalias." Her smile broadened at their surprised looks. "You look just like your father, Your Highness."

"A pity really," Jared said with feigned sorrow. "I would have much preferred to take after my mother. Her hair is a much more interesting colour than brown."

Arabelle whacked him lightly on the shoulder, but the Fair Lady only laughed, soft and musical. She looked even more lovely when she laughed.

"I do not believe that your father had quite the sense of humour that you do the last time we saw each other," she said.

Jared looked pleased. "Thank you."

"And how do you know that was a compliment?" Arabelle asked.

"Since when is having a sense of humour a bad thing?"

"And you," said the Fair Lady, turning her attention back to Derek. "You look just like Erianna."

Derek felt the breath catch in his throat. "Erianna," he said after a beat. "That was my mother's name? Her true name?"

The Fair Lady nodded, her face solemn. "Yes. I . . . I knew her well."

If you knew her so well then why did you cast her out? He wanted to demand. But instead, he clenched his jaw and kept his gaze fixed on a ladybug that was making its way across the floor.

"But I am afraid I did not come here for idle conversation and reminiscing," the Fair Lady said. "Not that long ago, I learned that three young Guardians would arrive at my borders and that they would come searching for something. Is this true?"

No one spoke. How could the Fair Lady possibly have known of this? Derek and the others had come into contact with a scarce few people on their journey and certainly no one who would know anything of their plans. Except for maybe, Durbash and his bandits, but Derek thought it was more than unlikely that they could have sent word to the queen of the wood elves.

Derek had a sudden thought of the elf mage he had met in Florinstone, Aurelia Blackwood. But no, she couldn't have been the one either. Derek had never told her what exactly he was looking for or that it would mean travelling so close to the Great Forest. In fact, Derek hadn't even known that they would end up coming to the Great Forest. He also never said anything about him being a Guardian and travelling with two others.

Then who could it have been?

It was Jared who spoke next."Who told you this?"

"That is not your business to know, I am afraid." The Fair Lady said not unkindly. "Is it true? Did you come to these parts in search of something? And I ask that you do not lie to me. If you do, I will know and I shall be forced to keep you captive here until you tell me the truth."

"You can't do that," Jared blurted out.

The Fair Lady arched one golden brow. "Perhaps you are not familiar with the treaty I signed almost seventeen years ago with your father? In it, it was stated that a Guardian would never come near our borders without forewarning or a written statement, signed by your king himself, explaining their presence. Since neither word nor letter has been provided, I am within my rights to assume you are here with malicious intent."

"Why would we be here with malicious intent?" Derek demanded.

"You three are too young to have lived through the war of years past. But your parents were not, nor their parents before them.

Many lives were lost on both sides during those times and many grudges were formed. Do not tell me that some of that bigotry was not passed down to the future generations, for I know that they were."

"His father, my *uncle*, helped put an end to the war once he took the throne," Arabelle explained, gesturing to Jared. "And he," she pointed to Derek now, "is half wood elf. How likely does it seem that we, of all people, would come all the way here because of hereditary bigotry?"

"Forgive me," said the Fair Lady. "But his grandfather," she nodded to Jared. "Was the one who started the war by trying to have me killed. Who sent the assassin that murdered my husband. How can I be certain the Prince here shares his father's views and not his grandfather's? And you." Her eyes turned to Derek. "Your mother was cast out for breaking one of our laws. She was shunned and despite the elf blood within you, you will never be acknowledged as one of us. Is it so hard to think that maybe you might also hold a grudge against my people because of that?"

It seemed that beneath the Fair Lady's beauty and musical laughter was a coldness that bordered on unpleasantness.

"Now, I will ask you again, did you come here in search of something?"

There was a look shared between the three of them. One that said that they all knew that there was no way to work their way out of this without admitting to the truth. Unless they wanted to become prisoners here.

"It's true," said Arabelle to the Fair Lady. "We did come here searching for something."

"And did that something happen to be the final piece of Milrath's amulet?"

Derek's heart lurched in his chest.

"I- I'm sorry?" Arabelle said after a moment, confused. "Milrath's . . . what?"

The Fair Lady tilted her head to the side. Strands of her golden hair brushing her fair cheek. "You do not know the tale? Milrath was one of the three daemon lords, son of Asmydionn, king of the daemons. It is said, that before they were banished from this realm, Milrath created an amulet out of three pieces that when brought together, could grant the wish of whoever wields it."

Silence. Derek didn't dare to look at either Jared or Arabelle. He knew that they'd be thinking on the words they had just heard and making the connections. And once they'd made the connections, there would be only two questions running through their minds, had Derek known? And if he had, why hadn't he told them?

"So the two of you did not know. But you knew." the Fair Lady said to Derek. "You knew from the very beginning what you were getting into. I can see it in your eyes."

Even without looking at them, Derek could feel Jared's and Arabelle's gazes on him. "I did," he said, not breaking the elf queen's gaze.

He heard Jared make a muffled sound of disbelief. Derek didn't see a point in lying or trying to wriggle his way out of this now. It was disconcerting, but somehow he got the feeling that the Fair Lady would see right through any untruths he might try to say.

"Even knowing that it is an artefact of daemonic origin, you still desired to seek it out." It was a statement, not a question.

Derek nodded. "Yes. I don't care if it's daemonic or not if it can give me what I want then that's all that matters."

"Even if the price is your life or the lives of your friends here?"

This gave him pause. "What?"

"I see," said the Fair Lady as if in response to a revelation. "So you did not stop to consider that a daemonic object might not really be so harmless?"

"That's not—I—"

"I once knew someone who sought the amulet of Milrath," the Fair Lady explained. "They had lost just something that was precious to them and was determined to get it back. They believed that the amulet would do this for them. But the result was not what they had hoped for."

"Did they die?" Arabelle asked, sounding as if she was almost afraid to hear the answer.

"No . . . They lived."

"Then that's fine," said Derek, rising to his feet. He suddenly felt far too restless to stay seated any longer. "As long as the price isn't death, then that's fine."

As long as I get my family back that's all that matters, he thought. *I'll pay any price to have them back.*

The Fair Lady closed her eyes and sighed. "There are worse

things than death, young Guardian."

Derek felt his lip curl in contempt. "Oh, believe me, I know."

"Since you have come all this way, I must assume that you already have the first two pieces? I am going to have to ask that you give them to me."

Derek froze. "What? Why?"

"I made a vow to myself that I would never allow Milrath's amulet to fall into another's hands." she rose from her chair and came to stand before Derek. She was quite tall, he realised as she practically towered over him. "Give it to me, Derek Draco. Please do not make me call my guards in here to use force."

Despite her warning, he did not move, only continued to glare up at her.

"Derek." He looked over at the sound of Arabelle's voice and found her watching him with a sad expression. "Just give it to her. Please."

Just give it to her? After everything, they'd been through? After how hard they'd fought to get here? When they were so close to the end of their goal, so close to having his family back. Now he was just supposed to give it up?

Derek looked from Arabelle's imploring face to Jared, who was not looking at him at all, and back to the Fair Lady, her expression resolute. He knew that unless he was really willing to fight his way out of this, then there was only one choice left to him.

With a sigh of deep resignation, Derek walked over to where their packs were propped up against the wall. He pulled out the amulet and carried it back over to where the Fair Lady stood expectantly. He kept his eyes on the floor as he placed it in the palm of her hand.

"Thank you," said the Fair Lady although she did not sound pleased. "I will be sending word to your king so that he can send someone to come and fetch you three. In the meantime, you shall remain here under guard." She strode across the room towards the door. "You may wander the village if you so choose, but you will have an escort at all times."

She reached for the door handle and hesitated. "I am sorry." She turned to look at them. "But this is for your own good." Her gaze was fixed solely on Derek as she said this. He turned his head away and he could feel her eyes lingering on him before she opened the door and was gone.

The silence that followed was almost oppressive.

"You lied to us."

Jared's voice was soft and somehow it still made Derek flinch as much as if he had yelled the words.

Outside, the sun had started to set and with no candles lit, the room had started to grow dark, casting everything in a greyish light.

"I never lied," said Derek. "I just didn't tell you what the amulet really was."

"That doesn't matter!" Jared's voice was much louder this time. "You still didn't tell us the truth! You let us come on this Goddess damned quest with you and you couldn't even tell us what we were really getting ourselves into."

Derek whirled around, matching Jared's glare with his own. "Well, it's not as if I asked you to come along! You both practically begged to come with me."

"I didn't want you to be alone," Jared snapped. "I wanted to be there for you in case you needed someone. I wanted to do that for you because that's what friends do. But you couldn't even be bothered to return the favour by being honest!"

In the years that Derek had known him, he had never seen Jared this angry and certainly not with him. If it weren't for the fresh wound in his side, Derek was sure Jared would be out of bed and most likely trying to strangle him by now. "What was there to be honest about? I told you that it was an amulet that grants wishes, which was the truth. No, I didn't tell you that it was actually a daemon's amulet. So what?"

"Daemonic artefacts are dangerous, Derek," said Arabelle as if she were explaining something to someone particularly thick-headed. "You say all this amulet does is grant wishes, but how do you know that's really all it does? What if using it could actually bring the daemons back? What if it could *kill you*?"

"And you would have dragged us along with you and we wouldn't have even known until it was too late," Jared added. "By the Goddess how could you have been so selfish?"

"Selfish?" Derek repeated heatedly. "I did what I did so that I could have my family back. Could you honestly say that you wouldn't have done the same thing if you were in my position?"

Jared snorted and muttered, just loud enough for Derek to hear, "And I'm sure they'd be *so* proud of you right now."

Something inside Derek snapped and a hot and blinding anger flooded through. "I never forced you to come on this journey with me," he growled. "In fact, one of you practically threatened me to let you come along if I remember correctly. If either of you ended up dying along the way then that's your fault, not mine."

Arabelle looked as if he had just slapped her and Jared's mouth fell open.

Derek knew his words were unfair and cruel even. He knew he was hurting them but he couldn't bring himself to care. He was too angry to care.

"You don't understand, neither of you do. You still have your families. You haven't started to forget what they looked like or what their voices sounded like. You haven't lived through the things I've had to live through. The two of you have no idea what finding this amulet would mean to me." Derek spun around. He made for the staircase, grabbing his pack along the way.

"Call me selfish or whatever else you want to call me, I don't give a shit. Allowing you both to come with me was the biggest mistake I could have possibly made."

Later, Derek lay alone in the loft on his bedroll. Aravanea and Sylvina had returned sometime earlier and by the sounds and smell of things, they had made dinner. No one had come up to offer him any and Derek was glad for that. He didn't feel like speaking to anyone.

Only a few minutes later, he heard the sound of footsteps on the staircase and the floorboards creaked, indicating that someone had come to join him. Derek looked over his shoulder to find Arabelle kneeling on the floor behind him, holding a lit candle in one hand, as well as a plate of bread and stewed vegetables.

"I thought you'd be hungry," Arabelle said stiffly. "So I brought you some food."

Derek didn't reply, only turned so that his back was facing her.

He heard Arabelle sigh behind him. "I don't really think you get a right to be angry here. Jared and I are the ones who should be upset since you lied to us."

Still, Derek said nothing.

"Or are you just sulking because the Fair Lady took the amulet away?" she asked. "It was for the best. You should have known better than to try dabbling in something daemonic anyway."

"And yet you were so keen on finding the rest of the amulet too, weren't you, Arabelle?" said Derek.

At first, she said nothing, then, "Are you going to eat or not?"

"You were so desperate to find the mother who abandoned you," he sneered. "But perhaps you're right, maybe it's for the best that the Fair Lady took the amulet. Because maybe there would have been no other explanation for why your mother left you other than that she just didn't want you."

He heard Arabelle get to her feet. "Fuck you, Derek Draco," she seethed before promptly storming down the stairs and leaving Derek alone once more.

He didn't touch the food.

Sometime later, when Derek was sure that everyone else was asleep, he got up from his bedroll and opened up his pack.

He fumbled around inside it until he drew out two items, one was a small black bottle and the other was Milrath's amulet.

Derek thought of the fake amulet he had given to the Fair Lady and commended himself for thinking to take those two potion bottles from Blackwood's magic shop in Florinstone all those days ago.

There had been two potions there that had caught his eye. One was a red, round bottle with a long neck. *'Duplication',* the label on the front had read. On the back, were instructions explaining that the potion would create a duplicate of any inanimate object it was poured on to. Along with the warning that if it was used to duplicate a magical object, then the duplicate would not maintain the original's magical properties. Derek had been sure to use the potion that same night when he, Jared and Arabelle had settled down to sleep in an abandoned barn.

He had thought that creating a duplicate of the amulet would be a good idea in the event that anyone ever attempted to steal it. Admittedly, it hadn't worked out when Durbash's bandits had caught him unawares holding the real amulet, but as it turned out, the duplicate had come in useful after all.

Derek slipped the real amulet into his pocket and turned his attention to the small, black bottle. The second potion he had nicked from Blackwood's. The label on the front read, *'Doorway'*. One drop spilled onto any solid surface and a temporary doorway would be opened. Derek had taken it, thinking it would come in handy in case they ever found themselves trapped somewhere.

Unstoppering the bottle, Derek carried it over to the back wall of the loft.

The Fair Lady said that they were to be kept here under guard and even with Sylvina and Aravanea around, Derek had no doubt that there were probably still guards keeping sentinel outside the front door. If he wanted to leave here undetected then this was the best way to do it.

He tilted the bottle and watched as a single black drop fell from the mouth and onto the floor.

A second later, a tall, arched doorway, with glittering edges appeared on the wall in front of him. Beyond it was the village. It was a moonless and cloudless night, making the darkness difficult to see through. Many of the windows in the trees were lit up, making them look like small yellowish spots against the near blackness of the massive tree trunks.

Gathering up his pack, Derek pulled out his ring . . . and hesitated.

He thought they would understand. He thought Jared, of all people, would have been more understanding. He thought Arabelle, who was also looking for lost family, would have been more sympathetic. But no, instead they had simply branded him selfish and a liar. Hurt and anger performed a chaotic dance inside of him.

He put on his ring, perhaps with a little more force than necessary, Changed and leapt through the doorway just seconds before it closed.

Blending in perfectly with the night, no one noticed as Derek slipped away.

* * *

The glass shattered as it flew across the room and struck the wall, spraying the floor with dozens of tiny shards.

"I gave you one, *one,* simple task," Durbash seethed. "And that was to find those Guardians, take back the piece of Milrath's amulet they stole and kill the whelps while you're at it and you couldn't even do that!"

Durbash cast about the room for something else to take his anger out on, when he found nothing, he settled for upending the table instead. It landed with a loud bang that reverberated through the house. The silver fruit bowl clattered to the floor, spilling oranges and bruised apples.

Lying broken and lifeless on the floor was Lustev, one of the only survivors from the failed mission to take back the amulet. He had been given the unfortunate task of delivering the bad news to Durbash and in response, Durbash had snapped his neck.

"Useless! You are all utterly useless," Durbash continued,

pacing back and forth like a caged beast, ready to tear apart anyone who got too close. His anger was a live thing inside of him. It was hot and it was overpowering and it made him want to snap more necks. He settled for breaking things instead. "I should just kill you all now and save myself the disappointment of having such inept people like you as the remainder of my crew." He picked up one of the fallen chairs and hurled it at the wall behind him.

Dahlia, Crane and Rall stood in a row halfway across the room. None of them had said a word or moved an inch since Durbash had killed Lustev.

There was a fresh bruise on Dahlia's cheek and she was still cradling a dislocated arm. Rall was without a shirt, showing off the crisp, linen bandages wrapped around his left shoulder. There were bags under his eyes and he looked paler than usual. Crane was the only one who had managed to come back completely unscathed from their little escapade.

"W-We're sorry, Boss," said Dahlia, finally breaking the silence. She was looking at him the way a kicked puppy might. She was clearly upset that she had failed him."W-We tried our best, Boss, but—"

"Well evidently, your best wasn't good enough was it?" He snarled.

Dahlia didn't say anything to that, but she looked even more miserable and ashamed.

"Children," said Durbash. "I set you up against a bunch of *children* and you couldn't even beat them."

Again, no one said anything. The rage was finally beginning to cool down and Durbash decided to take a seat on the one chair that had managed to escape his wrath. His right eye twinged painfully beneath the bandages. It had been a week now since the Bone Swamp and his eye was still as painful as ever. The elf girl hadn't been able to heal it, no matter how much Durbash tried to beat her into accomplishing it. Apparently, the damage was too great for a mage of her skill level.

"We would have done it, Boss," said Rall. "We would have taken the amulet back and killed those runts too if it weren't for those damn wood elves."

"You couldn't have even managed a few elves?"

"It wasn't just a few. There were . . . There were too many of them," Crane admitted. "They killed Jon and Luc and Flint in the blink of an eye and I wouldn't have been able to fight them off on my own."

"Yes," Durbash drawled, resting his elbow on his knee and his unbandaged cheek on his fist. "You ran away from a fight like a coward and Rall and Dahlia had their asses beat by a bunch of *children*. How lucky I am to call you three members of my gang."

None of them said a word. Crane looked impassive, Rall was scowling at the floor like a petulant child and Dahlia was flushed scarlet with shame.

All in all, Durbash probably shouldn't have been surprised that they had failed him, these three had never exactly been the best or brightest of his crew. Still, he wasn't about to excuse it and let them get away with their failure. He had to make sure that they understood what it meant to let him down so that it wouldn't happen again.

"We're sorry, Boss," Dahlia said again, her voice trembling. "Please forgive us. I promise it won't happen again."

Durbash sighed. "Oh, enough with your grovelling, Dahlia." He rose from his chair. Crane, Dahlia and Rall all took an instinctive step back as he came towards them. "Today is a lucky day. For all of you. As it turns out, I won't be punishing you for your failure."

They all looked more surprised than relieved.

"You ain't?" Rall asked quizzically.

"No. I'm not. Instead, I'm going to give you all a chance to redeem yourselves."

"How so, Boss?" asked Crane.

"We're going to get the last piece of Milrath's amulet," Durbash explained, a smirk curling the edges of his mouth. "I know where it is."

"Really?" Rall's tone was one of disbelief and it made Durbash's temper flare.

"Do you think me a liar, Rall?" He demanded, rounding on the man. "Or do you think me a fool who doesn't know what he's talking about?"

Rall opened and closed his mouth several times as he tried (and failed) to come up with the right response.

It was Crane who stepped in, a placating smile on his face. "Of course that's not what he meant, Boss. You know, Rall, he's never any good with words. I think what he was trying to say is that he's just . . . curious as to how you know that?"

Durbash snorted. "I had the slave girl perform another one of those locating spells. It showed me a cave, not too far from the Great Forest."

"But, if the last piece is near the Great Forest," said Dahlia. "Then that might mean that those Guardian kids already have it."

"That very well could be," admitted Durbash. "Which is why we are heading there now."

"*Now?*" Rall echoed.

"Yes, *now*," Durbash snapped. "So go and prepare yourselves. Ready everything you need and meet back here. Then, we leave."

They needed no further instruction. Once he was finished speaking, the others quickly filed out of the room, leaving Durbash alone.

Instead of going off to prepare right away, like the others, Durbash picked an apple off of the floor, considered it and took a bite out of it.

He had time, he thought. Plenty of time to prepare, but for now, just for a few short moments, he wanted to take it easy. He wanted to just imagine what it would be like once he finally had all the pieces of the amulet. Once he finally made his wish and watched it come true.

He couldn't help the slow, upward curl of his lips as he imagined it.

Soon the Guardians would be finished. They would be nothing

but ants beneath his boot. Durbash himself would be restored to his former glory and then some. And the Guardians would be ruined.

Durbash looked down at the apple clutched between his fingers. Slowly, he began to squeeze. His fingers dug into the soft skin until it broke and the juices inside began to trickle down his wrist. He kept increasing the pressure of his grip until the apple was nothing more than a squashed mess in his hand. He tossed the now ruined fruit uncaringly onto the floor.

He thought of the raven-haired boy with those defiant, blue eyes. That one especially, Durbash was going to enjoy ruining.

* * *

Darus's wings beat hard against the air. The forested landscape below him sped by in a greenish-grey blur. It was well into the night, but still, Darus did not stop. The tracking rune was throbbing. It felt almost as if there were a vice around his wrist that that was slowly cutting off his circulation. Somehow he knew that meant he was getting closer. Closer to Derek and Jared and Arabelle.

That's why Darus couldn't stop now. He had to keep going. Had to keep pushing forward.

He had to find them and finally bring them home.

17

The morning seemed to drag on longer than Aurelia would have liked.

She had been up early, concocting new potions to replace the ones Erianna's son had stolen. Usually, when Aurelia caught customers trying to nick stuff, she would either send them flying out the door or turn them into a toad (temporarily of course).

But she hadn't done that with the boy. Instead, she had simply allowed him to scamper off with the stolen items and let him believe that he was a clever little thief.

The rest of the morning was filled with plenty of customers coming in and out. Some just stopping in for a browse and others looking to purchase something.

Her last customer before she closed up for lunch, was a young woman with a pointed chin. She was after something that she could use to punish her husband for having an affair with the jeweller's daughter. Aurelia suggested either a potion that would make all of his hair fall out or one that would cause some rather embarrassing dysfunctions where he would least want any dysfunctions. The woman chose the latter.

Throughout the transaction, the woman also shamelessly flirted with Aurelia. However, she was forced to turn the woman down when she went as far as to invite Aurelia into her bed. Aurelia held very little desire for or interest in such things.

By twelve o'clock, she went about closing up the shop, she always closed early on the sixth day of the week. With a wave of her hand, the blinds were pulled all the way shut and the front door locked itself with a 'click'.

Upstairs she found Cora perched on one of the posts of her bed, asleep. As she crossed the room towards the shabby old wardrobe in the corner, her mind began to wander.

It had been doing that a lot lately and it always brought her to thoughts of Erianna's son and Milrath's amulet. She hadn't used her Scrying Glass to look for the boy since they had come face to face in her shop almost a week ago now. She wondered what had become of him? He should have arrived at the Great Forest by now and—if all had gone according to plan—the elves would have intercepted and detained them, like Aurelia knew, with absolute certainty, that the Fair Lady would have ordered them to.

Still, Aurelia couldn't help entertaining thoughts to the contrary—what if the elves hadn't been able to intercept them? What if they had but the boy had escaped? What if he had already found the last piece of the amulet?

What if she had failed Erianna?

She gave herself a stern mental shake at that last thought. *Stop that*, Aurelia scolded herself. *You won't fail Erianna because you never promised her anything. You always said that you were not going to get involved anyway.*

She pulled off her gloves and stripped out of her black tunic, leaving her upper body bare. Out of the corner of her eye, Aurelia caught sight of her reflection in the cracked mirror that stood against the wall to her right.

Her skin was pale, almost white. Her ribs and collarbones were just a bit too prominent. There was a thin slice of scar tissue that ran diagonally above her hip bone. But what really drew her attention in her reflection was her right arm.

Or lack of.

Just below the shoulder, where there should have been an arm made of flesh was one instead made of metal.

The prosthetic arm always reminded Aurelia of a skeletal one, but instead of white bone, it was made up of silver metal with gears at the elbow and wrist.

Eight years ago, Aurelia had tried to use Milrath's amulet and had lost her right arm in the process.

She had just learned of Erianna's passing and, desperate and grieving, she had sought out all three pieces of Milrath's amulet and after months of searching, she finally found them.

What occurred when she attempted to make her wish, Aurelia couldn't say even if she wanted to. The memory of what happened after she brought all the pieces together, was nothing but a dark void, followed by unbelievable pain, Cora's screeching cries and the stench of blood.

When she finally regained consciousness, days later, Aurelia had found herself lying in a feather-soft bed, in an opulent room. All the windows had been open, allowing bright sunshine and fresh air to filter through. Cora was perched on the headrest of her bed. The pleasant sounds of birds chirping just outside filled the room. She had also found that her right arm was missing.

They had told Aurelia that they found her lying unconscious and bleeding in her bedroom after hearing what sounded like an explosion, followed shortly by her screams. They had thought the Great Forest was under attack. When the guards had rushed in to help her, they had found the pieces of the amulet scattered around her body, bleeding from where her right arm had been.

They said that in the days she had been asleep, she had been close to death twice. But Aurelia hadn't cared about any of that. She didn't even care that her mother had not come to see her since she had been awake. All she cared about was that her wish had not been granted. Erianna was still dead—a quick look into her Scrying Glass had confirmed that—and she had lost an arm for it. And yet, she could not remember for the life of her how it had happened.

Two days later, the Fair Lady, Queen of the wood elves, had come to pay her a visit.

She had been dozing one afternoon and when she awoke,

Aurelia found the Queen sitting by her bed. She had looked as ethereal as ever, her golden hair even more so in the sunlight.

"Mother," Aurelia had croaked.

"You tampered with a daemonic thing," was all her mother said, elegant and fierce all at the same time. But more than that, she was cold. This was not the mother who would sing her soothing lullabies on sleepless nights when she was a child. That was when Aurelia truly realised the gravity of what she had done. "It is strictly against the laws of our land that anything of dark origin be brought into our borders. You know the punishment I must hand out to you." It was not a question.

"I know," was all Aurelia said. *And I do not care.*

"But before I cast you out, there is one thing I would ask of you."

"What is it?"

"Milrath's amulet. It is a dangerous object and I would be grateful if you helped me hide its pieces so that no one might have to suffer through what you have had to suffer through ever again."

Aurelia had had the urge to laugh and to tell her mother to do it herself, among other things. *You have not come to see me for two whole days. You say I am to be cast out. You have not even asked me how I am feeling. I am your daughter but you sit here looking at me as if I were some stranger to you,* she felt like screaming. Instead, she said, "How do you know I do not plan on taking the amulet with me and trying again?"

"You have already lost one arm. I do not think that you would be willing to risk another," said the Fair Lady flatly. "And despite everything, Aurelia, you are my daughter and I know you. I know that you will help me because it is the right thing to do."

Aurelia winced. *I am your daughter but you would still banish me for the rest of my life. You still seem content with never seeing me again for the rest of your days.*

But again, she did not say those words. Aurelia knew her mother and she knew that she would never go back on her decision, even for her own child. Not if it meant disregarding their laws. The laws that her mother clearly treasured more than she did her own flesh and blood.

"Very well," said Aurelia finally. "I will help you."

So, three days later, when Aurelia was cast out of the Great Forest, she set about scouring Aloseria to find places to hide the pieces of Milrath's amulet. She hid the third piece in the old earth elf ruins, east of the Great Forest and that was crawling with grems.

The second, she hid in Djedric's Tomb in the Bone Swamp.

As for the first piece, Aurelia had decided to keep it with her. As a reminder, of the mistake she had made.

After a few more months of travelling the land, Aurelia had found a metal worker in a small mining town and commissioned him to make her a prosthetic arm. Once it was finished, she had enchanted it with magic so that it would work just as well as any ordinary arm would. That too would serve as a reminder.

The distant rumbling of thunder broke Aurelia out of her

musings. Shaking her head, she pulled out a loose, crimson shirt from the wardrobe and slipped it on over her head.

Just then, the wind began to pick up, causing the half-open window to fly open further until it banged against the wall. The papers on her desk began to scatter and drift onto the floor.

Cora let out a startled squawk and left the bedpost to perch herself on Aurelia's shoulder, her ruffled feathers tickling Aurelia's cheek.

Stepping over to the window, Aurelia pushed it shut, pulling the latch into place.

The sky had been grey and cloudy all day, but now dark, ominous-looking clouds were starting to roll in over the rooftops of Florinstone.

"It looks like a storm is on its way," Aurelia noted aloud, just as a loud crack of thunder split the air. *And a big one at that.*

* * *

Darus had never seen the Great Forest up close before. When he was younger, during the war, he had heard tales from those who had fought just beyond its borders. How it was an eerie place, home to the monstrous wood elves. That to enter would mean to never come out alive again. As he got older, Darus had dismissed the stories as being nothing but lies spun to perpetuate fear of the wood elves. However, as he gazed up at the giant trees looming over him, against the backdrop of the storm-darkened sky, he could see how one might believe those stories.

Whether they're true or not doesn't matter, he told himself sternly. *Derek, Jared and Arabelle might be in there and I won't let anything keep me from them.*

Darus steeled himself and took a step forwards.

"Halt!"

Darus froze at the sound of the voice calling out over the wind and rain. He looked up towards the trees and spotted a person, wearing a green half cloak, standing on one of the lowest branches of one of the trees.

It was a wood elf and he had a bow and arrow trained directly on Darus. It didn't take long for Darus to spot others, appearing from behind tree trunks and bushes and dropping down from foliage, like silent forest spirits. They were all wearing the same green uniform and all with bow and arrows at the ready.

"Turn back now, human," said the dark-haired elf that had called out to him before. "Or we will open fire."

Darus held his hands up to show that he meant no harm. "My name is Darus Flynn," he explained in a loud, steady voice. "I am a Guardian and I wish to speak with you."

This statement didn't seem to relax any of the elves, not that Darus had expected it to. Still, he hoped that it would make them listen to what he had to say instead of shooting him full of arrows.

"First, prove to us that you really are a Guardian," demanded the elf.

Darus produced his ring from his breast pocket and held it up for the elves to see, before slipping it onto his finger and Changing.

His transformation didn't garner much of a reaction from the elves, although he saw one that stood behind a cluster of ferns, take a slow step backwards. Darus watched as the dark-haired elf murmured something to elf standing next to him, before stowing away his bow and arrow and climbing down the tree with a practised ease that no human would ever be able to master.

Darus Changed back as the elf came to stand directly in front of him, but still with a considerable distance between them. The rain was pouring down now, soaking right through Darus's clothes. He fought the urge to shiver, especially since the elf standing before him seemed completely unperturbed by the downpour.

"You are here to collect your young ones, yes?" said the elf. "We did not expect someone to arrive so quickly."

Darus could feel his heart beat begin to quicken. "Young ones?"

An almost irritated look crossed the elf's elegant features. "The three young Guardians that arrived in our Forest yesterday. Our queen sent word to your king about their arrival." The elf spoke as if Darus were being purposefully daft.

But Darus did not care. He didn't care about the elf's tone or the arrows still trained on him or the heavy rain. Right now, there was only one thing he cared about.

"Take me to them."

* * *

When Jared awoke, the first thing he was aware of was the pain in his side. from the arrow wound. The second thing was the sound of voices.

He had slept wretchedly the night before. Every time he moved, a jolt of pain from his wound would run a fiery path up his torso.

However, the pain wasn't the only thing that kept him awake. The argument they had with Derek kept repeating itself in his head. The hurt and betrayal and anger he had felt at finding out that Derek had been lying to them all this time.

How could Derek have done such a thing? How could he have known that the amulet posed such a danger and not told them about it? How could he have abused their trust like that?

But as Jared had lain there, trying to fall back asleep and listening to the sound of Arabelle's even breathing beside him, he'd remembered what Derek had said to him in Jared's bedroom when he'd first told him about the amulet.

"I don't expect you to understand, but I can't just ignore an opportunity like this. I have to have them back. I have to . . . I need *this.*

Derek was just so desperate to have his family back. While it didn't excuse what Derek had done, could Jared truly fault him for wanting to be reunited with his parents? Would he have done anything differently if he were in Derek's position?

A crack of thunder startled him enough that his body jolted on the bed. A sharp twinge from his wound drew a low groan from his lips.

He felt the bed dip beside him and cracked open his eyes to see Arabelle's face hovering above him. Strands of her golden hair falling down around her face. Her expression was pulled into one of gentle concern.

"How are you feeling?" She asked softly.

"Like I was shot with an arrow."

The corner of her lips twitched up into a small smile. "So in other words, you're doing just fine?"

Jared knew that she was trying to joke with him but it fell flat. There was a troubled set to her brow and a nervous edge to her voice.

The voices he had heard when he woke up were getting louder and more urgent. He lifted his head from the cushion just enough to spot the elves, Sylvina and Aravanea standing by the front door, along with two other elves. These ones wore polished silver armour and green capes, their faces obscured by helmets.

Something about the way they were speaking in rapid elvish gave Jared the impression that something wasn't right.

"Arabelle," he said. "What's going on?"

He watched as his cousin chewed at her bottom lip and after a moment's hesitation, she said, "It's Derek. He's gone."

18

The storm set in just as Derek arrived at the mouth of a cave.

After following the compass's directions all night and for the better part of the day, he had wound up here, at the top of a steep slope in the earth, looking down at the entrance to a cave. Two craggy, stone statues, stood to either side of the entrance. They looked like elves. Not wood elves though, they looked stockier, their legs shorter and their ears much longer.

Earth elves, Derek realised. He was standing at the entrance to one of the few earth elf ruins across Aloseria.

Derek looked down at the compass to confirm that that was where he needed to go. Surely enough, the needle pointed straight ahead.

He pocketed the compass and Changed before making his way down the grassy slope, now made slippery by the heavy rain.

The inside of the cave was a narrow passageway. A strong

smell of damp clung to the rocky walls. Ahead of him, the tunnel stretched into a void of darkness.

Fortunately, Derek's dragon vision meant he could see perfectly well within the dark. As he made his way through the tunnel, roots dangled down from the ceiling, sometimes hanging so low, they brushed the top of Derek's head and back. The sounds of the howling wind and the pouring rain outside grew more and more distant the further he went.

Derek eventually came to a stop when he felt something hard crunch under his paw.

When he looked to see what it was, it took him a few seconds to realise he had just stood on what could only be a piece of bone.

It was too small to be a human bone, it was no bigger than a twig and it was not the only bone that he found. Pretty soon, the ground, which had been covered only with rock and dirt up until now, was littered here and there with bits of white bone.

Animal bones, Derek realised when he spotted what was unmistakably the cracked skull of a bird by the cave wall. He even came across half of a ribcage, bits of it broken off in some places and it was large enough that he found himself wondering whether it was from some large animal or a person?

The presence of so many bones was starting to put him on edge, but he pressed on. His desire to find the next piece of the amulet far outweighed his apprehension.

It wasn't long before he spotted something, moving and making noises, up ahead.

It was a grem. Vicious creatures with an aversion to light that forced them to inhabit only Aloseria's darkest places.

Derek remembered hearing the story from his father as a child and then, more extensively, from History classes at the Academy. That hundreds of years ago, back when the daemons still wandered the land, the king of the earth elves, Ulmrak, stole a piece of treasure from the daemon lord, Zathral. In retaliation to their pilfering, Zathral placed a curse upon all earth elves. Turning them into foul, hideous little monsters that would forever walk in the shadows.

With that curse, the race of earth elves was wiped out and the race of grems was born.

The grem before him sat with its back to him, hunched over and making awful grunting and growling noises. Although Derek had never actually seen one up close before, he knew that grems were only about the size of a small child, but that it didn't make them any less deadly. A grem's real danger lied within their numbers.

With only one in sight, Derek didn't think he was in too much danger.

Slowly, he crept closer until the grem stopped what it was doing and turned around to look at him. It had mottled, grey skin stretched over a long face with a wide mouth and pig-like nose. Two, beady, orange eyes and long, pointed ears protruding from either side of its head. Its mouth was covered in blood from feasting on the torn body of the dead possum in its clawed fingers.

When its eyes locked onto Derek, the grem opened its mouth,

revealing rows of jagged little teeth, and let out an awful, piercing shriek.

Guardians were forbidden from using their fire to kill. However, Derek didn't think that rule would apply to inherently dark creatures like grems. Leaping forward, Derek opened his mouth and released a stream of flame that lit up the dark cavern.

The grem squealed as the dirty rags it wore around its body caught fire, the flames licking at its skin. The creature continued to scream as it tried unsuccessfully to put out the flames on its body before finally turning and fleeing in the opposite direction.

Derek chased after the grem just in time to see it disappear down a wide crevice at the end of the tunnel.

From the edge of the crevice, Derek watched as a light that was the burning grem, grew smaller and smaller before finally disappearing into the absolute darkness. Even with his keen dragon eyesight, Derek could not see what lay beneath.

Across the crevice was a sight that almost took Derek's breath away. It was a city, made entirely out of white stone. Stone houses, stone walls and stone pathways. Some of these stone structures were event built upon huge stalagmites that rose from the ground.

Pale shafts of light filtered in through cracks in the roof of the huge cavernous space. Not a tree or blade of grass was in sight. But even from here, Derek could see that this underground city had fallen to ruin and decay. Across the crevice, Derek spotted the broken remains of a bridge. There would be no using that to get across.

Spreading his wings, Derek leapt off the edge and glided across the wide opening of the crevice, landing lightly on the other side. He made his way into the city.

There was something incredibly eerie about walking through a city that had been practically abandoned for hundreds of years. Everywhere he looked, there was disrepair. Cracks in the stonework, broken down doors, smashed in windows. Dark stains were spattered across the walls and the ground. They looked suspiciously like dried blood. There were animal bones scattered around here also.

The silence was almost oppressive. Not even the sound of wind or birdsong could be heard from this deep underground. Although every now and again, Derek thought he heard the sounds of hissing and scuffling. He thought he saw movement in a gap between two houses but when he looked, there was nothing there. He knew this place was probably infested with grems, but, for whatever reason, they seemed to want to keep their distance from him.

He stopped when he came to the centre of a wide courtyard, just before the ruined statue of what Derek could only assume was the earth elf king, Ulmrak, judging from the crown that was carved atop his head. There was a large chip taken off the end of his curly beard and the tip of his crown. His right arm was missing and there were several, long cracks running along the body.

Derek gazed up at the statue and felt a flicker of resentment for the king. To think that an entire people had been destroyed and cursed to live as monsters, all because of one king's greed.

Looking around to make sure he was in no imminent danger of a grem attack, Derek Changed so that he could consult the enchanted compass once again. This time the needle was pointing east.

So he continued his way along the winding pathways of the city. It wasn't long before the compass led him to the front steps of a castle, made of the same featureless, white stone as the rest of the architecture in this city. Still, it managed to stand tall and proud amongst the rest of the buildings, despite the obvious destruction that had been wrought upon it.

Derek climbed up the front steps and entered cautiously through the towering archways. He scanned the bare, towering foyer for any signs of grems but found only smashed up bits of furniture and what looked like a shattered chandelier.

There were three more archways in the foyer, one to his left, one to his right and one in front of him. Derek looked back down at the compass and found that once again the needle was pointing north, straight ahead.

He walked through a long, wide corridor, taking care not to trip over on the mess of broken cabinets, picture frames and shattered vases. All along the walls were deep claw marks. Toward the end of the corridor was a large painting that was still hanging, albeit lopsidedly, on the left wall, despite half of the frame being missing. Although it had been torn almost to shreds, Derek could tell by the remains, that it must have been a family portrait.

He looked up into the round face of a little boy with long,

pointed ears, beaming with childlike happiness and innocence. That boy would have been turned into a grem along with the rest of his people. Derek wondered what it must have been like, had it been an instantaneous transformation? Or had it been long and painful? Did the child suffer? Had he been scared?

Shaking his head of such thoughts, Derek turned away from the ruined portrait.

Derek stepped through the archway at the end of the corridor and found himself standing in a large, open room made of grey stone floors, walls and ceiling. Three tall windows lined the walls to either side.

Walkways, with crumbling parapets, lined the walls from above, supported by two stone pillars against each wall. At the very end of the room, was a raised dais and upon that dais stood a throne made of white stone.

The throne room, Derek realised, turning his head this way and that in search of any grems. Again, he didn't spot a single one. He couldn't help but find it strange that he had yet to spot a grem since that one he encountered in the tunnel. He had assumed that an earth elf ruin would be teeming with them.

Just like the rest of what Derek had seen of the castle, the throne room was in a complete state of disaster. The floors were littered with broken ornamentation and shredded clothing. The carpet had been torn up and massive tapestries that had hung up on the walls had been torn down.

Taking another glance at the compass in his hand, Derek found that it was still pointed north. At the dais.

His footsteps echoed against the stone floor as he approached the dais, walking up the three short steps until he was standing in front of the throne. Up close he realised that the throne wasn't actually made of stone, but of what he could only assume was marble. Jagged veins of pale grey crisscrossed along the surface.

He walked around the dais, looking down at the compass as he did so. Wherever he moved, the compass needle would just spin around to point in the direction of the throne.

Derek set about inspecting the throne, searching for any sign of hidden compartments. He ran his fingers all along the throne in the hope of finding some somewhere where the amulet piece could be hidden.

When that yielded no results, Derek took a step back to consider the back of the throne, rubbing at his chin thoughtfully.

What if the third piece was actually *inside* of the throne? He supposed he could try melting it down with his dragon fire, but what if he ended up melting the amulet piece along with it? *No, Derek decided. I won't be melting any thrones down today.*

But then where else could the third piece be? The compass needle was still pointing towards the throne.

A whisper of doubt began to creep in from the back of his mind. What if the compass was wrong? What if the final piece wasn't really here? What if Derek had come all this way for nothing?

Feeling suddenly weary, he slumped against the back of the throne with a frustrated sigh—and nearly stumbled backwards.

Righting himself, he turned around and was surprised to find that the throne had actually *moved* forward a couple of inches. And there was something underneath it.

Placing both hands on the back of the throne, Derek pushed and found it was surprisingly lighter than he would have expected. It made a low scraping sound against the stone floor that echoed throughout the room. He pushed it as far as it would go and once the throne was completely out of the way, Derek found himself looking into a shallow, rectangular pit full of hidden treasure.

Derek knelt on the floor and began searching through the small treasure horde. There were coins of gold, gemstones of rubies, emeralds, sapphires and garnets. Amongst it all, he also found a dagger made of solid gold. A diadem of sparkling, white gems, several bars of ingot and a book with a cover inlaid with silver and amethyst.

"Shit," Derek hissed when he felt something sharp cut into his finger. He snatched his hand back, blood welling along the thin scratch on his index finger.

Half buried beneath all of the gold coins and gemstones, Derek spotted what looked like a circular object with triangular points lining the outer edge. It was a dirty bronze colour. The same colour as—

Derek's hand shot out, reaching for the third piece of Milrath's amulet.

It was bigger than the other two pieces. Nothing more than a bronze band with four, sharp points running along the outer rim and a chain attached to it. It was so plain and unassuming but to Derek, it was probably the most important thing in the whole world right now.

He reached for his pack, opened it and pulled out the first two pieces of the amulet. Finally, after weeks of searching and hoping and wanting, Derek finally held all three pieces of Milrath's amulet in his hand. Finally, he could wish away all the bad things that had happened to him over the years.

Finally, he could have his family back. He could have his life back the way it used to be.

All he had to do was fit all the pieces together.

So why was he hesitating?

"— it's a daemonic object. It's daemonic magic. That's the worst form of magic there is. That makes it highly dangerous and not to be trusted." Darus's words.

Why was he thinking about that now?

"What if using it could actually bring the daemons back? What if it could kill *you?"*

Why, at the last second, at the final hurdle, was he thinking about all of this now?

"As long as the price isn't death, then that's fine."

"There are worse things than death, young Guardian."

"By the Goddess how could you have been so selfish?"

Had he really been so selfish? When Jared had first said it to him, Derek had only reacted in anger. He hadn't thought about whether Jared was right or not. Now he couldn't help but wonder.

This whole time, Derek had been telling himself that if there was a price to be paid in using the amulet to make his wish come true, then he would pay it. That as long as he had his family back, then it didn't matter what the price was. But what if the price really had cost him the lives of his friends?

What if he really had nearly gotten Jared and Arabelle killed? What if he could still get them killed by using the amulet? What if it didn't matter that they weren't here with him?

Was he really willing to risk it?

Derek growled in frustration. His free hand coming up to run through his hair and grip the strands so hard it caused a twinge of pain. After all this time, *now* was the time for him to really think about all this? He'd been so caught up in trying to find all the pieces, in the idea of being reunited with his parents, he hadn't even stopped to think about the possible ramifications of using the amulet. Even when others had tried to tell him, he hadn't listened— hadn't *wanted* to listen. But now . . .

"Well well, isn't this a surprise?"

A deep voice echoed throughout the room and Derek's head snapped up to find four familiar figures, standing at the entrance to the throne room. Rall, Crane, Dahlia . . . and Durbash.

Derek's stomach plummeted. How did they find him? And so quickly?

Durbash began to stride forward, hands settled comfortably in the pockets of his trousers. The last time Derek had seen him, the ogre had been dressed in nothing but boots and a pair of baggy pants. This time he was covered neck to toe in brown boots, trousers and a jacket that looked as if it were made out of some kind of leather. Only his head was left bare. Showing off the white bandages that covered his right eye.

"I see you've gone and collected all the pieces for us," he said pleasantly.

"Stop right there," Derek ordered. He was on his feet now and holding his ring up for them to see. "Or I'll burn you where you stand."

Behind Durbash, Derek saw Dahlia reach for the axe at her back, Rall placed a hand on the hilt of his sword and Crane raised his crossbow. Durbash, however, made no move to reach for his weapon. He did stop, though, halfway across the throne room, an amused grin twisting his features. "I thought that was against your rules, little Guardian?"

Derek shrugged. "We're quite deep underground. I'm sure I'd have no problem hiding your charred remains."

"And here I thought all Guardians were nothing but a bunch of boring assholes."

Even at this distance, Derek could see the pinkish patches of skin on Durbash's face where they weren't covered by bandages; the bridge of his nose, the lower, right side of his face. He could only imagine what the damage was like underneath all the bandaging.

"And here I thought your face couldn't get any uglier," Derek responded wryly. "Those scars look like they must've hurt. And I can't imagine your shoulder feels any better either."

He had the brief satisfaction of watching Durbash's features twist in anger before he quickly reined his expression in. "I wear each and every one of my scars with pride, boy. These are no different," he said, gesturing to his face and then placing a hand on his right shoulder. The same shoulder where Derek had run him through with his sword.

"If telling yourself that helps you deal with the fact that you were bested in a fight by a boy, then whatever you say."

Derek knew he'd struck a chord by the look on Durbash's face. The ogre growled and said, "Enough of this. Hand over the amulet and I'll give you a quick death."

"How convincing," Derek muttered, then louder, "And if I don't?"

"Then there will be nothing quick about your death."

Of course, Derek thought. It appeared there was no way he was going to get out of here without a fight.

"If I give you the amulet, what do you plan on wishing for?" When no one answered, Derek added, "If I'm going to die here then surely there's no harm in telling me? Are you going to use it to make yourself king or something?"

"No, being king seems like such a bore," said Durbash. "Do you know what it's like to be forced to live in the shadows, boy? To be persecuted and hunted everywhere you go? It's exhausting."

"Then maybe you should have chosen your professions a bit

more carefully."

"I had it all once," Durbash continued as if Derek had never spoken. "I was the most powerful man in the world of criminals. I had wealth, I had respect and influence. I was living better than any king could ever dream of." His expression darkened. "Then you Guardians took that all away. Took my business, my *empire*. You took nearly all of my crew and forced me to ride and hide for these past three years. So when I get my hands on that amulet, I'm going to wish that everything that was taken from me be restored. I'm going to wish myself even more powerful than a king. I'm going to make myself even stronger than all of the Guardians combined." There was a manic edge to Durbash's tone and expression now. "I'm going to crush you all into the ground. I will make each and every one of you regret the day you dared to contend with me. Now *hand over the amulet*."

Derek looked down at the amulet pieces in his hand. He considered what Durbash had just said and what would happen if Derek gave the amulet to him. He thought about Jared and the rest of the royal family, being forced to kneel at Durbash's feet. He imagined Arabelle, being cut down by Dahlia's axe. Darus being shot down by Crane's crossbow. He thought about Ember and the rest of Aloseria being taken over by Durbash and his cohorts.

Because that's what would happen if Derek gave up the amulet. That's why it was so easy for him to look Durbash in the eye and say, "No. I don't think I will."

Durbash grinned.

And charged towards him.

Derek slid the amulet pieces into his pocket and Changed, leaping into the air.

A gout of orange flame burst forth from Derek's mouth, hurtling straight for Durbash.

As the flames rushed towards him, the ogre didn't even try to get out of the way. He stayed where he was, raising his arms to shield his head as the flames washed over him.

Derek expected to find Durbash as nothing more than a burnt-out husk, but as the flames died away, he was left stunned to find that Durbash still stood, whole and unharmed. His clothes weren't even singed.

Durbash lowered his arms and grinned nastily up at Derek. "Did you really think I would come here, expecting to battle with you, unprepared?" He said. "My clothing has been made fireproof. Your pitiful fire won't work on me now, boy."

As if that mattered. If Derek couldn't burn him, then he'd just settle for tearing him limb from limb.

With a growl, Derek dove down towards the ogre, claws extended and teeth bared.

Durbash sidestepped him easily as he landed on the floor once more.

Derek whirled around, lashing out with one of his forepaws and tearing four diagonal lines across the front of Durbash's jacket.

Durbash responded by slamming his fist into Derek's snout.

Derek ignored the pain in time to avoid the wicked-looking

blade being swung his way.

Durbash struck out at him with his knife a few more times before Derek managed to knock the blade out of his hand with a swipe of his claws.

The knife went flying, spinning through the air and Derek took Durbash's momentary shock to tackle him onto the floor.

They rolled and grappled with each other as both tried to pin down the other. Derek left a few more claw marks along Durbash's suit and the exposed skin of his face as they struggled.

No human could ever hope to contend with a Guardians in dragon form in a physical fight, but with his impressively large stature, Durbash was more than a match for Derek.

Finally, Derek managed to pin Durbash down. Durbash's elbow pressed against his throat, a hand gripped his jaw hard and a knee dug into his belly, as the bandit tried to keep Derek from completely bearing down upon him.

Derek's face was only inches away from Durbash's face. His completely exposed face.

Durbash's suit may have been fireproof, but his face wasn't.

Derek sucked in a breath and he felt the beginnings of fire lick at the inside of his throat.

Durbash managed to get his free leg underneath Derek and boot him hard in the gut.

Feeling as if a boulder had just been thrown into his stomach. Derek yelped, the fire in his throat dying out and his body going momentarily slack with the shock of pain. But that was all the moment's distraction that Durbash needed.

He kicked Derek again, forcing him off completely. This time, he managed to wrestle and pin Derek to the floor, grabbing him from behind. One arm went around Derek's throat, the other wrapped around his front legs. Durbash hooked one of his own legs around both of Derek's hind ones, effectively holding him in place.

The arm around his throat started to squeeze. pressing tighter and tighter until it started to become difficult for Derek to breathe. He thrashed whatever part of his body he was able, trying to get at least one of his legs free, but Durbash held onto him too tightly. Even flapping the wing that wasn't pinned to the ground did nothing to help dislodge the ogre.

In a last-ditch effort, Derek Changed and was finally able to slip out of Durbash's hold.

"Don't think you can escape from me that easily."

Derek was still on his hands and knees, hadn't even had a chance to climb to his feet when Durbash's hand closed around his ankle and *pulled*.

Derek grunted as his chin hit the stone. His fingernails tore along the floor, leaving bloody smears as they desperately searched for purchase—something to keep him from being pulled along by Durbash—that wasn't there.

Durbash yanked him off the floor completely and Derek soon found himself being suspended in the air above Durbash's head.

"It's time to pay you back for what you did to me at the Bone Swamp," said Durbash just before throwing Derek to the floor.

Derek's temple cracked against the hard stone. So hard that he was sure he actually blacked out for a second.

There was a ringing sound in his ears. Lying there, dizzy and disorientated, he felt as if he would be sick at any moment.

When he saw the blurred image of Durbash striding towards him, Derek tried to push himself up, but he was too unsteady. The ground felt as if it were tipping sideways beneath him. He was just struggling to his knees when Durbash kicked him in the ribs.

Derek rolled onto his back. The urge to vomit was even stronger now.

The tip of Durbash's boot caught him in the face, snapping his head to the side. Fire erupted beneath his skin and blood poured from his nose and into his mouth.

Durbash reached down, gripping him by the hair and lifting him half off the ground, only to slam his head back down.

It was astounding that Derek didn't pass out. A part of him wished that he would, so then maybe he could escape this brutality.

Durbash reigned more blows upon him. Derek couldn't keep count of just how many, all that he could register was the bright, burst of pain that came with each hit.

He was on his back now, his vision was blurring and everything was spinning. The throbbing in his head was tremendous, like nothing he had ever known before.

But he did his best to ignore it, in favour of reaching for his sword that was still sheathed at his hip.

But Durbash wouldn't allow him that. He grabbed at Derek's right hand, the one reaching for his sword, pulling his arm out straight and slamming it onto the ground. With his free hand, Durbash pulled out another large knife from his belt and drove the blade down into the palm of Derek's hand.

White-hot pain tore through his hand and up his arm. He was distantly aware of himself crying out. He felt the warm, wetness of blood well up around the wound. Derek's first instinct was to pull his hand away, but couldn't. Durbash was still holding onto the handle of the knife embedded in Derek's palm and he looked to be in no hurry to take it out.

Durbash was looking down at him with a sort of deranged look of glee on his face. As if Derek's suffering brought him some sick, twisted pleasure.

"I must say," said Durbash, chuckling. "I thought you'd make this more difficult. I guess I overestimated you."

Derek only managed a half-hearted glare.

With his free hand, Durbash reached for Derek's pocket, where the amulet pieces were hidden.

Change, said a desperate voice in the back of his head. *You have to Change.*

But he couldn't. He couldn't focus. All Derek could focus on was the pounding in his head, the pain in his right hand and the throbbing in the rest of his body. It even hurt to breathe.

Durbash pulled the amulet from Derek's pocket. Rising from his crouching position, Durbash considered his prize with a pleased smirk.

He didn't take the knife out from Derek's hand. Instead, he placed one booted foot on the crook of Derek's elbow, as if to hold him in place.

"You did it, Boss," breathed Dahlia in awe. She and the rest of the bandits were now grouped around Durbash. "The amulet is finally yours."

"Hmph, was there ever any doubt?"

"No! Of course not," she hastened to say. "Never any doubt, Boss. I just—"

"Stop talking." Durbash slid the amulet pieces into his own pocket.

Then, as calm as can be, Durbash reached down and pulled his knife from Derek's hand. Having the knife ripped out was just as painful as when it went in. Before Derek could even move, Durbash slammed his boot down on top of his already aching stomach, drawing a poorly repressed groan from Derek.

"I told you there would be nothing quick about your death if you refused to hand over the amulet willingly." Durbash hummed consideringly. "Let's see now, where should I start? Your shoulder? Maybe I should cut out your eye? Ruin it like you did mine."

Death had never been something that scared Derek. He'd never wished for it but nor did the thought of it really frighten him. What did, however, was the thought of the kind of torture he would have to endure before death came for him. It was that that made sweat break out along his temples and his heart to beat a panicked rhythm in his chest. That, and the predatory, almost joyful, look in Durbash's eyes as he looked down at Derek's struggling form.

Durbash raised the hand wielding the knife, the tip of the blade pointed down towards Derek's—

"Boss! Look ou—"

Durbash cried out as something drove into his knife-wielding hand from behind. The knife fell and clattered to the ground, inches from Derek's face.

"*Boss!*"

An arrow. It was an arrow that had pierced straight through Durbash's hand. Rivulets of blood were already running down his hand and dripping onto the floor. By now, Dahlia, Crane and Rall were at their leader's side.

Just managing to move his head enough so that he could see past the huddle of bandits, Derek saw the group that had gathered at the entrance to the throne room.

There was Sylvina standing at the front, already nocking another arrow to her bow. There were six other elves, dressed in the green uniform of the elven guard. Next to them was Arabelle, her tail lashing behind her and her lips curled back into a snarl.

And striding to the front of the group, pulling his sword from his scabbard, was Darus.

His expression was murderous as he pointed his sword at Durbash and said, "Get away from my son."

19

"Get away from my son."

My son.

Of all the things Derek could focus on right then, it was those words.

In all the six years that Darus had been his adoptive father, had he ever actually called Derek his son before? He must have. But if that was so, then why was Derek filled with such astonishment at hearing those two words come from Darus's mouth.

Durbash shoved Dahlia, who was fussing over his wounded hand, away and turned to face the new arrivals. "Darus Flynn," he growled. "So this is your whelp? I should've known."

"Surrender now, Durbash," said Darus, his voice ringing throughout the room with authority. "Before this has to get ugly."

"You think I'll make it that easy for you?" With quick, sure movements, Durbash snapped the stem of the arrow that was lodged in his hand and pulled out both ends without so much as a grimace.

It was Dahlia made a whimpering sound and looked as if she were just barely restraining herself from plastering herself to her Durbash's side.

Durbash flung the broken arrow pieces to the ground and started stalking towards Darus and the others.

"Do you think you can just give me a command and I'll obey like a dog?"

"Stay where you are," ordered Darus.

"You think you can just order me around?" There was a frenzied edge to Durbash's voice now.

"I said stay where you are!"

"I am finished!" He reached into his pocket. "I am finished running and I am finished hiding. From now on, *you* will live in fear of *me*."

The only warning any of them had was a low whistling sound before something split the air and Crane reeled back as an arrow struck him squarely between the eyes.

He stood still as a statue for a drawn-out moment, a look of shock stamped across his face before he finally crumpled to the ground.

"*Crane!*" Rall shouted. Then to Darus and the others, "How dare you?!"

But Darus, Arabelle and the elves looked just as shocked.

Because the arrow that had killed Crane and not been fired from an elf's bow.

A shrill, garbled cry tore through the stunned silence.

Derek looked up to the walkways above and saw a grem standing on the parapet. It held a crudely crafted bow in its hands, raising it above its head as it released another cry.

It was like a pot boiling over. Suddenly multiple grems were spilling over the parapet and even through the broken windows of the throne room. Like a roiling wave of hissing, snapping grey bodies. Dozens of them, pouring down the walls and onto the ground.

"Elves, fire!" Sylvina shouted in elvish and the elves fired their arrows at the oncoming grems in perfect unison.

There were squeals and howls as the arrows found their marks, but it still did little to impede many of the other grems and it wasn't long before they were upon them.

Derek's world became a blur of sound and movement as the bandits, the elves, the Guardians and the grems clashed.

He heard Sylvina calling out orders to her guard from amidst the snarling cries of the grems. Derek managed to roll himself onto his side and push himself up onto his knees before another wave of dizziness hit him and he nearly toppled over.

Two of the grems caught sight of Derek, unguarded and on the ground and ran towards him, their makeshift pikes and daggers raised above their heads.

Before they could descend on him, a huge figure with a broadsword was there, stabbing one through the chest and decapitating another. Blackish blood spilled onto the stone floor as the grems fell and Derek looked up to see Durbash standing in front of him.

But if Derek had any illusions that Durbash was protecting him out of a sudden change of heart, they were erased when Durbash turned to look at him from over his shoulder. There was such a look of abject hate in his eye that made Derek realise that the only reason Durbash had saved him, was so that he could finish him off himself.

"Goodbye, little Guardian," Durbash's words were barely audible above the clamour going on around them. Still, Derek heard them just before Durbash hefted his newly blood-stained sword, ready to cleave Derek in two.

A dragon's cry echoed above the noise and only seconds later, a familiar, yellow dragon, barrelled into Durbash, knocking the ogre off his feet. Durbash was quick to get back up again and gather his sword before Darus was attacking him again.

More grems had started to notice Derek on the ground, apparently picking him out as an easy target, and were rushing towards him. Once again, someone appeared to stop them.

Arabelle leapt over the heads of the grems and planted herself between them and Derek. Breathing fire in their direction, the grems scattered, many of them turning to flee only to find their path blocked by elves, who cut them down with deadly efficiency.

"Derek," said Arabelle as she Changed and fell to her knees beside him. "By the Goddess, what did they do to you?" She looked at him as if she couldn't quite believe the state of him.

I must look pretty bad, Derek thought a little dazedly.

She caught sight of his hand, that was still bleeding and, wasting no time, Arabelle tore off a strip from the hem of her white shirt and began wrapping it around his hand.

"Arabelle," Derek began, his voice sounded strange and distant to his ears. "What are you doing here? How did you—?"

"Don't worry about that for now," she told him not unkindly.

"Hurry and get him out of here," he heard Sylvina say. She was standing in front of them and shooting arrows at the attacking grems. Derek realised that she and four other elves had set up a kind of defensive circle around him and Arabelle. Keeping any and all grems from getting past them. "The two of you must leave this place. Now."

"But Durbash has the amulet," Derek protested. The dizziness was starting to recede somewhat, but the throbbing in his head was still persistent. "We have to get it back."

"I am sure Darus Flynn will retrieve it." Sylvina pulled an arrow from her quiver and used it to stab a grem in the eye. It howled and she kicked it to the ground with the heel of her boot. "Now, get—"

A shout caught their attention and Derek saw the elf standing to their left, fall to his knees, an arrow protruding from his shoulder.

"*Etran!*" Shouted a female elf but she stayed in position.

Another arrow bounced off the stone floor, just inches away from where Derek and Arabelle were.

"*Nwye gaen faethyr!*" Sylvina called out as she stabbed a grem in the head with the dagger that was strapped to her thigh.

"They have archers!"

More arrows started to fly. They were coming from the upper walkways.

"Derek," Arabelle grabbed him by the shoulder, forcing him to look at her. There was an urgent, questioning look on her face. He knew what she was about to ask him.

"I'm not leaving," he told her firmly.

Her expression changed then. Hardening with resolve and understanding. "You take care of the grems up above," Arabelle spoke with a fierce authority he had never heard from her before. "I'll handle the ones down here." She Changed, leaving him so that she could dive into the sea of grems. It wasn't long before he saw plumes of flame and heard answering squeals of terror.

Sylvina barely avoided an arrow to the head as she continued to fend off grems and Derek decided to quit wasting time, Changing, he flew up towards the walkways.

Several grem archers lined the west walkway, firing arrows at will upon the party of humans and elves down below. When the nearest grem noticed Derek's approach, it let out a garbled cry, alerting its fellows. This made little difference, however, as Derek breathed a stream of fire upon them. Shrieks were heard over the roar of the fire as the grems closest came into contact with the flame and those standing furthest scrambled to get as far away from it as they could.

One grem, whose ragged clothing had now caught fire, pitched itself off of the ledge and fell into the crowd below, quickly dispersing the grems that were nearby.

It didn't take long at all for Derek to dispatch the archers, their abject fear of fire was almost pitiful as they rushed to get away from him. Down below, Arabelle was having similar results as she breathed fire upon as many of the grem horde as she was able.

Derek even saw that many were now starting to flee up the walls and pillars and disappear into gaping cracks in the ceiling and out of the broken windows. Sylvina and the other elves were now having an easier time dispatching the grems that remained.

Further down, near the entrance to the throne room, Derek spotted Dahlia and Rall, battling a group of ten or so grems. Rall was hacking away at them with his sword, his face and clothes stained with black blood. Dahlia, however, did not seem to be faring quite as well. She swung wildly with her battleaxe. Wisps of blonde hair had come out of its topknot to fall into her face. The left leg of her tights was stained red with blood.

As she swung her axe, one of the grems ducked under and plunged its blade into her thigh. Dahlia screamed, momentarily stilling her movements. That was all it took for another grem, which had snuck up behind her, to sink its own knife into her back. The axe fell from her hands as Dahlia cried out and dropped to her knees.

Before Derek could even move to help, the rest of the grems were on her. Her cries rose to shrill screams as she disappeared beneath the grey bodies.

Derek leapt from the parapet and descended towards where Dahlia was being attacked. A few bursts of flame in their direction was enough to send the grems scattering. Abandoning Dahlia, as well as some of their weapons, and raced through the archway and out of sight.

Dahlia lay motionless, her clothes torn and soaked in blood. Her eyes glassy and staring unseeingly off to the side.

Even more of the grems were starting to flee. Many either retreated in fear of Derek and Arabelle's fire or were cut down by Sylvina and her elves.

Derek had just chased off a pair of grems that had made an attempt to ambush Sylvina while she defended her wounded comrade when he saw Darus and Durbash, still battling each other, now all the way at the steps of the dais. The bodies of dead grems lay scattered around them.

He saw Durbash move with astounding speed as he deflected Darus's sword and used his own to slice open Darus's shoulder. Darus didn't even cry out, he just staggered back as his wound started to bleed freely. With a boot to the chest, Durbash sent Darus tumbling down the steps.

Rage sang through Derek's veins as he launched himself across the room.

Durbash had hurt Darus. So Derek was going to tear his throat out.

He was halfway there when he saw Durbash pull out the amulet pieces.

He was three feet away when Durbash brought all three pieces together.

And Derek was upon him just as everything went dark.

When Derek next opened his eyes, he found himself gazing up at a red sky.

As he came to his senses, he spun in a slow circle, taking in his surroundings. He appeared to be standing in the middle of an unfamiliar, barren landscape. There was no grass, no dirt. No forests or rivers. Just an endless expanse of ash grey, desert. Rocks and boulders dotted here and there and what looked like the burnt, shrivelled remains of a tree standing alone on a hilltop in the distance.

And then there was the sky, that looked as if it had been painted in blood.

There was no sign of any grems or Sylvina and the elves. There was no Arabelle and there was no Darus.

He did, however, see Durbash, standing a little ways away from him. Upon closer inspection, Derek could see that Durbash had a long bloody gash on his right arm and a torn and bloodied lip. The ogre didn't appear to be paying any attention to Derek at all, instead, he was looking around with a strange fervour as if he expected something—or someone—to appear from any direction at any moment.

Then there was a voice. *"What do you want?"*

The voice was unlike any Derek had ever heard. It was horribly raspy and deep at the same time. There was something about the sound of that voice that sent a chill up Derek's spine. He glanced around, trying to find a body to place to the strange voice, but there was no one around. Only Durbash and himself.

Durbash perked up. "Are you the daemon, Milrath?" he asked.

"I am," drawled the voice, Milrath, after a beat. *"Who wants to know?"*

"My name is Durbash and I want you to grant me a wish."

"Oh?" Milrath sounded almost pleasantly surprised. *"And what wish would that be?"*

"I want what was taken returned to me," Durbash announced. "I wish to be returned to my former glory but also to be more powerful than I ever was before. I want to be mightier than any king and I want to be strong enough to crush the Guardians into oblivion!"

No, Derek thought. He had to stop this. He couldn't allow Durbash to have his wish granted. He had to—

A horrible, rasping laughter echoed around them. *"Clezka! Such pathetic creatures with such pathetic dreams."*

"What?" Durbash looked as if he had just been slapped.

"You really think I, a high lord and commander of legions, would spare what little I have of my powers just to grant your poor excuse of a wish?" More laughter.

Derek saw Durbash's fingers close into tight fists at his side. He could practically feel the rage radiating off of him, like heat from a burning coal.

"Oh, you clezka are all so wonderfully foolish!"

"ENOUGH!" Durbash roared. He thrust out his arm, which held the amulet between tightly clenched fingers. "*I* have the amulet! *I* summoned *you* and you *will* obey me! Now grant me my wish, daemon!"

The silence stretched on for long enough that Derek thought that perhaps the daemon had left. Perhaps it had grown bored? Perhaps Durbash had offended it?

But the voice returned and in a chilling voice, it uttered one word, *"No."*

There was a hum in the air before Derek saw Durbash's body seize as if he had been caught in the grip of some large, invisible hand. He made a choked sound as his body began to tremble and convulse. The amulet fell from his grasp and into the grey sand.

It was a surprisingly horrifying sight to watch and it was made even more so as Durbash's body began to wither away right before Derek's eyes. Durbash's grey skin grew paler and paler by the second, the colour draining away. Lines started to appear on his skin, like cracks in stone.

Durbash, let out a long, agonized scream before collapsing into a crumpled heap on the ground. He didn't move again.

Hesitantly, Derek approached Durbash's fallen form. Dazedly, he thought that Durbash looked like what a skeleton might look like if it was still covered in flesh and clothing. His body which had once been bulging with muscle was now nothing but skin and bones. His leather suit hung off of him almost like a child wearing their parent's clothes. His cheekbones were two sharp points on his face and his skin was a dirty, white colour with deep black lines running all over it.

But what really shocked Derek the most was that Durbash was actually still alive. His uncovered eye, now bulging in its sunken socket, was wide open but unfocused. Derek could hear the soft, rattling sound of his breath through his parted lipless mouth, his body just barely rising with each breath.

"Ah," came the deeply satisfied voice. *"It has been far too long since I fed on a clezka soul. The last one to call upon me using my amulet had put up much more of a fight than I had anticipated. I didn't even get the chance to finish her off. It was quite disappointing."*

Derek stared at the shrivelled remains of what was once, one of the most fearsome men in all four lands, before he finally summoned the strength to say, "What did you do to him?"

"As I said, foolish child, I devoured his soul. Oh, clezkas have such delicious souls."

"Clezka. You keep saying that word. What does it mean?"

"It is what we daemons call your kind. Mortals."

"His wish," Derek said, still reeling from what he had just seen. "You didn't grant his wish."

Milrath chuckled in a way that made him shiver. *"I never do. You clezkas really are such imbeciles. You truly think that I would spare my powers to make your stupid little dreams come true? No, this amulet was never anything more than a tool to lure victims to me. So that I might still feed upon your delectable souls even while I am no longer within your realm."*

In a way, it should not have come as a real surprise, but Derek still felt blindsided by the revelation. *It was all for nothing?* he thought. Running away from home, risking his life and the lives of his friends had all been so that he could end up here? Trapped in some strange, dead land with a near-dead criminal?

He thought of his mother and father. How he had hoped that he would get to see them again. The hope he had carried like a flame in the wind suddenly snuffed out and he felt weak from the loss of it.

"And how lucky I am, to have been brought not one, but two clezka souls."

Derek barely had time to register the words before his body seized. All the air left him in a rush and something lurched painfully inside him.

This was it. The thought raced through Derek's mind as he gasped for breath. He was going to have his soul devoured. Devoured by an invisible daemon. He was going to end up just like Durbash. He was—

There was a flash of blinding, red light in front of him and all at once the air flooded back into his lungs and that terrible pull inside of him vanished. Dizzy, Derek fell to his knees, panting and every muscle in his body trembling.

"What's this?" rumbled Milrath in a displeased tone.

Something was glowing beneath him. No, not beneath him. *On* him.

A dull, red light pulsed faintly from underneath his shirt. He lifted the hem of his shirt and was shocked to find a symbol he had never seen before, stamped on his chest. The symbol was no bigger than his fist and consisted of three circular patterns with smaller, jagged lines cutting through them. It almost looked as if someone has pressed a hot brand into his skin. Only there was no pain and no smoke rising from his skin, only the faint red glow.

"Wh- What . . ." Derek gasped. The dizziness was starting to return and he could taste bile in the back of his throat.

"There's something in the way. I cannot touch your soul. Could it be . . ?" The voice trailed off for a moment. *"No matter. Our time is near. We daemons will return and when we do, I shall look forward to devouring your soul then."*

Before Derek could ask what the voice meant, or about the symbol on his chest, he was falling back into the darkness.

". . . erek. . ."

". . . wake up . . ."

The sound of someone calling to him was the first thing he heard as consciousness drifted back to him.

"Please . . . Come back. . ."

He knew that voice. It was a familiar voice. A safe voice.

"Derek."

The next thing he became aware of was something around him. Arms and a body. Holding him. Keeping him warm and protected.

Da, he thought instantly.

"Derek, *please.*"

No. It wasn't Alexander Draco holding him. Not Alexander calling to him with such desperation and fear and love.

Slowly, Derek opened his eyes. Everything was blurry at first, but soon enough, he was able to make out the face hovering over him. His hair hung down in messy tendrils. His face was pale and stained with blood and grime. His eyes were wide and red-rimmed, as if he had not slept in days . . . or as if he had been crying.

Derek had never seen his adoptive father look so haggard.

With a croak in his voice, he said, "Darus."

Darus's face underwent a multitude of different emotions before finally settling on painful relief.

"Thank the Goddess," he breathed and the arms around Derek tightened in a strong embrace. His body twinged with a dull pain, but he didn't struggle or protest.

Darus held him close for a long while, whispering prayers of thanks and Derek just closed his eyes and luxuriated in the comforting feeling of Darus's arms around him.

When Darus pulled back, Derek took a look at their surroundings. They were outside, the air growing cooler and the light growing dimmer with impending nightfall. They were perched on a branch of one of the giant trees of the Great Forest. Darus was kneeling down with Derek cradled against him.

Standing nearby were the elves of Sylvina's guard. He spotted Arabelle hovering around him and Darus. She looked at Derek with a mixture of concern and relief. Standing beside her was Sylvina. Both women looked slightly worse for wear but otherwise uninjured.

"What happened?" Derek asked. "What are we all doing out here?"

The worried frown was back on Darus's face. "You don't remember anything?"

Derek furrowed his brow, trying to think back. "I remember the fight in the ruins. The grems. I remember seeing Durbash wound you and then try to use the amulet and I went to stop him, but that's it."

"When you tackled Durbash, there was this loud bang that split the air," explained Arabelle. "I thought for a second that he'd gone and blown himself up somehow and taken you with him. But then everything stopped, even all of the grems just . . . stopped. When I looked over there was this dark cloud of mist where you and Durbash had just been."

"Something about it must have frightened the grems because they all fled," said Sylvina. "We tried to get to you, but there was something in the strange mist that kept repelling us."

"But then the mist just disappeared and we saw you and Durbash, or . . . what was left of him at least, just lying there on the floor," added Arabelle.

"So we picked you up and got out of there as fast as we could,"

Darus added. "You scared the shit out of me, Derek."

"Did everyone make it?" Derek couldn't help but ask. "Was anyone—?"

It was Sylvina who answered. "There were a few injuries but we all made it out alive. Two of Durbash's bandits were killed and one managed to escape."

"What about Durbash?"

The others seemed reluctant to answer. Finally, Darus said, "Durbash is alive but—there was something wrong with him. I've never seen anything like it. He won't speak or move or show any sign of acknowledgment." Darus shook his head. "And his body— it's almost like he's just . . .wasted away."

"Some of the elves left to take him back to their village," said Arabelle. "See if they can heal him somehow."

"Derek," said Darus. "Can you really not remember anything that might have happened when you and Durbash disappeared?"

Derek shook his head. "It's all a blank. I must have fallen unconscious right away."

Darus nodded but he was still frowning as if Derek's answer had just made him even more apprehensive. Still, he didn't appear to be in any hurry to press the matter.

"But, how did you find me in the first place?" Derek asked him.

In answer, Darus lifted his right arm. The cuff of his blood and dirt-stained sleeve fell down just enough to reveal the faded design of a tracking rune on the inside of his wrist. "I've been following you for weeks now," he explained. "Thanks to this tracking spell. I arrived here in the Forest this morning. Just in time to find out that you had just been discovered missing. Once I'd checked to make sure Jared and Arabelle were all right, the queen herself ordered Sylvina here to gather who she could of her guard and we came racing after you."

"You came all this way just to find us?" Derek asked the question as if it were something incomprehensible.

With a tired smile, Darus leaned down rested his forehead against Derek's. "Derek, I'd travel all over the four lands to find you."

Derek felt weighed down by the sudden burgeoning guilt inside of him. How many times had he thought that Darus only felt a sense of responsibility to him out of pity? Yet here he was, tired and injured, covered in dirt and sweat and blood, after having followed Derek and the others almost halfway across Aloseria. He remembered that day, what felt like years ago now when Darus had struck him during their argument. The look in his eyes back then. He had thought that Darus hated him then. Had thought it for days now. He had thought that maybe Darus would feel relief when he realised that Derek was gone. That he would be better off without him. But when he looked into Darus's face now, the weary, but gentle, smile on his lips. The way he had looked when Derek first opened his eyes, it made him wonder if perhaps he had been wrong all this time.

"But . . . why?" Derek couldn't help but ask. He felt strange. He felt weak and he felt vulnerable and in need of assurances that he wouldn't allow himself to ask for under normal circumstances.

Darus's grey eyes were shimmering and Derek wasn't sure if it was just a trick of the light, or something else. "Why?" he huffed out a laugh. "Why do you think? I missed you and I wanted you back. Because I love you, you dumb brat."

And that was it. The words Derek had never realised he needed, finally spoken from Darus's own lips. Words that finally put to rest any doubts he'd had on Darus's feelings for him. Three words that comforted him beyond measure.

"I'm sorry," said Derek. "I'm sorry," he said again, this time looking past Darus at Arabelle, who he had spoken cruel words to the night before. He saw her eyes widen in surprise before her expression softened in a way that let Derek know he was forgiven. "I'm sorry for running away. I'm sorry for lying. I should have listened to you. I just . . . I—"

I just wanted my mum and da back.

Darus just hushed him and pulled him in close so that Derek's head was resting against his uninjured shoulder. Darus's hand came up to gently wipe the wetness from underneath Derek's eyes. He hadn't even realised he was crying. "I know," he said softly. "I know."

And just like that, despite all the trouble he had caused, Derek knew that all was forgiven between the two of them.

So he let himself be held and rocked gently like he remembered Darus doing to him when he was younger and had just woken from a nightmare. And just like back then, Derek felt completely and utterly safe. Like nothing could hurt him while he was in Darus's arms.

20

Ember was as vibrant and busy as ever on the day they returned home. Plenty of people were out and about, enjoying the bright afternoon sunshine on this first day of autumn. The weekly open-air market was in full swing and Derek, Jared, Arabelle and Darus were making their way to the palace.

"I know it's only been a month but it feels like we've been gone for so much longer," Arabelle was saying.

"I'm sure your parents feel the same way," said Darus from where he walked two paces ahead of them.

Jared moaned despairingly. "My mother's going to be so angry. She's going to *murder* me."

"You've survived bandits, aracnas and being impaled by an arrow," said Derek. "I'm sure you can survive your mother."

"You've never seen her when she's really angry. I think I'd rather have to fight off ten Durbashs all at once than face my mother when she's mad."

"Oh, Jared," Arabelle sighed. "Now you're just being ridiculous."

"It's the truth, I say!"

After the battle against Durbash and the grems in the earth elf ruins, they had returned to the elf village. It was almost nightfall by the time they made it back to Sylvina and Aravanea's home and when they did they had been greeted by an anxious Aravanea (who had flung herself into Sylvina's arms almost as soon as she had stepped through the door) and Jared.

Almost as soon as he had seen them, Jared had gotten up from the bed and limped over to them. Derek had expected Jared to make for Arabelle first and he had only just started to form an apology in his head when Jared had come to stand in front of him. He watched Jared take in his bruised face, the bloodstained cloth wrapped around his hand and as he opened his mouth to speak, Jared pulled Derek in for a hug.

"I'm sorry," Jared had said and he had sounded so sincere as if he were the one who had wronged Derek and not the other way around. "I'm sorry I yelled at you and I'm sorry I called you selfish. I should have understood why you did what you did. I thought about it and I get it now and I'm sorry I got so upset at you for it."

"No," said Derek slowly returning the hug. He and Jared never hugged. Jared had always respected Derek's personal space. He never so much as poked Derek in the arm without making sure it was all right first. What they were doing now was uncharted territory. "You don't have to be sorry. I'm the one who should be apologising. I never should have lied to you and Arabelle like that. You could have been killed because of me. *I'm* sorry."

Darus, Aravanea and Sylvina all smiled at the scene while Arabelle shook her head and muttered fondly about how odd boys were.

They had been forced to stay for a few more days in the Great Forest, at least until they were all healed enough to make the journey back to Ember. Even though Derek had been ready to finally go home, he had enjoyed the time he got to spend among his mother's people, swimming in the rivers and relaxing on the grassy hills with Arabelle, Jared and some of the elf youths.

Derek never went to see Durbash, who was kept somewhere in the Fair Lady's residence and treated by healers, but he knew that Darus did. Until on the third day of their stay, they received word that Durbash was dead. Whatever had happened to him in those ruins had been too extensive to heal. He never found out what they did with his body, and Derek found that he didn't particularly care either.

He had also been made to pay the Fair Lady a visit, to apologise for deceiving her with the fake amulet and for causing her and her people so much trouble. Fortunately, she had not seemed all that upset about the matter. All she had said to him was, "You are forgiven, Derek Draco and I am glad that you are alive." Again, she had looked at him with that strange look that gave him the feeling that there was more that she wanted to say but, for whatever reason, did not.

On the night before they were to leave, Sylvina came to him and said, "I knew your mother, Erianna, although I believe she called herself Erica when you knew her? We grew up together. I was deeply saddened when I learned of her passing."

It had been strange but pleasant, to hear of his mother spoken by someone who knew her long before Derek did. Just like it had been when he first came to Ember and he had met King Jonathan.

"You look just like her," said Sylvina. "But your eyes are just like your father's. I knew him also. Not as well as I would have liked, but I knew he was a good man and that I am sure he would have made Erianna very happy."

Now, as Derek and his small party walked through the gates to the palace, they were met at the front steps by a tall, broad-shouldered young woman, with short, brown hair and was wearing the golden armour and blue cape of a Crown Guard.

Her eyes widened when she caught sight of Jared. "Your Highness!" She dipped her head in a quick bow. "You've returned!"

A princely smile slid onto Jared's features. "Good to see you too, Beatrice. Did you miss me?"

"Of course, Your Highness. Everyone's been so worried," said Beatrice. "The Queen and Princess Julianna are waiting for you inside. Along with Captain and Lady Aloria. This way, please."

They were escorted up the steps, through the wide double doors and into the grand foyer with its marble floors and high ceiling. An ornate table stood in the centre with a vase full of daisies and red begonias. Beatrice the guard left them there to ascend the staircase go and inform the Queen of their arrival.

They weren't left to wait long. Derek saw the Queen first, appearing at the top of the staircase. She was dressed in a simple pink dress, her hair was down and looking slightly disarrayed as if she hadn't thought to comb it properly. Julianna was right behind her and then came a broad, barrel-chested man with the same red-brown hair and bronzed skin as the Queen, and a tall, slender woman with deep brown skin and glossy, black hair. Arabelle's parents.

The four of them stood frozen at the top of the stairs for a moment and Derek could practically feel the nervousness coming off of Jared and Arabelle in waves. Then, the tension snapped and there were exclamations of, "Oh, Jared!" and "Arabelle!" and the Queen and the Princess and Victor and Amara Aloria were flying down the steps towards their children.

Derek and Darus both took a step back as Arabelle was engulfed by both her father and step-mother in a tight embrace and Charlotte threw her arms around her son.

"Oh, Jared, you foolish boy!" cried Charlotte, her voice full of tears. "How could you just leave like that? Do you have any idea how worried we were?"

"If you ever run off like that again, I'm going to kill you," said Julianna. She looked as if she were trying to maintain an angry face while barely managing to keep herself from crying.

""I'm sorry, Mother. I'm sorry, Jules," Jared said, returning his mother's embrace. "I didn't mean to scare you. I'm all right though. Really."

Charlotte pulled back and gave her son a stern look. "Except for an arrow wound!"

Jared smiled guiltily down at his mother. He was almost a head taller than her. "It's nearly all healed up," he said. "I can barely even feel it anymore."

Charlotte managed a smile, a few rogue tears spilling down her cheeks as she cupped her son's face with both her hands. "Just promise me you'll never scare me like that again."

"I'll try my best." And the two were hugging again. Charlotte, looking as though she never wanted to let Jared out of her arms again and Derek ached. Even though Darus was standing beside him with a hand on his shoulder. After all these weeks of believing he would finally get to have his parents back, and then realising that it was never going to happen, well, it had almost felt like losing them all over again.

Then Charlotte did let go of her son, releasing him to his sister's embrace, and came to stand in front of Derek. For a moment, he expected her to yell at him. To tell him off for dragging her precious son and niece off on such a dangerous quest. Maybe even to forbid him from seeing Jared ever again. But the look on her face was the farthest thing from anger as she examined him from head to toe, taking in the still fading bruises on his face and his bandaged right hand.

"Oh, Derek," she said softly and there was a catch in her voice.

"Are you all right, sweetheart?"

"I . . ." He felt disarmed by the way the Queen was looking at him as if his response would determine whether or not she would shed more tears. "I'll be fine."

Ever so gently and slowly, so as if to give him time to pull away, Charlotte took Derek into her arms. She held him just like she had held her son moments ago. "I'm so glad you're home safe," she told him and Derek felt like a fox cornered by hounds. His hand twitched at his side. Should he return the embrace? Would it be rude of him not to? Some sort of breach in royal etiquette?

But then he realised that this was the first time anyone had hugged him so tenderly. So maternally. Not since he was a child, had he felt an embrace like this.

Not since his mother died.

Derek's bottom lip trembled, any hesitations he had crumbled away as he placed his own arms around the Queen and pressed his forehead against her shoulder.

"I'm sorry." He felt like he'd been saying that a lot lately.

Charlotte just stroked a hand down the back of his head and pressed a soft, motherly kiss to his temple and continued to hold him.

When Darus brought Derek home, they were greeted by Daisy bounding down the stairs to throw herself at Darus and smother him in wet kisses and a stern, but relieved, Lila.

"You idiot boy," she told Derek as she pulled him into a tight embrace. "If you ever run off like that again, I swear I'm going to toss you into the prisons myself."

"Please don't scare him off, Lila," said Darus, toeing off his shoes while trying to fend off Daisy. "I just got him back and it was no easy feat."

After hearing a quick recount of events from Darus and fussing over Derek some more, Lila finally left to give the two of them some time to rest.

Darus moved into the kitchen to pour himself a glass of water and sat himself down, heavily at the table. Daisy, having finally finished giving Derek his own enthusiastic greeting, padded over to him and curled up on the floor at his feet. Content to be near her master again after so long.

Derek stood in the doorway and just let himself look. He took in the familiar foam green walls of the kitchen. The floral patterned curtains on the windows. The dent on the skirting board by the doorway that Derek himself had put there a few years ago by trying to kill a spider with the broom handle. It all spoke of a familiarity that one could only associate with their home.

Because this was his home. Not the cottage back in the Valley where he had spent the first few years of his life living peacefully with his mother and father. Not anymore. It was here. In this unassuming little house in Ember.

It was with Darus and Finn and Daisy.

Finn.

He was just beginning to wonder where his cat was when he felt something bump against the back of his leg. He looked down into the familiar pair of round, green eyes gazing back up at him.

Finn mewled and Derek took that as the cat's way of saying, "welcome home."

"I would have thought you'd gone up to have a wash by now," Darus said.. "Or do you just like standing in doorways now?"

"Am I your son?" Derek asked.

Darus blinked. "Excuse me?"

"Back in the ruins, when you showed up while I was fighting Durbash. You said, 'get away from my son.' Did you mean it? Am I your son?"

Darus looked a little taken aback by the question. "Well, legally speaking, yes, you are my son—"

"But do *you* really see me as your son?"

Now, Darus looked uncharacteristically flustered. He reached up to rub the back of his neck. "I . . . Yes. I suppose I do."

Derek let that sink in and fought the urge to smile. He wasn't about to give Darus something to be smug about.

"What about you?" Darus asked. "Do you see me as a father?"

"No," said Derek, bending down to pick up Finn, who had begun winding around his legs and meowing. "You're more like an annoying uncle."

"Aw, that hurts my feelings, *son*."

Derek winced. "You're going to be insufferable about this now aren't you?"

"Of course I am . . . *son*." Darus's grin was wicked.

"I'm leaving now."

"But we were having such a lovely moment," Darus called out to him. "Son!"

Bright and early the next day, Derek, Jared and Arabelle found themselves standing in the throne room, before the King and his three Advisors.

The last time Derek had seen King Jonathan, had been the day before, shortly after they'd first arrived at the palace. He remembered Jonathan striding into the sitting room they had relocated themselves to. He remembered how Jared had gone rigid at the sight of his father, more so than when he had seen his mother and sister like he was expecting his father to start blasting his ears off right then and there.

But Jonathan had simply crossed the room to where Jared had stood and enveloped his son in what looked like a back-breaking hug. Then, without letting go of Jared, he held an arm out to Arabelle and Derek.

Arabelle had gone with no hesitation but Derek had been a little more diffident.

"Derek," the King said softly and Derek had been stunned to see tears falling from his eyes. "Come here, son."

And so Derek had stepped forward and allowed himself to be pulled into Jonathan's crushing embrace, listening as the man whispered prayers of thanks to the Goddess for bringing the three of them home safe and sound.

Derek thought it was the only time he had ever seen the King show vulnerability and it had been so strange to witness. Stranger still to know that he had been partly the cause of it.

That vulnerability was long gone now.

As he looked down at the three of them from where he sat upon his throne, Jonathan's face was a mask of indifference and authority.

"The three of you knowingly broke the law." The King's voice echoed throughout the hall. "Guardians are not to leave the city walls without having first been granted permission from the crown. That law especially applies to three, young and inexperienced Guardians such as yourselves."

The King's eyes landed on his son as he said that last part and Derek felt Jared stiffen minutely beside him. After all the tearful embraces, they had all gotten an earful from their families for their actions, but Derek suspected that Jared might have copped the biggest one from his father.

Jonathan continued, "If you had been gone for an even longer than you had, I would have had no choice but to label you three as deserters. I believe that you are all aware of the punishment that befalls deserters?"

They did. The punishment for a Guardian who had deserted their home and duty was a prison sentence. Often ten or more years spent in one of the cold, dark cells of Black Rock prison. Derek had once heard a boy at the Academy say that their great-great-something-granduncle had been executed for desertion. He wasn't entirely sure how credible that story was though.

The King wasn't considering locking them up in Black Rock was he? Surely he wouldn't do that to Jared, his son and second in line to the throne. And Arabelle was his niece. Derek was the son of his once close friend, but would that make much of a difference? Maybe he'd lock just Derek away for a while, while Jared and Arabelle were forced to polish the palace floors as a punishment.

Derek saw the corner of the King's mouth twitch into a reluctant smile and he felt himself relax a fraction. "But you are not deserters, so you will not be imprisoned," He said. "Instead you shall be suspended from active duty, without pay, for three months starting today."

That's it? Derek almost said aloud. He looked to Jared and Arabelle and they both looked just as surprised, yet relieved as he did. Clearly even they had also not been expecting to get off so lightly.

The only one who did not look pleased about this was Elias Decorus. "Pardon me, Your Majesty," he said. "But are you sure that this is truly a fitting punishment? For the Prince maybe, but I believe that Miss Aloria and Master Draco should be dealt with a bit more harshly."

Derek shot the old man a dirty look. *Bastard.*

Jonathan looked at Elias consideringly. "And why is that, Elias?"

"It is as you said, they broke one of our laws, not to mention they dragged the Prince along on their foolhardy adventure and put his life at risk."

One of the other Advisors, Albert Thorbone, chuckled. "The last time I checked, Elias, I believe the Prince joined them willingly. Isn't that right Your Highness?"

"That's right," Jared said firmly, back straight and head held high. "I joined Derek and Arabelle by my own volition. Whatever punishment is handed down to them should be given to me also."

"There you have it, Elias," said Thorbone cheerfully.

Elias grumbled under his breath.

"No, you are right, Elias. Their punishment should be harsher," said Jonathan. "So they will be suspended for four months instead of three."

Elias did not look as if that sentence pleased him any better than the last. He opened his mouth, likely to voice another objection, but the King raised his hand. "My decision is made." His voice brooked no room for argument.

"Of course, Your Majesty."

Jonathan's green-eyed gaze returned to the three young Guardians before him. He smiled. "After all, I'm sure their families have their own punishments they'd like to hand out as well."

Derek heard both Jared and Arabelle gulp in tandem and knew they were concerned for the punishments their parents would come up with.

He couldn't say he was excited about finding out just what

punishment Darus had in store for him either.

It had been a week since their return home and things were slowly starting to return to normal. For days, Derek, Arabelle and Jared had been the talk of the city.

If one were to ask anyone in Ember they would tell you that the Prince and his two companions, who had snuck out of the city one night in search of some mythical amulet, had left everyone in the palace in a worried frenzy. That on their quest they encountered Durbash, who had also been looking for the amulet and fought him. They never found the amulet (probably because it never really existed in the first place), but they had managed to slay Durbash (good riddance) and a few of his cohorts while they were at it.

Some might even say that they were young heroes. They had killed Durbash, notorious slave trader, bandit and murderer. They deserved a reward of some sort.

Others would say that they were suicidal fools and deserved the deserters' punishment of being locked up, except for the Prince of course. Some would even say that Arabelle Aloria and Prince Jared were not to be held accountable at all. That it was all that Draco boy's fault, it was the elf blood in him, made him too mischievous and a bad influence on others.

The first few days after returning home, Derek had even decided not to leave the house, so as to avoid all the murmuring and not-so-discreet finger-pointing in his direction. It was all very reminiscent of the days when he had first come to live in Ember.

On one sunny afternoon, Derek found himself sitting under the shade of one of the apricot trees in the palace gardens, with Jared and Arabelle sitting across from him. Every once and a while a leaf would fall from its branch and land either on the ground or on their person. The Queen's dogs, Spot and Lucie were running amuck, chasing and yapping at each other, while old Beth was dozing peacefully on Derek's lap.

He stroked the fur of her back with his right hand, which was now almost completely healed. After returning, Darus had taken him to the Healing House, where one of the mages who worked there had done what he could to make sure there would be no permanent damage left. All that was left now was a scabbed over cut along his palm that would likely leave a scar.

"And Wilda is merciless, I tell you," Jared was saying, referring to the palace's head maid. "She won't let me rest until I've cleaned every speck of dust. And she yells at me when I'm not quick enough. If she were allowed a whip, I'm sure she'd use it."

"You're being overdramatic," said Arabelle, who was leaning against Jared's side, with a pencil in her hand and a notebook open in her hand, happily sketching away.

"I am not. You're just lucky your parents gave you a light punishment."

Arabelle scoffed. "Light? I'm not allowed to leave the house after five o'clock at night for the next four months and while I'm suspended from active duty, I have to work with Amara in the Healing House cleaning out bedpans."

"At least you two get to sleep in," Derek said, reaching for the bowl of blueberries that sat in the middle of them on the grass. "Darus has me up at dawn every morning to do all kinds of training exercises for hours."

"I thought you liked to train?" said Jared.

"Not before the sun's up, I don't."

"Ah, is that why you're crankier than usual lately?" asked Arabelle with an amused quirk of her lips.

There was something about Arabelle's smile that Derek couldn't help but find . . . charming. He thought that the way it lit up her face reminded him of the way the sun lit up the sky at dawn. Even her eyes seemed to shine brighter in those moments.

I like it. Her smile, Derek thought and was immediately mortified at himself for even thinking such a thing.

"I am not cranky," he grumbled, popping a blueberry into his mouth.

"Just a tad," said Jared.

"In an adorable way," Arabelle added brightly. "Like a cranky baby."

Jared laughed.

Derek scowled. "I don't like this topic of conversation."

"Too bad," said Jared around his laughter.

Arabelle said, "As your friends, it is our solemn duty to tease you."

"Because we love you."

Derek felt a rush of warmth steal over his cheeks. With his pale

329

skin, he knew the colour must be showing on his face and unfortunately, it did not go unnoticed.

"Oh, Derek!" Jared leaned over with a wide grin on his face. "Are you blushing?"

Derek turned his face away. "No."

"Yes, you are."

"I'm not."

"You are! Your cheeks are pink."

Derek glared. "It's rude to point, idiot," and he threw a blueberry at Jared's face.

"Hey! Damn it, Derek, that nearly got me in the eye!"

"I'll throw another one at you if you don't shut up."

"No food throwing," warned Arabelle hunching protectively over her notebook and glaring at the both of them. "If you get food stains on my drawings I'll kill you."

"No you won't," Jared said. "You'd miss me too much."

She shrugged. "I'll have Derek to keep me company."

"But it wouldn't be the same because he's not your cousin. And I'm your favourite cousin, after all."

"I'll have you know, Julianna's my favourite cousin actually."

"Oh please," huffed Jared. "Julianna's boring."

"I wouldn't say that. She has plenty of *interesting* childhood stories of you to tell."

"Did she tell you about the bathroom incident?" Derek asked.

Jared gaped at him. "Wha—"

Arabelle laughed. "Yes, but my favourite was the one about him getting stuck in the—"

"All right, that's enough!"

Jared complained indignantly.

Arabelle laughed at his expense.

And Derek smiled.

EPILOGUE

Aurelia was awoken from her sleep by the sound of someone breaking into her shop . . . again.

This is starting to grow tiresome, she thought as she got up from bed, dressed herself with a magical flick of her fingers, and made her way downstairs.

Halfway down the stairwell, she heard Cora's shrill caw before the sound was abruptly cut off. She frowned and hurried her steps, summoning a ball of fire in her left palm and throwing open the back curtain.

The scene before her was of Cora, wings spread wide, talons extended and frozen in midair. Standing only inches away from Cora's sharpened talons was a man with short, black hair and a close-cropped beard. He wore a dark trench coat and a dark hat that shadowed his face. From what Aurelia could see of it, however, she thought he looked as if he were in his early thirties.

There were wisps of red light, flickering around Cora's immobile body. Aurelia could sense something . . . strange in the air and knew it had to do with the spell that had been cast on Cora.

Was he a mage? He had to be. But he was certainly unlike any mage Aurelia had ever encountered before.

"Release her," Aurelia growled.

The man looked from the raven to Aurelia, completely unfazed. "Only if it won't attack."

"She won't attack unless I do . . . Or you do."

The man nodded. He waved his hand in front of Cora and the spell came undone, the red light disappearing. As soon as she was free, Cora soared across the room and landed on Aurelia's shoulder. She could feel Cora's distress thrumming through her from the contact. She imagined it couldn't have been pleasant to be frozen like that. To feel trapped inside of one's own body.

Aurelia glared at the intruder. "Good. Now get out, before I burn you where you stand."

The man stepped forward, heedless of Aurelia's threat. "I did not come here to fight. There's only one thing I'm looking for and you give it to me then I'll be more than happy to leave."

"If all you are looking for is to buy something, you should come back in another few hours when the shop is actually open."

"I prefer to conduct my business when no one is around to see. Surely you understand that."

"And how do you know I have whatever it is you are looking for?"

"Well I wouldn't be here if I wasn't," was all the man said.

After a few moments of hesitation, Aurelia lowered her hand, snuffing out the flame. She came out from around the counter, snapping her fingers and suddenly the shop was illuminated by candlelight.

"So?" she said in an almost bored tone. "What is it you're looking for?"

"A bit of glass, actually," he said.

"Glass?" Aurelia folded her arms across her chest, a sense of unease began to settle over her. "I believe you might have to be more specific than that."

The man chuckled. "Right. It's a reflective piece of glass. Looks as though it might have been broken off of a mirror. Probably no bigger than your forearm."

Ah, Aurelia thought with dread. That *bit of glass.*

"I see." She tried her best to keep her tone neutral. "And what exactly does this piece of glass do?"

The man tilted his head up just enough for the candlelight to catch his eyes. They were red. An unnaturally bright red. "I'd rather not say."

She had been trying to think of a way to rid herself of the mirror shard that still sat locked up in the backroom for weeks now without any luck. Perhaps this was the solution to her problem? But when she looked at this stranger standing before her, she had the gut feeling that handing the shard over to him would not be a good idea.

"Then I am afraid I can't help you," said Aurelia. "In any case, I do not have anything here that fits the description of what you are looking for. Might I suggest trying the Magical Menagerie? They have a rather wide variety of objects there. Nothing of the same quality as what I sell, of course."

The man smiled in a way that lacked any warmth or humour."You're lying."

Aurelia's brow lowered. "It is rude to call someone a liar you know. Especially someone you hope to do business with."

"I know the glass shard is here. I know you know what I'm talking about. You can either hand it over or I'll take it by force."

Aurelia smirked. "I'd like to see you try."

The man took a step forward and those red wisps returned, coming off of him like tendrils of smoke. Aurelia felt that same strangeness in the air that she had felt earlier, only more intense this time. It wasn't just a strangeness she felt but something *wrong*. Something sinister.

Aurelia swallowed. "Who are you?"

"No one," he answered.

"And if you had the shard, what would you plan on doing with it?" she asked.

"I'm afraid that's no concern of yours."

Of course not. Aurelia could just hand over the mirror shard. She had been meaning to find a way to get rid of it for a while now anyway. Then this strange man would leave and she could go back to bed. But over the last few years, Aurelia found that whenever she was faced with making the choice between a right decision and a wrong one, a voice would whisper in her head, usually taking on the sound of Erianna's soft lilt.

It whispered to her now. *You do not know what that shard is truly capable of. If you give it to him who knows what kind of damage he could cause? It might become a situation for the Guardians to deal with. What if Derek becomes involved? What if he's put in danger?*

But why does it matter so much? She wondered. *I always said that I would not get involved. That you wouldn't want me involved with your child.*

But if it means keeping him safe . . .

Aurelia sighed, her decision was made. "Like I already told you, I do not have it."

The man closed his eyes and shook his head as if he were dealing with an obstinate child. "I hoped you wouldn't say that."

Cora launched herself from Aurelia's shoulder and straight towards the man.

He flung out his right arm and with a startled cry, Cora went flying, as if batted away by an invisible hand. She crashed into the display of Scrying Glasses on the far right wall, falling to the floor and lying still.

Before Aurelia could even blink, the man was right in front of her. A crackling red aura surrounded his hand.

When he made as if to punch her with it, Aurelia was just quick enough to sidestep the attack and counter by summoning a gust of wind that sent him staggering back a few paces.

Conjuring a ball of fire so hot it burned blue, Aurelia sent it hurtling straight for the man. He held out both of his hands, stopping the fire in its tracks.

Aurelia held out her own palm, willing the ball of fire forwards as the man fought to hold it back.

With his face illuminated by the fire's glow, she noticed the hard set to the man's eyes and that's when Aurelia realised that he wasn't just trying to block her spell, but was trying to take control of it. Very rarely had Aurelia seen or heard of such a thing. It was next to impossible to take control of another mage's spell, it took too much power. The only viable options for combating a mage's spells were to avoid them, block them or counter them with another spell.

Just as in the back of her mind, Aurelia began to think of how foolish the man was for attempting such a thing, she started to feel her control over the fireball weaken. Unmistakably, she could feel her magic being pushed back, replaced by another's.

The flames began to turn from blue to red.

And just like that, her hold snapped and the man turned what was once Aurelia's spell against her.

The fireball roared back towards her. Aurelia managed to turn the fire to ice before it could even reach her.

The now frozen ball of fire fell to the floor, where it shattered, scattering glimmering, crystalline pieces everywhere.

The man summoned red, coils of chains to his side without so much as flicking a finger. They jangled loudly as they shot out at Aurelia with frightening speed.

Aurelia leapt to the side just in time to avoid being struck.

Her elf blood lent her the ability to expertly dodge and manoeuvre herself out of the way as the chains lunged and slithered after her like a pair of snakes.

She landed lightly on the table with the display of potions when the man seemed to appear out of thin air right in front of her.

This time, Aurelia wasn't quick enough to avoid his hand, once again covered in that red aura, as it jabbed her in the middle of her chest.

The red light travelled over her body and she felt every single one of her muscles seize and lock up. An uncomfortable numbness spread throughout her body and there was nothing she could do to stop the man from placing a kick to her midsection that sent her crashing onto the floor.

The table toppled over along with her, potion bottles shattering all around her, their contents spilling onto the floorboards in clouds of smoke and dust or puddles of liquid.

She tried as hard as she could to move. Her hand or her foot, or even her big toe, but try as she might, her body just wouldn't obey her.

She tried to reach for her magic, but found that was just as impossible.

Aurelia saw the man's booted feet land lightly on the floor beside her head.

"Now," he muttered to himself. "Where is that shard?"

He clapped his hands together two times, the sound ringing out louder than it should have. Moments later the sound of muffled thumping could be heard from backroom followed by an explosive bang and within seconds, the large, wooden box came flying into the man's outstretched hands.

The man reached inside it and pulled out the mirror shard, still wrapped up in its thick layer of cloth.

A pleased smile crossed the man's face. He tucked his prize into the inside of his coat before turning his red-eyed gaze onto Aurelia.

"It was a pleasure doing business with you," he said, tipping the brim of his hat.

If Aurelia was in control of her facial muscles she would have given him the dirtiest look she was capable of.

She saw his eyes flick minutely to her right arm, which was flung out to the side.

Moving with what seemed like inhuman speed, the man lunged forward, bringing his foot down on her right arm with enough force that Aurelia felt it shatter to pieces.

Aurelia's heart stuttered in her chest and if she could have moved she would have opened her mouth on a gasp.

She saw the sleeve of her nightshirt fall flat against the broken pieces. Saw the gloved hand roll forward an inch, now completely useless.

Her arm was broken.

Her arm was gone. Again.

"Goodbye, Miss Blackwood," said the man as he turned his back on her and made for the front door, with a casual stride. "I doubt we'll be seeing each other again."

The meaning of his statement became clear when he snapped his fingers and a spark of fire lit itself on the floor behind him. The flames spread quickly and the stench of smoke became overpowering. She could already feel the room growing hotter by the minute.

Cora . . .

The man didn't even spare her one last glance as he stepped out the door, closing it behind him.

Aurelia was left unable to move a muscle or even to shout for help. It had been a long time since Aurelia had felt helpless and she *hated* it. Hated that she was unable to do anything for herself. Hated that man for doing this to her.

As she felt the flames draw nearer, Aurelia closed her eyes. Because what else could she do?

All she could do now was lie there as everything burned down around her.

Printed in Australia
AUHW021421240122
358679AU00019B/121

9 780645 092806